THE
MANHATTAN
STING

THE
MANHATTAN
STING

A SPENCER MARLOWE
ADVENTURE
ONE MAN, TWO CENTURIES

Kelvin White

This book is dedicated to my beautiful wife Jenny. Without her literary advice, input and encouragement, The Manhattan Sting would not have happened.

CONTENTS

PROLOGUE — 1

CHAPTER ONE — 9

CHAPTER TWO — 24

CHAPTER THREE — 31

CHAPTER FOUR — 34

CHAPTER FIVE — 40

CHAPTER SIX — 48

CHAPTER SEVEN — 52

CHAPTER EIGHT — 58

CHAPTER NINE — 64

CHAPTER TEN — 75

CHAPTER ELEVEN — 82

CHAPTER TWELVE — 87

CHAPTER THIRTEEN — 91

CHAPTER FOURTEEN — 93

CHAPTER FIFTEEN — 106

CHAPTER SIXTEEN — 115

CHAPTER SEVENTEEN — 125

CHAPTER EIGHTEEN — 127

CHAPTER NINETEEN — 141

CHAPTER TWENTY — 143

CHAPTER TWENTY-ONE — 146

CHAPTER TWENTY-TWO — 154

CHAPTER TWENTY-THREE — 162

CHAPTER TWENTY-FOUR 167
CHAPTER TWENTY-FIVE 171
CHAPTER TWENTY-SIX 173
CHAPTER TWENTY-SEVEN 183
CHAPTER TWENTY-EIGHT 191
CHAPTER TWENTY-NINE 193
CHAPTER THIRTY 198
CHAPTER THIRTY-ONE 208
CHAPTER THIRTY-TWO 222
CHAPTER THIRTY-THREE 228
CHAPTER THIRTY-FOUR 236
CHAPTER THIRTY-FIVE 242
CHAPTER THIRTY-SIX 251
CHAPTER THIRTY-SEVEN 253
CHAPTER THIRTY-EIGHT 259
CHAPTER THIRTY-NINE 266
CHAPTER FORTY 268
CHAPTER FORTY-ONE 272
CHAPTER FORTY-TWO 276
CHAPTER FORTY-THREE 284
CHAPTER FORTY-FOUR 290
CHAPTER FORTY-FIVE 295
EPILOGUE 297
CHAPTER ONE 302
CHAPTER TWO 305
ABOUT THE AUTHOR 310

PROLOGUE

Savannah had the day off school to recover from a bout of influenza. She had begged her father to allow her to help in the store. After all, the Great Depression was still on. Dwindling, sure, but still ruining lives all over the United States. When she could, Savannah always helped out.

'Please, Dad, I'm just about better, please, please?'

'That girl twists you around her little finger,' June Steele remarked, something she often said to her husband.

'Yes, I know. But she's a delight to have around and the customers just love her.'

The day was as normal as every other and it was business as usual at the Steele's hardware store. Sales of tools, hammers, nails, seed and paint were despatched to the customers, often with sage words of advice from Fred Steele.

'Sav, go to the back of the store and grab a gallon of white gloss paint, there's a good girl.'

Savannah could have navigated the rabbit warren of a store with her eyes closed. It was her personal playground. She found the paint and darted back along the aisle filled with hammers, nails, gloves, glue, flowerpots, and the mix of scents you only find in hardware stores.

'There you are, Dad,' she announced. Savannah gasped. The man at the counter wore a bandana pulled over the lower part of his face. All she could see were his eyes, cold and merciless, but also something else. Each eye was a different colour; one blue, one grey. She also noticed a tattoo, a faded blue anchor, high on one cheekbone. In his hand he held a 0.38 Smith and Wesson revolver.

'Open the register. Give me the money … now!'

Her father stood rigid, saying nothing.

Give him the money, Dad, please.

'Give me the money.'

Still Fred Steele did nothing. Whether he was scared or just plain stubborn, Savannah never knew. The 0.38 barked twice. Fred Steele collapsed in a heap. He coughed once, then again. Savannah watched a dribble of blood run down his stubbled cheek. A bigger pool of blood gathered under him.

She screamed. The gunman casually moved behind the counter and opened the register. Forty-eight dollars and twenty-six cents. He missed the bundle of notes that'd been stuffed into a hessian bank bag sitting amongst a wooden box full of screwdrivers, rivets and nails.

Law enforcement didn't find Fred Steele's killer; the description offered by a young girl was quickly forgotten. The case was relegated to a bottom drawer at the Pierre Police station.

And then life just … continued. That day turned into another, and another. Days became weeks.

June Steele never completely recovered after her husband's murder. She sold the hardware store. Savannah grieved, and went on grieving, but her focus and resolve changed. Once she had imagined a life as a teacher or a nurse. Now she was going to do something about those who stole and murdered.

Four years passed. Savannah did well at school. June Steele went through the motions of caring for her daughter, but to Savannah, it seemed as if her mom was just filling in time until she died.

One afternoon, Savannah was hanging out with friends after school. They sat in the drugstore drinking cokes and eating ice-cream. Through the open door, Savannah noticed a dusty Studebaker with Alabama plates pull up at the diner next to the drugstore. A man and a woman climbed out and made their way to the diner.

The lady wore a tight skirt and tottered on high heels. Her scarlet lipstick was a slash of colour, her cheeks heavily rouged. The man wore a conservative double-breasted suit, crumpled from hours spent behind the wheel travelling.

Savannah stared hard. What was it? There was something inexplicable she couldn't quite put her finger on. She excused herself and strolled to the diner.

Savannah paused at the front, her breathing short and sharp. She went inside, where the proprietor stood attentively behind the counter. The diner was full. Savannah hardly noticed the busy tables. Savannah strode up to the proprietor. Al Arbuckle was a kindly man. Big, bluff, with a cheery red face.

'Hi there, Savannah, what can I do for you?'

'Could you use me as a casual waitress sometime, Mr Arbuckle?'

'Sorry, Savannah, not at the moment.' Mr Arbuckle didn't need another waitress.

Savannah positioned herself to see the newcomer's face. An anchor tattoo … the odd coloured eyes. She blanched.

'Bye, Mr Arbuckle, thanks anyway,' she mumbled. Savannah strode out of the diner, looking neither to the right or the left, her face set hard. The man glanced casually as she exited the restaurant. There was no recognition. Savannah was no longer that little girl in the hardware store. She was a young woman.

Savannah ran headlong down the street. Bursting through the front door, she tore inside as if being chased by demons. The screen door banged behind her.

'Savannah,' her mother called out from the kitchen. 'What on earth is your hurry, girl?'

'Nothing, Mom.'

Savannah raced to the dresser in the living room, reverently removing her father's old service pistol, a Colt 0.45 semi-automatic. Fred Steele had shown Savannah how to operate, load and fire the cumbersome weapon. She remembered her father's words: 'Remember, Sav, guns are only as bad as the people using them.'

Her hands shook as she pressed the release and checked the magazine. Full. Eight rounds. She grabbed her winter jacket off the coat stand and sprinted back to the diner.

The dusty Studebaker was still there. Savannah paused momentarily on the pavement, as she regained her composure. Her fingers explored the cold metal of the Colt, like a braille reader. Savannah knew from this moment on, her life would never be the same.

As calm as the judge of truth, Savannah stepped into the diner, her hand clasped around the gun in the pocket of her winter jacket.

'Back again, Sav?' Mr Arbuckle's face registered mild surprise.

Savannah faced her father's murderer. 'You probably don't remember me.'

Henry Kelly looked up at the young girl. He saw no threat. His female companion saw things differently. 'Piss off, you little twat.'

'Ethel, behave yourself, she's a bit young for me.' *On the other hand, maybe not.* 'Hi there, sweetie.' Henry gave a smile that incubated a leer.

Reaching into her coat pocket, Savannah pulled out the Colt and pointed it at Henry. 'You killed my dad.'

Kelly laughed. 'You're kiddi—'

The firing pin hit the cartridge primer of the First World War pistol. Perhaps it was just the Midwestern way of always doing a job properly. But for whatever reason, Henry's lifeless corpse lay with seven more slugs pumped into it. Somewhere between the first and the eighth shot, Ethel began screaming.

The report of the murder threw the sleepy sheriff's office of Pierre into a frenzy of unwelcome activity. Things like this didn't happen in their part of the world.

The wail of the police siren destroyed the serenity of the South Dakota summer day as the sheriff and his deputy roared up in their highway patrol Chevrolet.

The deputy had his gun drawn as he burst through the doors, only to be met by the sight of a calm and composed girl and a violently sobbing Ethel, who pointed a finger at Savannah and screamed, 'That's the little bitch, right there. She killed my Henry. In cold blood.'

The sheriff calmly surveyed the scene. He was an unflappable man and nobody's fool. There was something solemn swimming in his eyes as he unhurriedly assessed the carnage before him. The diner was now empty save for Savannah, Ethel, a white-faced Mr Arbuckle and a dead man identified as Henry.

'Chief, this's Savannah Steele. She's just a kid. Do I handcuff her, or what?' the young, inexperienced deputy asked.

Savannah had calmly waited for the sheriff. She had no regrets. No feeling of guilt. Henry's corpse now had a red checked tablecloth thrown over it. Savannah couldn't help thinking, *I hope they wash it before they use it again.*

The sheriff plonked down heavily on a bentwood chair and took off his peaked cap, throwing it onto a table. Leaning forward, his hands on his knees, he sighed. 'Why did you do it Savannah?'

'He killed my dad.'

The sheriff scratched his head as he fixed his gaze on this unlikely killer. He motioned the deputy to join him. 'See what's inside the Studebaker with the Alabama licence. It might throw some light on things.'

The deputy discovered a Thompson submachine gun and four handguns. Further investigation revealed a cotton bag marked Fidelity State Bank Arkansas, containing $10,000 in cash.

More enquiries were made. The Studebaker was stolen. The late Mr Kelly fitted the description of a masked man who'd held up a bank in Eureka Springs in Arkansas recently. Annoyed when the teller was a little tardy, Henry had shot him in the head. A reward of $5,000 had been offered for information leading to the identity of the murderer. Fourteen-year-old Savannah went from cold-blooded killer to heroine in double quick time and was the grateful and surprised recipient of the $5,000 reward. She became the toast of the town; in fact, the whole state. When it was discovered that Kelly was also wanted for crimes in other states as far away as Florida, she was interviewed on the television news. The TV reporter asked what her future plans were and sniggered when Savannah said she planned to go to college, then join the FBI. The reporter winked at the television audience. Everyone laughed. Savannah was not comfortable with her new-found fame. The experience could well have deterred a lesser person. But for Savannah, it created an implacable resolve to be on the frontline of crime fighting. She knew there were many Henry Kellys out there in the world. From that time on, Savannah learnt how to box. And later she learnt judo and jiu jitsu. But her special skill was the handgun.

MANHATTAN RHYTHM '55
Oh…
The hustle and bustle of people on the street,
Well-heeled women with tap-tap feet.
Gloves, hats, handbags; high-end design,
Nipped-in waists, fashions sublime.
Arm-in-arm strolling, immaculate ladies,
Kiss-kiss, shopping bliss, Barneys, Saks, Macys.

Skyscrapers, billboards, Manhattan Bridge looming,
Times Square, Theatre District, yellow cabs zooming.
Greenwich Village beckons with tempting wares,
Pizza, coffee, burgers; a myriad of fares.

Italians, Jews, Irish and Greeks,
A meld of cultures, harmonious on the streets.
Sightseeing trips to Ellis Island and more,
Lady Liberty shining to finish the tour.

But…
Street gangs, petty crime, underbelly of suffering,
Light/ shade, Yin/ Yang, down and outs shuffling.
Undercurrent, subculture of violence, thrill killing,
Mafia, bribes, money laundering; corrupt cops willing
To be paid off, take a bribe, look the other way.
Concrete shoes, so long pal, buried in the bay.

The scorpion aims its tail
And stings till you are dead,
Manhattan comes to life,
Be wary where you tread.

~Jennifer White

CHAPTER ONE

DEJA VU

The subway from Queens to Manhattan was crowded, a sea of humanity, dense and motley. A man sat hunched in a corner seat, leaning back against the chromed metal-panel partition. This didn't arouse the interest of the other passengers. This was New York and in the Big Apple, you didn't display too much interest in other people. Spencer Marlowe stirred in a moment of consciousness. He glanced around at the collection of subway passengers. The gaudy and the gorgeous. The officious, the timorous, the sophisticated, the bemused.

Where am I?

With a hiss and a clank of brakes, the subway train ground to a halt. The denizens of New York shuffled to the doors that opened wide and spilled onto the platform.

Spencer followed the teeming throng, looking for something familiar. *This isn't right.* He found himself surrounded by grey walls. Grey above. Grey below. Grey faces. A black tunnel. Yesterday's news, cigarette packets, candy wrappers and overflowing trash cans. He winced at the rancid odour of stale urine and unwashed bodies. A suspicious look, a sideways glance; were the faces of the city staring?

Where are the mobile phones? Everybody has a mobile. What on earth's going on? And the clothes! The hairstyles! Men with hats? Please, please, not again.

Spencer clambered up the subway stairs, his sense of foreboding increasing with every step. A light, drizzling rain greeted him as he emerged onto the sidewalk. Unaccustomed to the light, he squinted at the sign, *Canal Street Subway Station.* He was in New York.

Spencer peered in disbelief at his image reflected in the mirror of a furniture shop display. His check shirt looked fairly new. A chocolate-coloured creased and faded leather bomber jacket looked old as did the pleated nut-brown trousers and well-worn tan Oxford shoes. His apparel suggested another time. Clothing that had been a part of another life. *A life where? Did I have a life here in New York? For God's sake, who am I? Where have I been? Do I have family, friends, lovers?*

As he took shelter under an awning from the intermittent rain drops, he noticed a police officer studying him with some degree of interest. The officer's hand hovered menacingly over his 0.38 Smith and Wesson revolver. Navy blue peaked cap, navy blue shirt and tie. Law enforcement with a sixth sense for crime and criminality. *Time to move on, I guess. Why do I think that? I'm not a criminal.*

Spencer shuddered as he waited for the dream to end, inhabiting a twilight zone where sight, sound and smell existed in an ethereal nightmare. His survival instincts told him to move along … play the game … *It's not going to last. We're going out for breakfast. Michiyo said she wants to see Grand Central Station. I'd like to walk across the bridge to Brooklyn. There's just so much to see.*

But still the dream persisted like a nagging toothache that hammers away constantly, reminding you all's not well. Strolling along Canal Street, Spencer turned right into Broadway. The welcoming bright lights of a shop advertising Rolex watches grabbed his attention. He glanced at his wrist. No watch. *I had a Rolex.*

A moment of triumph as a sliver of memory returned to him. It was gold … and stainless steel; nice. A present. Someone important gave it to me.

A cold sweat beaded on Spencer's brow as he rummaged in desperation through his pockets. *This just isn't right. I must have something; papers, a passport?*

Nothing. Digging deeper, his hand wrapped around something hard with the crisp touch of paper. Spencer pulled the object out. *Curious; a money clip. Don't know how this got here, but thank God, I won't be starving any time soon. Over a hundred US bucks by the look of it.*

He quickly stashed it back in his pocket and out of sight. Then, his fingers tentatively touched a small metal object. *Silver. It looks familiar.* Spencer turned the object over and over. *I know this, I know it.* He was puzzled by the significance of what appeared to be some sort of lucky charm, but it felt strangely comforting. Slivers of memory gradually filtered through his mind. *It's going to come to me. It feels like I'm in a fog, a haze … as if … around the next bend the fog might lift. It is going to lift. Look. Yes … it's lifting. Things are a little clearer.*

Spirits now temporarily buoyed, Spencer kept walking although where he was going, he really didn't know. He began to pay more attention to his surroundings. *Well, it's definitely New York. But what am I doing here? How did I get here?*

Blarp, blarp. The harsh sound of a taxi's horn made him jump.

'Well, ya hoid dat, didn't ya?' the driver yelled in a broad New Jersey accent at a hapless pedestrian.

The unfamiliar, bulbous shape of the yellow Chevrolet cab caught Spencer's attention and he gazed, confused, at the sight of the vehicle. *What sort of car is that? Maybe it's some sort of special promotion? Looks like a cab, but it's old.* Spencer spotted the New York taxi medallion riveted to its bonnet. *Yep, definitely a New York cab. I don't get it.*

As he walked further along the street the rich smell of sauerkraut, onions, ketchup and mustard wafted temptingly towards him, making his mouth water. He soon noticed a street vendor selling hot dogs. *Nothing new there. Same old, same old.*

On the next corner a pretzel seller leaned out from his shoddily constructed stainless steel cart with its colourful umbrellas, to serve eager passers-by. Spencer felt some measure of comfort in the presence of these street traders, who might just as easily have belonged to his century. *But something isn't right, it's not a dream, it seems so real. Please, please, not again.*

His attention was grabbed by a day bill advertising *The New York Times* with the headline, 'Albert Einstein Dies'. Peering closer at the banner he could read the date, April 18, 1955. His mind whirled as he tried to find meaning in a sea of confusion.

Spencer continued to walk. He glanced at a sign, 'West Broadway'. He found himself in La Guardia Place. He paused again to gaze at the facades of the buildings, buildings that raced each other to touch the soft blue sky. Life here seemed upbeat and moving, a constant throng of people all set on going about their lives. *Keep walking, just keep walking. Maybe this New York dream will end.*

He felt the bite of a sudden chill wind and a shudder shot through his body like a small electric shock. He pulled his bomber jacket tighter around his chest. *This isn't a dream. Surely you don't feel cold in a dream?*

Now grasping the frightening truth, Spencer stumbled into Bleecker Street. The style of architecture had subtly changed from that of Broadway. This was different, more residential and with more restaurants. Spencer had no idea when he had last eaten, but by now he was very hungry.

Seventy years in the past.

Antonio's place looked inviting. A vibrant, multi-coloured canvas awning extended over the sidewalk. Bustling waiters dressed in black trousers, white shirts, black bow ties and aprons lent an aura of professionalism and class to the establishment. The blackboard menu boasted today's special, 'Reuben sandwich and coffee, bottomless cup only $1.99'. *Perfect.*

Spencer sank gratefully into the wicker chair on the sidewalk. Welcoming coals smouldered in the wrought iron brazier next to his table. He leant over, warming his hands. The simple experience of being at a restaurant and knowing a waiter would acknowledge his presence, in some way helped him regain his equilibrium. He was a person. Someone was going to attend to his needs. The panic that had threatened to overwhelm him started to subside, but he still felt as if he were riding an emotional roller coaster lurching between a dizzying sense of anxiety and a crushing loneliness … an unfathomable feeling of loss.

'Yes, sir, what'll it be?'

'The special please, with black coffee.'

Spencer smiled so warmly; the unsuspecting waiter immediately tensed, and his expression changed. Maybe the waiter thought he was a nut. After all, Greenwich Village had more than its fair share of crazies who thought they were Jesus Christ or the reincarnation of Abraham Lincoln.

The waiter smiled his professional smile, then whispered to a busboy, 'Hey Santo, just watch out for that beatnik, yeah, the one with leather jacket.' Spencer blinked; the waiter wasn't trying to keep quiet in the slightest. The waiter then cautioned a nearby server as he placed Spencer's order, making a twirling motion with his finger around his ear, like *watch out for poco loco there.*

Spencer shrugged as he heard the waiter's stage whisper. He had bigger things on his mind. Memories were slowly starting to filter through Spencer's mind, like shadowy figures darting in and out of his consciousness. At first just snippets, tantalising snatches of events. He remembered gazing out of the window of an aircraft as it descended into JFK. Michiyo peering excitedly out the window, straining to catch her first glimpses of the Big Apple.

'Spencer, just look, I can see the Statue of Liberty, I can't believe it. Over there, is that the Chrysler Building?' Michiyo, as always, was captivated by different cities and the new experiences and knowledge they brought her.

He remembered going through customs. Walking to the taxi rank. The taxi was a Nissan van. The driver had dreadlocks, a crocheted Rasta cap in colourful green, yellow, red and black layers. Friendly and chatty, he referred to his Caribbean birthplace in reverent tones. Spencer remembered the rhythmic cadence of his speech. 'Hey mon, where you goin'?' followed by a smile as wide as the Brooklyn Bridge. 'My name Winston.'

Spencer had winked at Michiyo, both of them intrigued by the language of this cheerful Rastafarian. 'We want the Langham please … Midtown.'

'A wah ya baan?'

'Sorry … come again?'

The driver had laughed. Spencer remembered his laugh; long, low and musical. 'Sorry mon, dat Rasta speak, where you from eh?'

'We're from Australia.' It'd been Spencer's turn to laugh.

'It still amazing to mi dat the iron bird can fly inna di sky suh easy.' The driver whistled.

The friendly Winston had peppered them with questions about Australia. Michiyo had given Winston a ten-dollar tip on the thirty-five-dollar fare.

'Praise, Jah.' Winston had beamed.

Spencer remembered a light drizzling rain falling as they had stepped out of the cab. The traffic, the people, the advertising, the relentless energy of the city that never sleeps. The city representing more things to more people than any other city in the world; fashion, the arts, the high finance of Wall Street. New York seemed like the centre of the universe.

A moment of blankness. *When was this, think, think, then what came after that?*

Once again, the feeling of dread, of terror as he'd thought, what's happening to me? Staccato drops of rain, puddles, the rumble of traffic. *The Langham, porters, bell boys, a tip, how much? Not sure.*

As Spencer thrust his hand into his pocket, seizing the silver *cornicello*, a torrent of memories swept through his consciousness ... *Oh no. Oh, my God, Michiyo.* With a jolt, memories flooded back. He'd flown to New York with his wife Michiyo in the year ... what year, 2014, maybe 2015? He couldn't quite remember. Spencer felt his stomach turn. Little by little chunks of memory, like pieces from an elaborate jigsaw, tumbled into place.

Spencer was so absorbed by his returning memories that he hadn't paid attention to the black Cadillac limousine that had glided silently up to the restaurant. The driver pulled slickly into an available space. Two muscular, heavy-set men of swarthy Italian appearance stepped out. Their watchful gazes appeared to scan the street like radars, searching for potential threat. One of the men opened the rear door of the limo. An impeccably groomed middle-aged man, also of Italian appearance, alighted. He glanced in Spencer's direction, a look of annoyance crossing his smoothly shaved face. He whispered to one of the two men. As if programmed, they strode purposefully to Spencer's table, exuding muscles and menace. 'Scram bud, this is Mr Romano's table.'

Spencer turned his attention to this unwanted intrusion. He was hungry, unhappy, and certainly in no mood for this thuggish-looking man telling him to move. His memory was returning and his predicament was becoming more apparent with every second.

Spencer fixed the thugs with a baleful stare. Right at this moment, his sandwich and coffee had become the centre of his universe. It was his Christmas, birthday and Thanksgiving all rolled into one. These overfed Italian popinjays, who had strutted up to his table throwing their not inconsiderable weight around, were rapidly moving into dangerous territory. Spencer glanced again at the friendly glow from the coals in the brazier. *Clearly this is where the big shot expects to be sitting. Well … not today.*

Under normal circumstances Spencer was affable, friendly and obliging. He stared at the scowling apparitions before him and saw two muscular, stout, well-dressed, overbearing gangsters who were used to getting their own way. Spencer mentally labelled the heavyweights 'Thug One' and 'Thug Two'. He ran a jaundiced eye over Thug One: big, but running to fat, confident, eyes flat and lifeless like a hammerhead. This man, Spencer decided, was someone so steeped in violence, the casual act of murder wouldn't raise a sweat or the merest twinge of remorse. A loud pinstripe double-breasted navy-blue suit, black and white Oxford shoes and a hand-painted tie featuring a well-endowed lady in a hula skirt, was in a word … what? Spencer thought for a moment … In a word … mobster. He laughed inwardly, wondering fleetingly if there were a store somewhere advertising, 'We have everything for the well-dressed gangster'.

Casting a quick glance at Thug Two, the first and most distinguishing feature was a large nose, red, veined and lacking a solid formation, as if a lump of putty had been stuck on the face as an afterthought. Thug Two was equally large, loudly tailored and with the same flat, hard eyes. Spencer smiled at the garish gold ring with an ostentatious green stone on the thug's ring finger. Expensive yet tasteless, like the man himself.

Generally, it took a lot to get Spencer angry, but the well-dressed Mafiosi couldn't have picked a worse time to antagonise him. His eyes narrowed. 'Sorry, what's the problem?'

'This is where Mr Romano sits. Beat it.'

Spencer noticed Thug Two had joined his comrade, standing close in battle formation. Any normal person would have quailed at the sight. He noticed the bulge in their well-cut jackets. *Of course, they would have shoulder holsters. Don't do this to yourself pal, or you're going to have a very bad day.*

At any other time just maybe, Spencer may have complied. But today he was simply not in the mood. At that moment he had become oblivious to consequences.

'Guess what fellas? Today Mr Romano will have to sit somewhere else … but the good news is … tomorrow he can sit wherever he wants. Sadly, not now. Bugger off, cos I haven't had a great day and you're annoying me.'

'Hey, Nose, a scemo. Whadya reckon?' Thug one laughed at his partner.

'Yep, a *succhiacazzi*, One Shot,' the other man grinned.

Spencer rose from his seat, smiling companionably at the predictable insults. The man named One Shot aimed a powerful right at Spencer's jaw. He shifted sideways, grabbing the well-manicured fist, jerking it forward, using the thug's considerable momentum.

Spencer stifled a yawn. 'Really guys, is this the best you've got?'

A vicious kick to his right leg, and the thug dropped as if the ground had disappeared. As a coup de grace, a potentially lethal karate chop slammed onto his neck. The thug's eyes bulged, and then it was lights out. Right at that moment, Spencer didn't care if the thug lived or died. He was floating in an ethereal, twilight world where he still wasn't sure what reality was and what was fantasy.

For a moment, Nose seemed stunned by the sight of his comrade sprawled unconscious on the ground. Bellowing like an enraged bull, he lunged forward, only to be stopped in his tracks by Spencer's elbow, spreading his already malleable nose even further around his face. Nose hesitated as blood gushed from his mangled proboscis, spilling down over his exquisite tailoring. Spencer held up a warning hand. 'I can play this game for hours, pal, but I'd suggest that unless you really enjoy pain, quit while you're still standing.'

It seemed Nose did enjoy pain. With both paw-like hands outstretched, he lunged at Spencer's throat, roaring, '*Figlio di puttana.*'

Spencer couldn't help himself as laughter got the better of him. 'Oh, dear sweetheart, this just isn't your day, is it?'

Although not textbook and definitely not part of Spencer's karate repertoire, he blocked the lunging Nose, opting for a tried-and-true solid kick to the groin. Nose dropped to the ground with a sickening thud, at that point appearing to have lost all interest in prolonging the altercation.

Meanwhile, a mildly amused Romano observed the events unfold, watching his two bodyguards as they slowly came to their senses. Nose sat up awkwardly, scowling at Spencer and muttering unintelligible curses. His hand reached inside his coat.

'Don't be stupid Gino,' snapped Romano. 'Not the time or the place. Now get Louie up. Grab a cab. Beat it.'

'Sorry boss.'

Romano shook his head in disgust as the two bodyguards limped off in search of a taxi. Turning to Spencer he smiled and held out his hand. 'Tony Romano.'

'Spencer Marlowe.' Spencer gazed warily at the proffered hand.

'Mind if I sit?' Romano pointed to the seat next to Spencer.

'Sure.' Spencer shrugged, sensing no immediate danger.

Spencer warily summed up the crime lord. The musky, citrus odour of 4711 cologne glided into his nostrils. He paid closer attention to the subtle but expensive Brooks Brothers threads that also adorned millionaires in every board room and country club across the USA. Romano wore a single-breasted dark blue suit paired with a white silk shallow-collared shirt. The ends of the collar were fixed by a gold safety pin beneath the Windsor knot of the colourful hand-painted tie. The socks were grey silk and the expensive brogues were polished to a high lustre. Sadly, the look didn't quite cross the divide between corporate business man and well-dressed gangster.

Romano placed his black narrow-brimmed homburg with its wide claret ribbon carefully on a spare chair. His fawn cashmere coat he threw casually over the back of the chair. Fixing Spencer with a momentary stare, Spencer felt Romano's coal-black eyes bore right through his face and to the back of his skull. Romero clicked his fingers at a hovering server who stood nervously by.

'Yes sir, Mr Romano, what can I get for you?'

'What are you having, Marlowe?'

'The Reuben.'

'Good choice. They do the best Reuben in Manhattan here. I'll have the same and the coffee. Put it all on my bill.'

'Of course, Mr Romano.' The waiter bowed.

Spencer raised an eyebrow. Why would this powerful crime lord suddenly be turning on the charm? 'You don't have to pay for my lunch.'

'Think nothing of it. Look at it as a sort of apology.' Romano waved a hand.

'Apology?'

'Yeah, well my boys got a little out of hand,' he chuckled. 'They didn't seem to be a problem for you.'

In spite of his better judgement, Spencer found the Don to be effervescent and charming. 'As far as guarding bodies are concerned, maybe you didn't make the wisest of choices.'

'Well,' Tony shook his head, smiling ruefully. 'I thought up until now they were the best. But that's what I want to talk to you about.'

The waiter scurried back to the table with their order. Spencer had forgotten just how hungry he was. *When did I last eat?* The sandwich really was superb; rye bread, a particularly robust Russian dressing, paired with the nutty taste of Swiss cheese, chunky rough-cut corned beef and a subtle yet tangy sauerkraut. Romano watched on in amusement. 'You look like you haven't eaten in days.'

'Feels like a hundred years,' Spencer said through a mouthful of crusty rye.

For the next ten minutes both men made small talk as they enjoyed their food. Then Romano pushed back his chair, extracting a silver cigar case from his jacket and carefully removing a half corona. 'Cigar, Marlowe?'

'Thank you, no.'

The ever-attentive waiter sprang forward, cigar lighter and cutter in hand. Romano leaned back in his chair puffing contentedly. The smoke twirled heavenward. Spencer didn't get cigars. As far as he was concerned, the stench could best be described as Satan passing wind.

'Impressive.' Romano shook his head, continuing to study Spencer as if he was an exotic zoological exhibit. 'Yep, I've known some good street fighters, in fact, if I do say so myself, I was pretty good in my day … but you seem to have … I don't know what you'd call it, but it's a style of fighting I haven't seen before.' He pointed the Cohiba at Spencer. 'I've got a proposition for you.' With great relish he blew out a cloud of fragrant smoke.

'Go on.' Spencer drank the last of his coffee, puzzled at this turn of events.

'How would you like to work for me?'

'Doing what?'

The Don examined the glowing end of his cigar, carefully tapping the ash into an ashtray depicting the sartorially elegant Johnny Walker striding across its base. 'The way you handled Louie and Gino, like I said, it was pretty impressive. I thought they were the best and …' He shrugged, as if that explained thing.

'I beat up two of your guys and you want to hire me?' Spencer was incredulous. He couldn't help himself; he laughed out loud at the absurdity of the situation.

'I don't like being laughed at.' Romano's icy stare chilled Spencer to the core.

Spencer scrutinised the expensively clad and coiffured Don. *I'll just bet you've gone to a lot of time and expense to camouflage your humble beginnings and working-class mannerisms.* 'Sorry, believe me it's not personal, but surely you can understand the humour of it all?'

'My card.' It seemed that Tony Romano didn't have a sense of humour. He glanced at his Patek Philippe watch, a bleak expression on his face. 'Sleep on it and call me tomorrow. But I gotta tell you, I don't handle rejection well.'

CHAPTER TWO

A VERY WANTED MAN

Spencer studied the black card with its embossed gold lettering. 'Tony Romano—Imports and Exports' A phone number 'Business by Appointment only.' Just what exactly would he be importing and exporting?

Romano abruptly rose to his feet, peeling several bills from a substantial billfold, without a backward glance he strode purposefully towards his waiting limousine. The driver jumped out, flinging open the door. Spencer shook his head in bewilderment. *Stranger than fiction.*

Spencer's eyes followed the Cadillac as it silently sped off down the street, its tail fins looking like the dorsals of a white pointer shark. *Only in America. What now? Where to go? What to do?* Spencer enjoyed the sunshine that now bathed the brownstones and apartment blocks in a gentle apricot light. There was a reminder of the earlier rain with clouds swirling like gauzy curtains. Certainly, he decided the world looked a more cheerful with a full stomach and the comforting feeling of the money clip nestling securely in his pocket. And as for the crime lord and his lackeys? Out of sight and out of mind.

Spencer now turned his gaze to his surroundings. The restaurant, he decided, was definitely upper crust.

There was nothing out of place. Every flower was colour coordinated and arranged perfectly. Every blindingly white tablecloth pressed to an inch of its life. His hand strayed to his pocket, making sure his limited funds were still intact. Spencer was in no hurry, he had nowhere to go, and he was enjoying the ambience. Time to do some people watching.

Spencer was used to the casual chic of the next century. But here in New York 1955, silks, satins and furs abounded. Every man wore a hat and tie. One such man caught Spencer's attention. Sitting quietly at another table, also enjoying the pleasant spring weather, engrossed in the *New York Times* was a sober suited gentleman, a regular New Yorker, perhaps?

From his pork pie hat, his nondescript houndstooth three quarter length jacket, his pale fawn pleated chinos, check polo shirt, basket weave, loafer shoes and Argyle socks, he really could have been anybody from anywhere. *What am I missing? He just doesn't fit.*

'Could be a tourist from Nebraska taking in the sights?' he mused, 'No, hang on. A lawyer, I reckon that's it.' Spencer motioned the waiter for another cup of coffee. He figured since he'd been a guest of El Mobster, they wouldn't hustle him out too quickly. 'An accountant. Gotta be an accountant. Or an academic. Boring as batshit. Yep, gotta be.'

One could certainly imagine a life of academia. Studious. Unquestionably law abiding, a man unaccustomed to violence or the seamier side of life. He was average in the purest sense of the word. Average height. Average build. His light brown buzz cut, greying at the edges, suggested life in the burbs, the little woman at home and two point three obedient children. A man who frowned upon extravagance. In a word, forgettable.

Spencer observed as the man placed a quarter, nickel and a dime onto the check, now flattened in front of him. *Big spender here.* He climbed to his feet, stretched, ambling towards Spencer's table. 'Mind if I join you?'

Looks fit? He's gotta be selling something? Spencer ran his eyes over the casually dressed smiling man in front of him. *There must be something about me?*

'Be my guest.' Spencer indicated the chair vacated by the Italian-American crime lord.

Searching through his pockets the man produced a packet of Lucky Strikes and a battered stainless-steel Ronson lighter; he proffered the packet to Spencer. 'Cigarette?'

Spencer shook his head, continuing to appraise the new arrival. *This guy is trying to appear nondescript, but there's rather more here than meets the eye. He's trying too hard to be nothing.* Spencer waited patiently for the ritual of the cigarette to be completed, the tapping of the end. of it, the cupped hands stopping the breeze from blowing out the flame of the lighter. Then the obvious reward as the first plume of smoke was exhaled. As a red convertible with four teenagers crawled past, Spencer heard a soulful voice from the car radio warbling something about being a great pretender. There was a silence as the mystery man studied Spencer, his unblinking steel grey eyes were computing, dissecting and calculating. *I'm beginning to feel a little like the strange specimen in the zoo. I think his bullshit meter is running hard into the red zone.*

Spencer's antenna was now gaining focus. It's the eyes, he decided, hard and wary. He's not at all what he appears to be. Whoever he is, I don't think he's a threat. But as they say in Latin 'paratus' be prepared. Then abruptly there was a hand thrust towards Spencer, a broad smile appeared, as if he had miraculously received a CT scan of Spencer's inner workings and was satisfied with the results.

'Dale Fletcher.'

'Spencer Marlowe.'

'I was very impressed with the way you … neutralised Lou "One Shot" Palazzo and Gino "the Nose" Petrelli.'

It clicked; this guy was law enforcement. 'I didn't know their names. Obviously, you do. Why the interest?'

Fletcher chuckled, reaching into his coat pocket, producing a leather billfold. On one flap was a Department of Justice logo. In big bold black letters FBI and a photo of an unsmiling Dale Fletcher. Dale thrust the ID back into his coat pocket. 'As it happens, these guys don't exactly keep a low profile. Tony Romano is the godfather of the Romano crime family. Those two meat-heads are his loyal body guards; perhaps ex-bodyguards after you embarrassed them.'

Spencer leaned back, his arms folded, still appraising the affable FBI agent. There was no doubt in Spencer's mind that he was who he said he was, but why exactly the interest? Dale Fletcher had all the enthusiasm of a Boy Scout trying for his first merit badge. Spencer pointed to his cup. 'Waiter, may I have a refill?' He turned his attention to Fletcher. 'And you?'

'Please.' Fletcher nodded at the waiter.

So, it seems this is more than a desire to congratulate. 'I can feel a punchline coming.'

Spencer couldn't help reflecting on the difference between the attitude of the man who was the face of organised crime in Manhattan and this earnest Government man, trying to woo him by appealing to his better nature. All in all, Spencer decided Dale Fletcher was a lot less scary than the urbane Don.

Dale pulled his chair forward, glancing around to make sure no one was in earshot, leaning forward his arms on the table. 'How would you feel about working with us to take these guys down?'

'You're not serious?

'Serious as a heart attack.'

'I've only been in town a few hours and I've had two job offers, from both sides of the divide.' Spencer shook his head and for the second time broke into laughter.

As in his previous forays into the past Spencer felt as if an unseen hand was propelling him into events and situations that had danger written all over them.

'We've been looking for someone like you.' Fletcher lit up another cigarette and took his time exhaling the smoke. People here in the past rushed their lives a bit less, and Spencer rather enjoyed that. 'Do you have a job. What's your situation? You're not American.'

'No, Australian, and I could possibly be looking for a job. But something tells me that someone like Romano plays for keeps and I could wind up seriously dead.'

'We'd look after you. The pay's good.' Dale's enthusiasm was certainly infectious. Spencer gazed at the FBI man sensing that he was a decent honest defender of truth, justice and the American way, and every other appropriate cliché.

Spencer was still feeling disoriented, but minute by minute his memory was returning, a little like a thousand-piece jigsaw with some pieces still missing.

Dale changed the subject. 'How long have you been in New York? How long have you been in the States? What's your background? Have you been in the military? Do you follow the Knicks, the Giants, the Yankees or even the God damn Dodgers?'

'Hold on, hold on.' Spencer laughed again, holding both hands up. 'Look, right at the moment I have a few things to sort out. I really don't see myself as an agent for the FBI. But never say "never", ok?'

Dale appeared disappointed, draining the last of his coffee. 'Here's my card. Give it some thought. My number's there. Call me. I tell you; it was a tonic seeing you take down two of the toughest hoods in Manhattan.'

Spencer took the card. The two men parted with a vigorous handshake. Dale strolled unhurriedly towards Broadway. Spencer studied the card before sliding it into his pocket. He was well aware that a computer-literate marketing man from the twenty-first century had limited scope in 1950s America, and right now he needed to think about a job and getting a roof over his head.

This was now the third time Spencer had been transported back to the past. There wasn't quite the same sense of desolation he'd felt the first time when he'd to come to terms with being in the Australian Army in 1942. He'd come to learn he was completely on his own. He could confide in no one. His positive mental conditioning instilled in him by his *sensei*, Katashi, made it possible to adapt quickly to his changed circumstances. Katashi's training imparted not only superb reflexes but also mental conditioning, enabling him to deal with the emotional aspect of being thrust into another century, where he'd had to rely on his wits. The bad guys were real, death had been a constant companion.

With his memory restored, Spencer strolled from the restaurant and set off to explore bohemian Greenwich Village.

CHAPTER THREE

WHAT'S GOING DOWN?

'This is so exciting! New York City. I can't believe I'm here.' Michiyo had been delighted to be in the Big Apple. It was cold, damn cold. The 34th street hotel lobby was illuminated with a soft and welcoming light as visitors bustled around the reception desk. Suitcases, lots of suitcases. A small child wailed.

The bellhop chattered as the high-speed lift whisked them to their floor high above Manhattan.

'Michiyo I'm beat, I'm going to have a nap.' Her disappointment was clear.

'You go exploring, we'll meet up afterwards.' Spencer hastily assured her.

'Well, Spencer, my old man husband, if you can be boring so can I.' Putting her arms around his neck, she kissed him passionately.

'Never boring, but let's hear it.' Spencer had retorted with a grin.

'I'm going to grab that bloody hard taskmistress of mine, the laptop, and finish those reports and forward projections for work.' Michiyo shook her head in mock despair. 'I appreciate climbing the corporate ladder, but by God they want their pound of steak.'

'Actually, that's flesh. It's from the Merchant of Venice.'

'Who? What?'

'Shakespeare, famous author. Merchant of Venice and all that.'

Michiyo rolled her eyes. 'This may come as a surprise but Shakespeare did find his way to Japan. Anyhow, steak, meat, flesh, who cares?'

'But then if the little princess is still asleep, guess where I'm headed?' Michiyo held up a warning finger.

Spencer managed a weak smile.

'I'm going to Saks to buy some sexy lingerie'

She sauntered suggestively out of the room, laptop in hand, and blew him a kiss as she closed the door.

This was the last thing he remembered before the subway. And then despair, a numb feeling of helplessness, and the devastating pain of loss had washed over Spencer in waves. Bitterness was certainly an emotion to be dealt with. Sink or swim there was nobody to turn to.

Spencer walked with the leisurely gait of a man with somewhere to go, but was in no particular hurry to get there. His mind flashed back to his two previous sojourns into the past.

Cast back into 1942 Wartime Australia when he had found himself involved in a dangerous mission in Japanese occupied Singapore. There he'd met where he had the privilege of meeting and working with a youthful Lee Kuan Yew and the brave but troubled Trilby Lim.

His comrades had voyaged to Singapore on a captured Japanese fishing boat to join him. They teamed up with the resistance and had sunk enemy ships in Singapore harbour, thwarting an invasion of Australia.

With the war coming to an end, Spencer finally accepted he was probably stuck back in time forever, he woke inexplicably one morning in the correct time once more. He found himself returned to his century, back with the love of his life, Michiyo. He and Michiyo had decided to get married, a quiet and romantic affair on a beach in Hawaii.

Before their nuptials Spencer once again found himself in 1941 Hawaii, prior to the Japanese attack on Pearl Harbor. There in Hawaii he'd ended up in much the same situation, wondering if he would ever return to his soon-to-be bride. He'd once again gone to sleep, waking to find himself back with Michiyo. For Michiyo only one night had elapsed, yet for Spencer he'd been in the past for a year.

Spencer had hoped that his time travelling days were behind him. He knew he'd have to learn and learn quickly, how to survive, surrounded by a different set of rules. He knew to stay alive it was imperative to find allies.

CHAPTER FOUR

THE EMPEROR'S WRATH

New York, New York. Still not completely accepting he was here in the last century, and not knowing for how long, Spencer looked around, scanned his surroundings and spied a payphone. Its glass and timber construction looked like it belonged on the set of a Superman movie. He could imagine Clark Kent, saying, 'Excuse me but I have an emergency.'

He rummaged through the still unfamiliar coins in his pocket and found a nickel. *You can only deal with the cards you've been dealt.* He spent a few minutes examining the strange apparatus. *How in hell does this work?* Grabbing the handset, he dropped the coin in the slot and dialled. It rang twice.

'Talk to me.'

'Tony, I've given your kind offer of employment a lot of thought. Thanks, but no thanks ...' Silence, for a long time. 'You there Tony?'

'As I said, Marlowe, I don't handle rejection well.' More silence, then a click.

Spencer chuckled as he hung up the phone. Seriously, what a jerk. 'I don't handle rejection well.' Very sad, sunshine, but you're just going to have to get over it. I've got bigger problems than a petulant New York gangster.

Spencer set off to explore 1955 New York City. He strolled down millionaires' row: Fifth Avenue. He studied a display of new season spring wear and a range of Jacquard patterned sweaters in Saks, which probably cost a week's wages for the average working Joe. Glancing in the Tiffany and Bergdorf Goodman windows only increased his melancholy; he recalled he and Michiyo had intended to browse these famous stores. He felt more comfortable when he found himself in the more downmarket Greenwich Street and then Waverley. There in front of him stood Washington Square Arch. He found comfort at the sight of this historic piece of architecture, built in 1892 to commemorate George Washington's inauguration. *It's as if time has stood still. All of those years ago, it's still here. Time doesn't seem to have a lot of meaning, particularly for me.*

Dawdling through the Washington Square Park, he felt some of the angst washing away. He studied the other park visitors, watching as their city attitudes succumbed to a new world of elm, oak and a rolling carpet of lawn. this green enclave was a wonderful and welcome oasis in frenetic Manhattan. As if by magic, any moisture from the showers had disappeared. There were couples sitting on benches having lunch, others sprawled on the lawn, some sleeping or reading newspapers.

He paused to cast an eye over the statue of the Italian patriot Garibaldi. A group of chess players sat immovable, pondering the intricacies of the ancient game. A man stood playing a Brahms violin sonata, a bowler hat placed strategically in front of him. His ragged appearance in stark contrast to his obvious mastery of the instrument. He had the appearance of a down and out, clearly lost in his own world. The beautiful arias poured out of his battered violin. Truly a virtuoso, delighting passers-by with his interpretations of timeless classical pieces. As Spencer stood entranced. *What's your story, friend? Why aren't you in Carnegie Hall playing with the New York Philharmonic?*

Appreciative passers-by had already filled the bowler to overflowing with dimes, nickels and quarters. Spencer fished through his trouser pockets, finding a silver dollar and throwing it into the hat. The violinist, an elderly Italian gentleman, smiled in acknowledgement of the generous gratuity.

That's a dollar well spent. Absolutely awesome. The soothing sounds of Brahms continued to restore Spencer's wellbeing as he wandered out of the park onto Waverley Place. On the corner stood a hotel that clearly had seen better days. The Hotel Earle. The sight of this rundown hostelry dissipated the beauty of the music of Brahms, bringing his new reality home with a jolt.

Everything about this hostelry shrieked neglect and decay. Gingerly, Spencer entered. Of the two glass panelled entrance doors one pane had been smashed so that the sign that'd been etched into the glass now read *el Earle* the *Hot* being left to the imagination. Roughhewn ply had been hastily nailed over the broken pane. The reception had worn linoleum on the floor, its frayed edges creating a safety hazard. *Somehow, I don't think you can afford the Waldorf Astoria right at the moment.*

Behind the battered reception desk parked an oafish man, with a round unshaven chubby face and small beady eyes, that darted from side to side avoiding contact. He wore a dirty white shirt with a detachable collar. The shirt looked as if the collar had been detached some years ago. Stitched over the pocket was the faded logo, *Hotel Earle* and the extravagant promise, *Share a great experience.*

'Yeah really … aha, you don't say? Well, he's the boss, you're lucky you still got a job. So, tell me again, what's this klutz's name? Aha, yeah gotcha. Yeah sure, if I hear anything … you'll be the first. And tell me, your wife did what? Really?'

Spencer stood patiently as the big man didn't acknowledge his presence. An unlit stogie glued to his mouth, he was engrossed in his telephone conversation. 'Yeah, and you keep telling me your wife's an angel. You're lucky, mine's still alive. Yeah, yeah, really? It's your twentieth wedding anniversary. How about that.' He stuck his tongue out in a grimace, putting his hand over the receiver, grinning at Spencer. 'Twenty years. You don't get that for murder … Sorry Lou, gotta go … customer. You wanna room, huh?'

'Please.'

'Three bucks a night, two if you're staying a week. In advance, ok? Write your name in the register. Luggage?'

'No.'

'Lessee here. What's the name? Eyesight ain't what it was. Marlowe, huh?'

Spencer nodded and paid for a week.

'End of the corridor. Take the elevator. Fourth floor. Room 413.'

This really hit Spencer with a jolt. A grubby hotel and life in another century. No job and no prospects, unless you counted his job offer with the mob. This was the downside of Babylon. For those with little or no money it was a world far removed from Fifth Avenue and the land of luxurious hotel suites, with attentive staff seeing to your every need.

The antiquated lift, with its steel cage, rattled and wheezed its way to the fourth floor. Spencer jerked the worn wrought iron door open, before him a dingy corridor with a worn stained carpet runner. Voices raised in anger blasted from one of the rooms, the thin lathe and plaster construction no match for the angry voices. Spencer now regretted his choice of lodgings, it dawned on him that $100 was a tidy sum in 1955. *Perhaps next week something a little more salubrious?*

A radio, broadcasting Bing Crosby's dulcet tones crooning about Ireland, filtered through from another. Spencer wouldn't have known or even cared but the down at heels Hotel Earle had already played host to such luminaries as Dylan Thomas and Ernest Hemingway. And in years to come, the likes of Bo Diddley, Bob Dylan, even the Rolling Stones.

The seedy hotel drove home Spencer's predicament. He thought of Michiyo sauntering through Saks, examining exotic lingerie, lingerie he may never see. The pain he felt was physical, like a pile-driving blow to his chest, a pain that just didn't diminish. He momentarily braced himself against the mean-stained plaster wall, closing his eyes, telling himself this was his new reality. *You can only play the cards you've been dealt.*

Greeting Spencer was a single steel framed bed with a faded chenille spread and a pillow with a cover that looked like it'd never been washed. The linoleum was a rainbow of browns, with a path worn from countless feet from the door to the bed. A chipped enamel water jug sat on a scarred wooden dressing table, embellished with previous guests initials haphazardly scratched into the surface. He shuddered at the depressing surrounds.

At reception, the desk clerk was on the phone again. 'Mr Romano, this's Roy from the Hotel Earle. Friend of Louie. I'm real sorry to bother you … but Lou … Yeah … Lou said to call you direct. Yeah, yeah, Hotel Earle, Greenwich Village. That fella you were looking for has just checked in. Yeah, Marlowe, yeah, that's right. Tall guy. That's the one. Yeah, thanks Mr Romano, glad to help.'

CHAPTER FIVE

LET'S DO DINNER

Darkness descended. Greenwich Village came alive. Like a vogue model, hard, glittery, wanting to be heard. A modern Jerusalem. A thousand cultures, fighting, scrambling, for a piece of the American dream.

Realising hunger once again was causing tummy rumbles, Spencer wandered down Bleecker Street. *Oh boy, look at this and doesn't it smell appetising?* He'd managed to dredge up some of his old optimism. Everything, he reasoned, had a purpose. He knew for now at least; he had to try and compartmentalise his old life. Move on. This was real. *Someday, I just know this madness will disappear. Meanwhile, eat drink and be merry. Well merry may be a bit of a stretch.*

Spencer paused at the front of John's Pizza. Checking his money, he still had ninety-one dollars a quarter, two dimes and a nickel. *That'll pay for a pizza.* The fragrant aroma accelerated his awakening taste buds. The appearance of this homely Italian Pizzeria with its white aproned waiters bustling around was like a flame to his moth. He fell into a vacant seat under the awning at the front.

'Pizza calzone, please and a large, very cold beer.'

The calzone pizza in Spencer's view was seriously underrated. You had the ever-popular margarita and capriccioso, but a good calzone, well that was something else. This one was as good as it gets; pillowy dough folded over, concealing the mouth-watering combination of pepperoni and Mozzarella cheese.

This one had something special a subtle herb or spice that had a tang. Just the sight of this Mediterranean masterpiece sitting placidly on his plate waiting to be devoured was enough to dispel any feelings of gloom. The dough a perfect consistency, with tell-tale miniature burn marks on its outer edge. The wood fired pizza oven had been at just the correct temperature, the sight, the smell was … wow … *This is great, Michiyo would just love it.*

The beer was one Spencer had never heard of: 'Hamm's of Minnesota'. Spencer emptied the glass tankard in two big gulps. *There's no doubt about it, a nice meal improves your view of the world.* Finishing off with a double espresso Spencer felt more positive.

Strolling down Bleecker Street, certainly in no hurry to return to his squalid accommodation, Spencer was unaware of the Nash Rambler following slowly at a discreet distance. Lost in thought, he wandered off Bleeker Street into New York's no man's land.

Pacing resolutely behind him were two lean swarthy gentlemen wearing garish zoot suits, the latest addition to the well-dressed gangster's wardrobe.

Oblivious to his entourage, Spencer ambled into the dimly lit, bleak and narrow Mott Street. Rough cobblestones and decayed buildings made it look like a war zone. Even the trees seemed hunched, standing tired and forlorn. A chill wind stirred a miserable pile of litter, cigarette butts and newspapers, which added to the impression of urban decay. The odd streetlamp that worked, projected little circles of white light onto this street of despair. Spencer pulled his jacket tighter, his hands thrust deep into his pockets. A momentary feeling of unease—then the *clack-clack* of leather on stone—the determined stride of men in a hurry.

'How ya doin'?' A menacing voice growled.

Startled, Spencer's immediate instinct was to strike, but he realised a man in a garish yellow suit had a revolver pressed into his side. Another man in an equally outrageous purple suit also had a pistol. Spencer mentally cursed himself for this rare lapse in concentration. A saloon car bounced to a halt. Out strutted Gino the Nose, a conspicuous bandage covered his deformed proboscis. His two black eyes gave him the appearance of an unhappy panda cub. 'You're coming with us Marlowe.'

'I'm glad to see you brought your nose along, Gino. I need a good laugh.'

The hard flat eyes registered nothing. 'Get in the automobile.'

Spencer gazed at the two hard faces on either side of him. No joy here. Big. Stolid. Unflappable. Unimaginative and very dangerous.

Even with his formidable skills he knew with the revolvers jammed into his side there was no chance. 'Purple suit' opened the door. Spencer hoped the gangster might be distracted, leaving him the slightest window of opportunity to unleash fists elbows or even feet. The gunman's hand was unwavering. The demeanour suggested kidnapping someone off a New York Street was absolutely routine. Spencer's reflexes were extraordinary, but he knew the thug had only to squeeze the trigger and it would be game over.

The driver released the clutch and the Nash Rambler crept forward, the radio an indistinct blur in the background. 'Hey Frankie, toin up de radio,' the thick accent made "turn" sound like "toin", 'Yogi Berra's battin. I got a sawbuck on dis one.'

Spencer had piled into the back with a zoot-suiter on either side. The Nash headed in the direction of the Brooklyn Bridge. The men sat in silence, the only sounds being the clunk of gears changing, the squelch of the clutch and the low murmur from the valve radio. Spencer had no idea where they were, but he knew he was in big trouble. Neither Gino, the driver, nor the other thugs felt inclined to chat.

Spencer's mind raced furiously. If ever there was a good time to wake up from a bad dream this'd be it. He dwelt for a moment on what he'd arranged for the day. He and Michiyo had planned to do the sights. Go to the top of the Empire State building. Explore the magnificent Grand Central Station; stroll across the Brooklyn Bridge. If the weather was clement, he'd planned to go to Central Park and lunch in Loeb's Boathouse. *Instead, I'm travelling in a vehicle on my way to a very unpleasant experience. Perhaps a terminal one.*

Spencer tried to make sense of it. Romano hadn't seemed particularly upset about his bodyguards being made to look foolish. His main beef seemed to the fact that Spencer had declined his offer of employment. *Surely you don't kill a man just for that ...? Do you?*

There was total silence from the men in the automobile. The bright lights of Broadway only increased his melancholy as the Nash made its way across Manhattan. His hopes leapt as he spied two police officers astride their Harley Davidsons. Perhaps he could signal them.

'Don't even think about it.' The revolver was jammed even harder into his ribs.

Spencer thought the route they were taking was unnecessarily circuitous. *Is this to throw off someone tailing us?*

The Nash rolled along the bustling canyons of downtown, the luminous glow of skyscrapers shirtfronting each other.

Spencer was intrigued to see Times Square. The only things that'd changed from his century were the vehicles, the fashions, and the advertising: Admiral Televisions, Canadian Club Whisky and the latest movie, 'Blackboard Jungle' starring Glen Ford.

He'd been able to see the Chrysler Building. Up Fifth Avenue. The Flatiron Building, and Macy's.

Spencer remembered Michiyo was heading there to shop. This only served to increase his sense of despair. Glancing at his two back seat captors, he could see no hint of compassion in their hard faces. This he thought was just another day in the office. He could imagine them arriving home to the bosom of their families and the welcoming conversation: 'Did you have a nice day dear?' 'Oh, you know. Same old, same old. Had to drive a guy to Brooklyn and shoot him in the head.' 'That's nice dear. Put your feet up. Dinner will be ready in a minute.'

He knew whatever these men were planning was unlikely to be pleasant. He also knew if he had the slightest hint of an opportunity, he could very probably handle the thugs. But with the revolvers pressed resolutely into his side, it made any struggle pointless. Spencer leaned forward. 'Hey Gino, did you hear the one about the fella who said, 'And when they said *nose*, I thought they said *rose*, and I ordered a big red one.'

This amusing little parable elicited no response from the phlegmatic Gino. But Spencer thought he heard purple zoot suit snigger. *What the hell are they going to do?*

Travelling over the bridge with the lights of Manhattan receding into the distance, Spencer momentarily had a feeling of detachment. Once again, he was a pawn in a game controlled by, who, or what? The only thing he needed to understand was ultimately, his destiny was in his hands. *You can only play with the cards that you've been dealt.* The driver obviously knew where they were going. *I think he's done this before.*

The Rambler jolted over a rough potholed unlit road. A mist rose from the water, clothing the night in a clammy ethereal shroud. Spencer couldn't help reflecting that the setting looked like a horror movie: the scritch scratch of rodents scurrying, the hiss of feral cats.

'Hey Gino,' One of the zoot suiters grumbled 'Wind up the God damn window. It sounds like the Bronx Zoo out there.'

This was an industrial wasteland. The unwanted and unloved discarded relics of industries long gone. Draped in the cloying grey fog rolling in from the sullen waters, lapping relentlessly at a crumbling retaining wall.

Spencer shuddered. Was this where it all ended? An anonymous body, an unnamed John Doe with the cardboard tag attached to a big toe? in the city morgue? Then finally an unidentified corpse, despatched unlovingly, without emotion into a pauper's grave? Surely his life was meant to have more meaning than this? *What about Michiyo? Do I just disappear from her life? Do I just go missing while she frantically searches a city that she's unfamiliar with, pleading with disinterested police to instigate a search?*

He racked his brains to think of some tale that he could tell these thugs, to perhaps give him a second chance. He realised they were acting under orders, orders from a crime lord they feared. There was no compassion here. Certainly, the unlovely Gino would be relishing whatever it was they had planned for him.

The car lurched to a halt, the front wheel sinking into a water-filled pothole.

'Jesus Christ!' the thug in the purple suit exclaimed in disgust. 'Didja have to stop in the middle of a blasted lake? My new shoes are gunna get wet, sonofabitch.'

The Rambler had stopped in a quagmire facing a tract of water that because of the mist, Spencer couldn't determine if it was a lake, a river or the ocean.

'Get out.'

Spencer was still considering his options, but he knew his captors had the upper hand.

Gino spoke. 'Lucky for you, Marlowe, the boss likes you. If it was up to me, you'd be dead.'

Just as Spencer started to feel hopeful, Gino punched him hard in the pit of his stomach. The blow took him by surprise. The breath was driven out of him. This was quickly followed by another. Then another. 'This is just the start,' Gino snarled.

The other two thugs held him while Gino pounded into him. Spencer fell to the ground. He felt a crunch and knew it was a rib breaking. Then the kicking started. He heard laughter.

CHAPTER SIX

PAIN AND SUFFERING

Oh my God, what's happening? Can't move. Can't breathe. Chest hurts like hell, like fire. Red hot needles, jabbing into me. What's on my face? My fingers, why can't I bend them?

Consciousness flickered like a weak candle about to be snuffed out by the wind. In his brief moments of lucidity, Spencer noticed a conservatively clad woman. *A nurse, no, can't be.* Spencer's befuddled mind attached a disproportionate importance to the lady's garb. *Maybe she's a doctor? no stethoscope. Who the hell is she?*

***

'No visitors, ok?'

Savannah had been given the mind-numbing job of guarding the damaged mystery man Savannah wasn't informed by her immediate superior Dale Fletcher as to why the patient may be at risk from the New York mob.

'What about family?'

'As far as we can tell he doesn't seem to have any family. Hell, we don't even know who he is for sure. When I spoke to him at the restaurant he gave his name as Marlowe, Spencer Marlowe. He's an

Australian, that's all we know. God dammit! No papers, no passport, nothing. Anyway, if a wife or girlfriend or whatever turns up, he or she will have to clear things with me before they're allowed to see him. Got it?'

'How exactly do you expect me to stop Mario Mobster from forcing his way into the room?'

'You have a gun … shoot him, ok?'

Savannah nodded, surprised that Fletcher would suggest a female agent might actually use the weapon she'd been issued with. This was the first time he considered the magnum revolver strapped to her waist to be a weapon of destruction.

Savannah now viewed the man in her care with a little more interest. Badly bruised with a fractured skull, broken ribs and broken fingers taped together, he looked like he had been hit by a train. But even though badly damaged, Savannah could see he was unusually good looking. *What's your story, handsome stranger?' Why the interest in you, and do you have a wife or girlfriend?*

Savannah was immediately angry with herself, harbouring such unprofessional thoughts. Stop it this minute you silly girl. He's probably married with six kids and is a hit man with fifty kills to his credit for all you know. A feeling of guilt descended; after all Savannah was spoken for. Savannah had met Seth Alvah through friends. Seth was a paediatric nurse at Bellevue Hospital, New York, and was clearly dedicated. 'I just love kids,' he would say. 'I've always wanted a big family.'

Savannah welcomed the stability of a committed relationship. Seth was pressing her to get engaged but something held her back. 'I just don't think I'm ready.'

Savannah had been also given the task of laboriously jotting down on every word Spencer Marlowe uttered. While delirious, he'd rambled incoherently as Savannah furiously scribbled away. Most of what he'd said made no sense. Savannah heard references to someone named Michiyo. *Wife, or girlfriend maybe?* Savannah was curious. Michiyo sounded Japanese. *Surely no one would have a Japanese wife or girlfriend … would they?*

In 1955 the wounds of war were still raw. Hatred for the Japanese ran strong. It seemed as if everyone knew someone, who knew someone, who had a loved one who'd died at the hands of this brutal enemy.

So much of the man's delirious ravings were completely nonsensical. Savannah diligently wrote down everything. *What on Earth is he on about? None of this makes any sense.* She shook her head thinking, *what a waste of time. Nobody could understand any of it.*

The tall mystery man started to stir. 'Nurse, nurse,' His voice muffled by the oxygen mask was a painful but insistent whisper. 'Nurse, nurse.'

'I'm here. Do you need help?' Savannah leaned forward.

'Nurse,' the muffled voice whispered, 'Are my testicles black?'

Oh my God, what on Earth do I do now? Get a hold of yourself woman. You're an FBI agent, you've seen dead and mutilated bodies, inspecting his dangly bits shouldn't faze you.

Savannah gingerly pulled back the covers, undoing his pyjama pants. She tentatively examined his private parts. *Well, the family jewels seem to be ok.* Just as carefully she did up his pants, replacing the covers. She leaned forward, whispering. 'Don't worry. They're fine. Your testicles aren't black.'

The man painfully tore off his oxygen mask. 'That was very nice. But what I said was, are my test results back?'

'Oh, oh, oh dear, I'm sorry, I'm sorry.' Savannah put a hand to her beetroot face.

'For God's sake don't make me laugh, it bloody well hurts.' Spencer Marlowe chuckled a slow, wheezing sound.

Spencer was well on the road to recovery, but the ribs were still sore. He'd conversed with Savannah each day, who was puzzled at Spencer's apparent memory lapses.

Dale Fletcher had been a constant visitor to the hospital. He seemed to take a lot of interest in Spencer's ramblings, so diligently recorded. He took page after page away with him.

Spencer on the other hand now had perfect recall. He knew he'd once again been sent back in time. The other thing he knew as an absolute was, this was real. The danger was real, the wounds that were inflicted on him by Romano's thugs were a painful testimony to this uncomfortable reality. He desperately wanted to be back in his own century. Once again, he didn't know, was this going to be for a month, years, or even, and he shuddered at the thought. *Maybe for ever?*

CHAPTER SEVEN

DALE FLETCHER IS PUZZLED

'Hey, Spencer, you sound like a God damn kangaroo. Those crutches sure make a racket.'

The patients in the wards could hear Spencer as he clumped along the worn linoleum passageway. He'd made friends with a few of the sick and injured.

Spencer eased himself painfully on to the chair next to Irving's bed. Irving was a retired barber from Queens who'd just undergone an appendectomy. Spencer whiled away the hours playing chess with the amiable Irving, welcoming the chance to chat and once more feel a part of the human race.

'Irving,' Spencer retorted 'I'll just bet you don't know a whole lot about kangaroos.'

Irving grinned. 'What's to know?'

'Well, did you know kangaroos can jump higher than the Empire State Building?'

'Get outta town.'

'No, Irving, that's a fact.'

'Go on. I know there's a punch line coming.' Irving laughed.

'It's an oldie but a goody … you see, Irving, the Empire State Building can't jump.'

Irving laughed, his many chins bouncing happily.

Spencer had come to cherish his time with the affable ex-barber, a family man with an endless store of funny stories about his customers. Irving was a living, breathing, chunk of humanity and the only person on the planet with whom he felt any connection.

When they chatted or played chess, he could momentarily put aside the crushing feeling of loneliness and alienation.

Even with Spencer's previous sojourns into the past it took him a while to adjust to a world that went along at a snail's pace. In Spencer's world information and contact with anyone on the planet was either gratifyingly instant or at times annoyingly so. Right now, the thought of a computer or a mobile phone had him craving a screen in front of his face.

These thoughts and others were tumbling through his consciousness when Dale arrived.

'Nice to see you mobile.' Dale smiled. Spencer had been exploring the hospital on his crutches with an exasperated Savannah following, her hand never far from her 0.357 Magnum.

Dale sat at Spencer's bedside on the uncomfortable steel hospital chair, his arms draped around the backrest. He pushed his fedora further back on his head, searching his pockets for his packet of Camels and his Zippo. 'I'm not crazy about this brand but most of the doctors recommend them.' He shrugged as he lit up, glaring at the glowing end of his cigarette.

Spencer made his way painfully into his room. With Savannah's help, he managed to clamber on to the iron framed hospital bed. Reaching for the comfort of the oxygen mask, he took a few deep breaths. He closed his eyes as the pain shuddered through his body. He forced himself to focus on Dale Fletcher.

'Ribs still sore, huh? Romano's crew?'

'I think the ungodly, he of the deformed proboscis, Gino did most of the damage. Are you going to arrest him?' Spencer grimaced as another spasm of pain sprinted through his frame.

Dale rubbed his chin, glancing out of the window at a rainy Manhattan skyline, grey and bleak. 'Well, we could try to have him arrested. But we're the FBI and the 'F' stands for federal. We couldn't arrest him. It would have to be the NYPD. Given that in the Police Commissioners office, that's Commissioner Martino; Romano and Martino are both Sicilians from the same village.' Dale threw his hands in the air. 'There's a photo of Romano with an arm around the Commissioner's shoulder, probably taken at the Policeman's Ball or some other well publicised occasion. Romano is Godfather to Martino's son. Do you get the picture?'

'So, the corruption is fairly obvious.' Spencer winced as he spoke. Pain, it seemed still lurked in the hidden recesses of his body. Any movement or flexing of muscles unleashed spasms and tremors from bones broken and muscles and tendons that had been kicked and punched.

Dale laughed, a humourless sound. He stood up straightening as he gazed out of the window and the rain that bore down mercilessly upon the heart of the city. 'I don't know what's worse in New York, the stinking summers or the damn cold winters. Look at it! It's late April and it's still wet. Anyway, I'll get on with the story. Romano has the Commissioner, the

Mayor and several judges in his pocket. This is why the FBI is trying to use, shall we say … unusual methods to bring him down. That aside, I can guarantee the unlovely Gino will have a long list of impeccable highly placed witnesses who will be prepared to testify he was at the time doing charitable works or some such nonsense. We do have some plans I'd like to talk to you about, but first we do have a problem.'

Spencer tensed; he knew what was coming.

Dale pulled out a large pad, 'While you were delirious you said some really strange things to agent Steele here.' Dale nodded at Savannah. 'She was kind enough to write it all down. We'd appreciate it if you could explain.'

Spencer had a feeling of dread, but smiled disarmingly. 'Well certainly, I don't have any secrets,' he lied.

'Who's Dorothy?' Dale perused the first page.

'Who?' Now Spencer was perplexed.

'Spencer, I gotta tell you I've had the smartest code-breakers in the FBI going over these notes. Believe me these guys are so smart, it's scary. So, I'd really suggest you answer my questions. Who's Dorothy?'

'I'm not trying to be evasive, but could I have a bit more of a clue?'

Dale glanced at his notes again. 'You said, "Spencer Marlowe", that's you, isn't it?' Spencer nodded. 'You said "Spencer" then "hot mail dot com". Now I told you our guys are smart, didn't I?'

Spencer nodded again, trying hard not to smile.

'Our guys figured "dot" was obviously Dorothy, right?'

Spencer smiled sheepishly.

'And our guys figured you abbreviated her last name to Com, probably because the surname was a long one, in all likelihood European and you shortened it.' Dale had a look of triumph on his face.

Trying manfully to keep a straight face, Spencer admitted, 'Yes, that's Dorothy Comopoulos. Your guys really are amazing.' *Where in hell's this going to go?* Spencer's mind was racing. What on Earth had he said? What sort of answers could he dream up? *Dorothy Comopolous, really?*

'Now what I want to know, what exactly is this mail that's so hot? And while I'm at it. What exactly is "internet"?'

'Well, I'll tell you, Dale. But this is highly confidential.' Oh my God what the bloody hell can I come up with? I really don't need this.

'As long as it doesn't concern national security, it'll go no further.'

'I've been involved with a fishing company in Western Australia. Which is called "Internet". Which of course relates to international fishing … um … using nets … fishing nets, so therefore … it's called … Internet. And the hot mail Dorothy Comopoulos has sent me refers to … um … fishing rights. Awarded by the Australian Government. So … this mail … is really … hot … mail, it's um … highly confidential … because … ah … there's always competitors trying to get the jump on you to secure these … um … fishing rights.'

'Yeah, our guys thought somehow fishing was in there somewhere.' Dale nodded wisely.

Dale continued to wear that thoughtful expression as he continued to turn the pages of the notebook. 'One more thing. It's not that important, but what on Earth is Google?'

CHAPTER EIGHT

A DANGEROUS WOMAN

Spencer was bored and depressed he lay listlessly on the hospital bed, railing at his immobility. How long has it been? At least a month. *The hospital room is as devoid of beauty as I am of hope. The walls are simply cream, not dirt y, not peeling, just plain bloody cream. No decorations of any kind, the curtain is green, perhaps once the type of green that reminds people of springtime and hope, but it's now faded, insipid, depression clothed in a limp piece of cloth.*

The one sliver of joy was the delightful Agent Steele. Spencer had managed to prompt her into telling her life story while adroitly avoiding too much scrutiny of his own.

Savannah was certainly not classically beautiful, with her turned up nose and open features. There was something charming about her, Spencer instinctively trusted her. Here he decided was somebody with a very strong set of values. Her zeal and enthusiasm shone like a beacon.

Savannah was by and large a 'What you see is what you get' kind of lady. She was raised in a world that embraced homespun values: hard work, thrift, honesty, common sense and a suspicion of big city folk with their fancy clothes and liberal politics.

Spencer was aghast at the harrowing tale of her adored father's death at the hands of the psychopathic 'Henry the preacher' Kelly. As she told him of her decision to join the ranks of the FBI and the hurdles, she had to jump to gain entry to this elite organisation, a story that had a number of humorous and inspiring moments. *There's a movie script here.*

***

'Camels may be better for you but … honestly you can't beat these.' Dale opened a fresh packet of Chesterfields. 'Cigarette?' he asked, offering one to Spencer. After rummaging through his pockets for matches and finding the hospital-issue ash tray, he lit up, pausing for a minute as he drew on his cigarette. His gaze focussed on Spencer, as if he hadn't quite made up his mind what exactly he was dealing with.

He stood up, stretched, frowning at the grey Manhattan skyline. Spencer had the impression Dale was still not quite convinced about the man of mystery. 'Well … ah … do you ahh; do you remember the discussion we had at the restaurant in the village after you ah … persuaded Gino and Louie that you weren't going to skedaddle?' Dale chuckled at the memory.

'Yes.'

'The offer I made is still open. We've a plan to put all of these guys away for a long time. Interested?' Dale pulled up a chair and sat down, legs crossed and fingers intertwined over one knee.

'I guess you have a plan?' Spencer glanced at the FBI agent. He'd decided early in the piece that Fletcher was an honest man who could be trusted.

Over the next hour Dale went into detail, explaining the structure of the Mafia, the hierarchy, the main players, the role of the 'made men', the common soldiers and the wannabes. Spencer couldn't help but be impressed with Dale's obvious enthusiasm. His zeal and pugnacious rhetoric, rising and falling as he made his points. He was like an old-time fire and brimstone preacher, thundering hell and damnation to the evildoers of the world.

The plan was truly audacious in scope. The FBI had leased premises in Morton Street, Greenwich Village. The FBI was going into the restaurant business. Dale's enthusiasm was infectious. 'We're setting up a coffee, ice cream, sandwich shop. You and agent Steele, perhaps a couple of other staff if you need them, are going to operate the business.' He paused, looking like a kid who had just discovered his Christmas presents at the first light of day.

Spencer was incredulous. 'I don't know about Savannah, I mean Agent Steele, but I know nothing about running a restaurant. But I do know a bit about cooking. Italian mostly. I don't want to brag but my spaghetti and lasagne were pretty darn good if I say so myself.'

'Hey, let me tell you, this lady is a pretty mean cook. Minestrone, Buffalo burgers. My strawberry shortcake will have, em lining up down the street.' Savannah gave a thumbs up.

'Ok, I was going to say you'll have expert help if you need it, but it seems that's not necessary.'

'With all due respect sir, how on Earth does this have anything to do with taking on the mob?' Steele asked, eyes narrow. 'If Romano and his crew come in, do we poison them maybe?'

Dale glared at Savannah, drumming his fingers in a slow tattoo.

'Sorry. Just a joke. What's the object of the exercise, sir?' Savannah cringed glancing at Spencer.

'Well …' Dale rubbed his hands together still wearing a cat-got-the-cream expression.

'Greenwich Village is Tony Romano's patch. And, agent Steele, as I think I explained earlier, I can guarantee within a few days of opening, one of his gorillas will be around explaining the benefits of their comprehensive accident insurance policy.'

'Protection money, huh?' Spencer smiled.

'You got it.' Dale looked triumphant. 'There's simply no way these baboons are going to accept a new business on their patch not paying.' He sprang up, pacing quickly to the door and glancing down the corridor. 'Yep, the mob machine will swing into action and they'll be explaining the benefits of their policy to you.' He paused, waving a finger at Savannah and Spencer. 'You two are going to throw a spanner in to the works. Don't look so worried, we've a great plan.' Dale rubbed his hands together, his boyish enthusiasm not quite convincing the troops. 'Oh boy, I tell you we have the edge.' Dale glanced again at his two recruits noticing their lack of enthusiasm. He wagged a finger. 'Just wait till you hear what we've got.'

Spencer glanced sideways at Savannah, who shrugged.

'You're both going to love this,' Dale declared. 'There's more.'

Spencer almost expected Dale to add he was throwing in a set of steak knives.

'We've a brand-new science that the baddies know nothing about.'

Now Spencer's ears pricked up. He wondered just what this new 1955 science could be.

Dale glanced around again making quite sure no one was in earshot. 'You're not gonna believe this. We've almost every one of the cars driven by Romano's thugs, even Romano's car, fitted with hidden microphones. We can listen in to everything. We reckon we'll have advance knowledge of any moves they make on the restaurant. Now what do you think about that? Are you in?'

Spencer was silent.

'Come on. Say something.' Dale frowned.

'Something's bothering me.'

'Spit it out.'

'I will. If you can listen in to Romano and his merry men, what's to stop you recording incriminating conversations and then arresting them?'

'Good question. Eye on the ball. I like that. This, what would you call it? Science I guess, has been around for, God, I'm not sure, twenty years or thereabouts. But here's the thing, we've never been able to get a conviction based on recorded wire taps. The God damn lawyers say things like "That's not my client. Sounds a bit like him, but you can't prove it."

'And that's it. The judges don't like it. The juries don't like it. I tell you we're stymied. But then I came up with this doozie of an idea. Maybe we can't get a conviction, but if we can listen in on what sort of skulduggery they're planning, we can fix their little red wagon. And as a bonus the FBI will be paying your hospital bills. So, what do you say, huh?'

Well, I don't have a lot of prospects. 'It sounds like fun, Dale. But one other question: where am I going to stay? New York's expensive, and I'm not exactly flush. I do have some cash. Maybe Gino took pity on me?'

'It was dark and they didn't see it more like. I'm not sure pity and compassion are exactly mob attributes.' Dale grunted. 'Anyway, there's premises above the shop. You'll be paid forty dollars a week. Of course, you can eat for nothing at Spencer's.'

'Spencer's?'

Dale laughed. *'Spencer's coffee, cake and great grub.* Has a nice ring to it. Don't you think?'

SPENCER THE RESTAURATEUR

Yep, that's bloody impressive. Clad in a monogrammed black apron, and standing under the awning protecting him from the sun that'd had all winter to sharpen its teeth, Spencer paused from setting up tables and chairs, complete with snowy white tablecloths. He wiped his brow, gazing with satisfaction at the restaurant bearing his name. With its candy-striped awning adding a touch of Paris to its wrought iron chairs and tables now at the front of the shop, Spencer's looked like a French eatery in Montmartre.

Spencer had fallen for New York, hook, line and sinker. He'd spent even more time in hospital and then a period of rehabilitation. Days became weeks. Then finally the day had come. doctor examined him and grinned, 'Well Mr Marlowe. I reckon it's time. Get out of here. Be a regular tourist. '

Spencer had been enthralled by the Memorial Day Parade that travelled up Fifth Avenue, finishing in Central Park. Meanwhile a team of tradespeople had worked like beavers creating the restaurant Spencer's.

As promised Spencer had a room at the top of a rickety staircase. The floors were bare and the paint was in need of loving care. A sash window, its panes warped by time, afforded a view onto busy Morton Street. A lick of colour, a second-hand reading lamp, a bed, a print of Whistler's Mother and a bookcase already half filled with contemporary novels, and it felt like home.

Dale had supplied some eager young acolytes from the FBI training school to be waiters and kitchen hands when needed.

'Spencer, Savannah, meet your staff,' Dale said with a wink.

The two wannabe agents both looked like quarterbacks with ripped physiques and buzz cuts.

'Mr Marlowe, ma'am, I'm Dwayne from Wayne,' the six foot plus young guy held out a hand.

'Dwayne from Wayne?' Spencer laughed.

Dwayne laughed, 'yeah, I'm from Wayne, Indiana.'

'And I'm Rafael.' A swarthy, smiling Hispanic guy held out his hand. 'From the Bronx.'

'Mexican riffraff more like,' Wayne laughed, punching Rafael lightly on the shoulder.

'Indiana redneck,' Rafael retorted with a grin.

Spencer glanced sideways at a grinning Savannah. It was obvious the two trainees were keen and very likeable.

'Listen up everybody,' Dale cut in. 'Rafael, Dwayne, you're waiters, busboys, kitchen hands, that's it. You get to see how an FBI undercover operation works. You have to live the part. Be inconspicuous, got it?'

'Yes sir,' they replied in unison.

'I think you'll find there's a stack of dishes to be washed. Hop to it, guys.'

'So, Dale, if there's any action, are these guys armed?' Savannah queried.

'Negative, agent Steele, they haven't done their firearm training, they really are going to be just staff.'

'Just a few last-minute things to sort out. We'll be going full steam ahead before you know it,' Spencer explained.

Trucks and vans were now rumbling into Morton Street in the early hours. unloading the fresh produce. Restaurant supplies piled up in the storeroom. Tantalising fragrances of garlic, cheeses and fresh bread overflowed into the street.

Levi the jeweller, a small, sharp German immigrant with a wide grin and a mind like a steel trap, admitted while he spooned shortcake into his mouth, 'Spencer, I'm puzzled.'

'What's the problem, Levi?' Spencer felt nervous when inquisitive traders asked questions.

'*Gott in Himmel*, Spencer, where does the money come from? This must cost, ja? I know restaurant can be good business. But you are newcomer? You borrow the money? Who would lend?'

'No mystery Levi, I have wealthy parents in Australia. They own a big sheep station.'

'Station?'

'Ranch, Levi. In Australia we call it a station.'

Levi gobbled the rest of his cheesecake and grunted. 'Rich parents? Oy vey. I should be so lucky.'

The FBI had spared no expense in the stage production that was 'Spencer's. Along one wall was a row of booths for those who desired intimacy. Another wall featured a fresco, painstakingly painted by a local artist. Spencer gazed in wonderment at the scene of a sixteenth century eatery with colourful cartoon style characters with exaggerated features. Men with big noses, waitresses with impossibly large breasts, serving mountains of food at the same time appearing wanton and lascivious. The fresco just managed to cross the divide from pornography to art. The tables all had red check cloths. Candles placed in wicker bound chianti bottles added to this rakish Mediterranean bar, restaurant, cum diner. Not five-star dining but basic homely Italian style cooking. Gelato, sandwiches, pasta. And of course, coffee. Very good coffee.

Very classy, Spencer thought. His natural optimism had returned. Once again, he marvelled at the twists and turns of his life. He relished being busy as it helped him take his mind off Michiyo. His past experiences had filled him with hope. If he could survive the vindictive Tony Romano, he would eventually be transported back to his century.

Business was brisk from the start. The first person to walk through the door was Savannah's paramour, Seth Alvah, clad in his hospital whites. 'Spencer, I'd like you to meet Seth.'

Spencer's feeling of distaste was immediate. He found Seth's voice as sharp and invasive as a dentist's drill and as charming as a bag of rotten fish. Seth was tall and undeniably good looking, but all Spencer saw was a weak chin and furtive, empty eyes that flashed nervously around the room, never making direct contact with other people.

Seth was effusive, shaking Spencer's hand vigorously. 'Yo, Spencer, I've heard so much about you from Sav. This really is a pleasure, a great pleasure.

And you're an Aussie as well.' This said as if being Australian was to be part of an exclusive club. 'We'll have to get together some time, sink some suds, eh.' With that came a nauseating slap on the back.

Spencer nodded politely while trying to spit out some mindless platitudes. *This guy is like Ford's salesman of the year and Billy Graham all rolled into one.* Spencer feigned a smile feeling as if he wanted to slink away and wash his hands, he shuddered. *This guy makes my flesh crawl.*

He thought of the smarmy Lieutenant Beinard from operation DNA. Spencer's distrust and dislike was instinctive. He immediately castigated himself. *Savannah obviously loves the guy. He's a nurse, works with kids.*

Spencer had decided he liked Savannah. Her grit and determination to make it in the overtly sexist FBI he thought was truly inspirational. Because they worked such different hours, Seth often dropped in before or after his work to see Savannah, but no matter how hard he tried Spencer just couldn't warm to him. But annoying boyfriends were small potatoes compared to vicious New York crime lords.

Spencer awoke to a cool, pleasant June morning, with fleecy clouds scudding over the azure sky. The constant drone of the New York traffic was a reminder this was the city that never slept. The early morning rush had subsided.

Wearing his customary black apron Spencer again swept leaves off the sidewalk. The Silver Maple spreading its branches over the entrance of the restaurant was a handsome tree with its two-toned foliage and its shaggy bark, but it did seem to have an inexhaustible supply of leaves Spencer was constantly removing. A small price to pay for beauty, he decided.

The pay phone inside rang. Spencer leant the broom against the wall and bolted inside. It was Dale, his voice tense.

'Spencer, Angelo Fazio is heading your way. He drives a flashy red '53 Caddy. Look … Spencer, this guy will certainly be armed. He's a tough bunny. Do you need backup? I can get a couple of solid guys there in minutes. Spencer … what's it gonna be? I know you can handle yourself but …?

'Dale, Dale, remember, I have a 0.38. Savannah's armed, there's a couple of your cadets in the kitchen. Don't worry. A walk in the park, ok?' Spencer killed the call. *Well, well, well, it's started. We'll see just how tough the opposition is.* It occurred to Spencer; Romano probably had no idea who exactly was behind this new restaurant. The well-oiled mob machine probably swung into action the moment a new business opened its doors.

He took stock of the situation. as he gingerly flexed his muscles, he reassured himself. *Not 100 percent, but pretty darn close.*

The cherry red Cadillac, a 5000 lb chunk of Detroit metal and rubber, jerked to a halt and parked illegally next to a fire hydrant. Spencer smiled at the overweight Angelo Fazio with his loud pinstripe suit and even louder tie. Pushing the heavy door against the resistance of a solid hinge, he thrust his feet onto the ground. A swirl of wastewater eddied around his two-tone Oxfords. He clambered heavily out of the vehicle, carefully adjusting the knot in his garish neck apparel and tossing a cigarette butt onto the sidewalk.

It was all Spencer could do to not laugh out loud as the mobster swaggered into Spencer's.

Brash, arrogant, king of the walk. Earlier that week, figuring Romano would likely send Angelo around to the restaurant, Dale had read out Angelo's details from his extensive rap sheet to Spencer. Angelo Fazio led the good life: money, women and fancy cars. Being a "made man" in the Romano crime family appeared to be suit him well.

Angelo often re told his inauspicious start into a life of crime. 'I wanted to pray to God for a new bicycle, but even as a kid I figured he didn't work that way, so I stole a bike instead and asked for his forgiveness.'

He had started as an errand boy, then a runner for the numbers rackets. From there he'd graduated to car thefts and a few smash and grab heists. He'd served the mandatory spells in reformatory and prison and had now earned his rightful place in the gangster world. A man of respect, a man only a fool would argue with. But all was about to change …

Spencer lounged behind the counter. Savannah tried to look busy washing glasses in the sink behind. Under her loose jacket with "Spencer's" monogrammed on the front was her revolver in the custom shoulder holster.

'Yes, sir, what'll it be?'

'Tutti-frutti, in a cone.'

'Coming right up.'

Spencer deftly placed the scoop of ice cream into the cone and handed it over. 'That's a nickel.'

'Keep the change.' Angelo handed over a quarter. Spencer smiled.

'Nice shop you got here. New ain't it?'

'Open just a couple of weeks.'

'You know this is a pretty dangerous area. There are some tough customers about.' Angelo glanced around.

Spencer continued to smile.

'Yessir, then of course there are accidents,' continued Angelo.

'Really?'

Angelo Fazio was a confident man. His reputation and that of his employer preceded him. This was an easy assignment. Very few customers gave any trouble. The odd one who protested would eventually see reason, generally while they recuperated in a hospital bed. Angelo was quite proficient and creative when it came to convincing recalcitrant customers. He found some sharp blows from his trusty claw hammer usually did the trick. Nothing terminal, broken hands and fingers seemed to do get the required result.

Angelo leaned forward and with the air of a street side tout selling dirty photos. 'My name's Angelo ...' He paused as if Spencer somehow should know the name. Spencer leaned against the counter.

'What I'm offering is insurance. Thirty dollars a week paid in advance and we guarantee you won't have no problems.'

Spencer was quite impressed with the way this street thug was able to convey an air of legitimacy to an act of blatant extortion. Apart from the loud clothes, Fazio could well be an employee of a regular insurance firm.

Spencer gazed thoughtfully at the mobster in front of him. *You might have been a tough guy in your day, but I think the good life might have taken its toll.* Even the expensive tailoring couldn't hide the widening girth.

His heavy, sweaty jowls and the five o'clock shadow added to the picture of someone who'd done the hard yards and no longer felt the need to exercise.

'Ah … No thanks.'

Standing on the counter was a row of large glass jars containing confectionary.

'You see, pal, accidents happen so easily.' Grabbing a jar, he flung it onto the black and white tiled floor. The jar exploded like a bomb. Black aniseed balls bounced over the floor like miniature bowling balls searching for pins.

Spencer immediately seized a broom and scoop and handed them to the surprised mobster.

'I'm sure you're going to sweep them up … oh, and you owe me ten dollars for the jar and the candy.' Spencer smiled warmly as Angelo tried to grasp what was happening. Spencer found it hard to control his mirth. He felt as if he could read the hoodlum's mind: *What sort of boob is this guy? Doesn't he realise who I am, what I represent?*

'You won't be getting no ten dollars. And the insurance is now forty bucks a week.' Angelo snarled, grabbing Spencer's collar with both hands.

Spencer continued to smile. Which if Fazio had a few more brains, should have made him a little nervous. Spencer stood still, only because he hadn't decided exactly where he was going to hit the mobster. With Fazio's hands both occupied holding Spencer's collar, it left Spencer with too much choice. Finally, he decided on the heel of his hand thrust forcefully into Angelo Fazio's jaw.

Angelo Fazio's eyes glazed over as he collapsed onto the floor. Sprawled untidily on his back, he looked like he was asleep.

Spencer opened the mobster's coat, noting the automatic Colt in a shoulder holster. He decided to confiscate the weapon. At the same time, he fished out the thug's wallet, removing ten dollars from it, and placing the rest of the wad into a charity tin collecting for wounded war veterans. He then threw a pitcher of water into Angelo's face.

'Wakey wakey, darling.' Fazio groaned. 'Are you feeling, ok?'

'You sonofabitch.' Angelo thrust his hand on to his shoulder holster.

'I imagine you're looking for that nasty automatic, hidden under your jacket. Really, Angelo baby, tut. In fact, a trio of tuts. You could hurt somebody with that.' Spencer shook his head sadly. 'Now Angelo, I'd like you to pay careful attention … What I'd like you to do, is go back and talk to your nice Uncle Tony and explain to him … now you are paying attention, aren't you?'

Angelo didn't acknowledge he was paying attention, but Spencer was confident the message was getting through. 'Tell Uncle Tony I won't be paying insurance. And this bit is important. Tell Uncle if I have any more trouble, I'm going to get quite cross. Now, can you remember all of that?'

Angelo scowled at Spencer.

'This may come as a surprise, Ange, but I actually have a pretty good idea what's going through your mind at the moment. And of course, I do understand how difficult it'll be to explain this encounter to *numero uno*. Please feel free to start swinging with those nicely manicured hands and fingers of yours. But honestly, if you're planning to take me on, I'd suggest you bring some help. As they say, don't send a boy to do a man's job, ok?'

Angelo glared.

'Now,' said Spencer. 'Let me help you up.'

Angelo swore an obscenity in Italian. Spencer understood the language reasonably well. 'Angelo, dear me. That really isn't nice. And I can assure you my parents were married.'

Angelo climbed unsteadily to his feet, rejecting Spencer's help. As he stumbled his way out of the door Spencer added, 'By the way Angelo, in view of your more than generous donation to the veterans association, the next tutti-frutti is on me.'

Angelo grabbed his wallet and saw his sizeable wad gone. 'You sonofabitch.'

CHAPTER TEN

THE HITMEN

The restaurant door burst open and Dale Fletcher appeared.

'Savannah, Spencer, this you gotta hear. Do you mind closing up? I know it's early, but there are some things we need to talk about.'

Spencer yelled into the kitchen, 'Wayne, Rafael, you have an early finish, see you in the morning.'

Dale groaned under the weight of a Grundig tape recorder the size of a medium suitcase he'd lugged into the restaurant. 'Into the office, away from prying ears.'

Spencer scanned busy Morton Street before hanging out the closed sign, locking the doors and making his way to the rear.

'G'night boss, we're off to the movies with our gals.' Wayne gave him a jaunty salute.

'See you later, alligator,' Rafael added as the two would-be "G" men strode off in the direction of midtown.

Spencer gazed fondly at their retreating figures, their boundless enthusiasm and optimism he'd decided was a tonic. Spencer scanned busy Morton Street before hanging out the closed sign, locking the doors and making his way to the rear.

'Hey, this looks neat,' Dale said as he hoisted the Grundig onto a desk cluttered with invoices.

'The desk looks neat. Really?' Savannah chuckled as she shut the door.

'No, I mean the office. I mean it looks, *neat*. I mean it looks like an office should look.'

Hastily erected shelves creaked under the weight of recipe books. Two bentwood chairs, a lamp, a teak desk and a stack of Kelty and Son Tomato Paste in cartons resting in a corner completed the scene. A slice of late afternoon sunshine from the dusty skylight illuminated the tiny room.

'Did you see any of Romano's goons outside?' Spencer asked.

Dale shook his head. 'No, from what we've gleaned from the tapes, that's not what they're up to.' Dale plugged in the machine.

The tape recorder clacked and whirred into life as they listened to the enraged voice of Tony Romano yelling abuse at someone; presumably his unfortunate lieutenants, Angelo, Gino and Louie.

'Morons. Fucking morons. In my day we'd have this prick sorted. Piss off, the both of you.'

'Boss, how about we take some of the boys, shoot up the joint. Maybe some dynamite?'

'Dumb and fucking dumber. We don't want to destroy a business. The business makes money and we want our fucking cut. Now fuck off, I'll sort it out.'

'He doesn't sound at all happy,' Savannah said, doing a very good impersonation of the fabled Cheshire Cat the way she was grinning.

Dale switched the recorder off. 'I won't bother you with the rest. I reckon he's going to get more desperate, and more violent. This's going to get messy.

If you want out, I understand.' Dale looked worried. It seemed to Spencer that Dale suddenly realised it was no longer a 'boys own adventure'. It wasn't a game.

'I want to take this thug down,' Savannah snarled.

'Likewise,' said Spencer.

Dale stared hard at Spencer, then turned his gaze to Savannah. 'All my instincts tell me Romano wants to get rid of the problem. I mean … period.'

'Yeah, well just let the bastard try,' Savannah hissed.

Dale raised his eyebrows at the unexpected passion from this lady FBI agent.

'Ah … yes … that's the spirit, Agent Steele.' he said hesitantly.

Spencer watched on silently.

***

BOOM.

A car had backfired, making Spencer jump. Savannah swore and grabbed her revolver.

'Bloody hell that was loud,' he said. 'I tell you, just waiting for something to happen is driving me nuts.' It was several days since Dale had played the conversation in Romano's office. They were getting jumpier with each passing day.

'You're not kidding. Did you see that young college kid yesterday, the one who parked his Model A Jalopy out the front?'

'The kid who bought the tub of ice cream?'

'Yeah, that's the one. A more unlikely gangster I've never seen … when he reached into his jacket for his wallet, I almost grabbed my gun and shot him. I mean, he was all of seventeen. I just wish they'd hurry up and do their worst. The suspense is driving me nuts. Honestly, everyone on the planet is starting to look like a damn thug.'

***

Tuesday started like any other, not overly busy but steady. Spencer had just served a pleasant middle-aged couple from Iowa with coffee and sandwiches. They were keen to get information on what to see in The Big Apple. The FBI recruits were due to start their shift.

'You must visit Central Park, and of course the Empire State Building.' Spencer pointed out the landmarks on the map the man had spread before him on the table.

'Oh, ya! And I must go to Macy's,' the lady piped up. She had a pleasant, rounded face with chunky horn-rimmed glasses. The squared shoulders of her heavy grey wool jacket seemed a little dated to Spencer's untrained eye.

'Now Doris, doncha know we ain't got taame to strut all over this darn town.' The man winked at Spencer. 'The name's Cyrus.' He held out a calloused hand, veined and speckled with age. He had a white goatee that reminded Spencer of Colonel Sanders. The check sports coat with rounded notch lapels and two very large square pockets suited him perfectly. Spencer grinned and shook the proffered hand.

'Nice to meet you both, and Cyrus, Macy's have a great selection of guns.' Spencer smiled conspiratorially at Doris.

Spencer could just hear Dwayne and Rafael clattering in the kitchen.

Outside, a black Lincoln with Detroit plates slid stealthily into a vacant parking space. Spencer watched two heavy-set men wearing overcoats climb out, the taller man nodding to his shorter companion. *A little warm for coats.*

'Would you please excuse me?' Spencer strode to the counter where Savannah was arranging cakes on a display stand. He glanced around at the customers; the Iowa couple and one other couple who were poring over their menus. 'This could be it,' he whispered.

Savannah moved to a table close to the entrance, pretending to wipe it down. Spencer tensed behind the counter ready to duck, a loaded 0.38 within reach behind a box of serviettes. He knew he was a lousy shot. Even at relatively close range, unless you were an expert, revolvers were not accurate. Spencer felt nervous, not entirely for himself, but also knowing Savannah had little exposure to this type of operation. The 0.38 felt cumbersome and foreign in his hand. Opening the loading gate as Savannah had shown him, he checked. Six rounds.

The two men sauntered casually into the restaurant, both silent. One, tall and blonde, certainly didn't look like mafia, in his fawn cashmere overcoat and black homburg. The other was short, swarthy, with a dark old-fashioned herringbone coat and no hat. A pleasantly ugly man who gave the impression he could well be somebody's favourite uncle. The tall blonde man would have been handsome if it wasn't for his watery blue eyes.

Spencer had no way of knowing these men were true professionals, contract hit men in the employ of the Purple Gang from Detroit. Isaac Goldman, known throughout the underworld as Isaac the Jew and Ambroos Bakker, known as Dutch Ambroos.

The man in the dark coat nodded to his partner. Simultaneously reaching into their overcoats, they each pulled out a deadly-looking sawn off shotgun. The lady from Iowa, about to enjoy her coffee and cake screamed, the piercing noise reverberating around the restaurant.

Both men aimed their sawn-offs at Spencer, who threw himself on the floor behind the counter. In unison, the shotguns exploded. The spray of buckshot ripped through the glass display cabinet, sending shards of glass and strawberry shortcake across the floor and wall, like the aftermath of a school children's food fight.

The hit men disregarded the inconsequential serving girl standing near a table. Her shapeless jacket hid her custom spring-loaded shoulder holster. Savannah, with speed that would have put old time western gunfighters to shame, drew her formidable Magnum. The powerful .357 round was deafening as it ripped into the tall man. The slug entered under his arm, killing him instantly. He collapsed like a rag doll, the shotgun bounced on the tiled floor. Savannah was using hollow point ammunition and it had been messy. Blood and bone spread over the far wall. The second man gawped, staring down the barrel of Spencer's 0.38 and the serving girl's revolver.

'Probably a good idea to drop your gun. What do you reckon?' Spencer asked.

The gunman seemed to agree, dropping his weapon. It clattered harmlessly on the tiled floor, his eyes like silver lightening, flashing from Spencer to

Savannah and the body of his comrade lying lifeless in a pool of pulp and blood. The four customers scrambled for the door.

'Get down on the floor, on your back, legs crossed, hands on your head.' Savannah kept her weapon trained on the man while Spencer collected the shotguns.

'Sure, babe, sure.' The gunman appeared to have recovered his equilibrium, even as he obeyed the command.

Spencer glanced at the dead thug and shuddered. *It seems I didn't need to be concerned about Savannah.*

'Hey babe, do you mind putting that cannon away? You're making me nervous.'

In your dreams pal, Spencer thought grimly. Savannah surprised him.

Well ok then. If you promise to behave yourself.'

'Yeah, sure doll, you got me fair and square.'

What on Earth are you thinking?

The moment Savannah slotted her weapon into her shoulder holster, the man's right hand dropped from his head and dived into his coat. Savannah's hand flew to her holster; the spring-loaded fast action holster. The gun leapt into her hand.

The gangster's hand stopped in mid-flight. He smiled nervously. The smile disappeared as he looked into the merciless eyes of Agent Steele. In a flash he seemed to know he was looking into the eyes of one of his own—a remorseless killer.

Savannah stared at the open-mouthed man, his odd-coloured eyes bulging in terror. In the milliseconds before he died, Isaac may have wondered at Savannah's words, 'Goodbye, Henry.'

CHAPTER ELEVEN

TAKE NO PRISONERS

The shot echoed around the now empty restaurant. The man's head was unrecognisable. His brains spattered like grey paste over the tiled floor. The hollow point round had made a hole the size of a fist going in, and an even bigger one as it exited.

Savannah surveyed the scene with smug satisfaction. While Spencer turned his back, searching the street for any sign of more thugs, Savannah surreptitiously reached into the hitman's jacket, grasping his 0.32 revolver. She slipped the weapon into her coat.

Spencer's face was deathly white when his gaze returned to Savannah.

'Jesus, Savannah, what … what in hell?'

'You saw it. He went for his gun.'

Rafael stood in the kitchen doorway, open mouthed, plates of pastries in hand, staring in horror at what he'd just witnessed.

'You ok, Rafael?' Spencer asked.

'Yeah sure. That was …' He retreated into the kitchen, face white.

Spencer was disturbed at Savannah's brutal execution of the hitman. He realised he'd misjudged her and her motivation.

It seemed to Spencer the death of Savannah's father at the hand of small-time villain Henry 'the Preacher' Kelly had awakened a hatred in her for the killers of this world.

After the crime scene was contained by the NYPD, Dale Fletcher stepped in to make sure there were no embarrassing questions. Apparently, it was business as usual. The NYPD had a fairly relaxed attitude to it all. They had a breathless account from the Iowa tourists who'd returned when the police had arrived. The old lady, who had been tucked away in a booth and hadn't got to consume her coffee and cake, confirmed the story.

The leading detective surveyed the carnage. 'What a mess. Isaac the Jew was never a pin-up boy. But seriously, this is some splatter. It looks like you used a Thompson at three feet and emptied the whole drum into him.'

This was directed at Spencer, who shrugged. He was having trouble keeping his breakfast down.

The other detective didn't seem to be particularly disturbed by the gory scene. He stood over the corpse smoking a cigar and rather indelicately Spencer thought, dropped ash over the gruesome remains, chortling, 'Oh dear, poor Isaac, rest in pieces.'

Dale was not at all concerned at the death of the bandits. Spencer decided Savannah's brutal handling of the situation would remain their little secret. As Dale debriefed Savannah and Spencer, Savannah naturally offered a slightly different version.

'Yes sir, I couldn't believe it. Without warning he reached for his gun even though I had him covered.' She shook her head, managing to appear distressed.

Spencer watched the interaction between Dale and Savannah, finding it difficult not to laugh.

'Please try not to blame yourself, Agent Steele. You did what you had to do. Just remember, it was him or you, ok?'

'Yes sir,' she muttered, a wan smile on her face.

Spencer gave her a wink. *There's a job for you on the silver screen, I reckon.*

***

Peace and quiet reigned for the next week. Trade had dropped off a little. 'I guess people don't really want to get caught in the crossfire,' Spencer reflected one hot humid afternoon as he went about preparing lasagne from a recipe he remembered from his late Italian mother.

Dale sauntered into Spencer's, all smiles. He was thrilled at the disruption to Tony Romano's crime empire, explaining to Spencer and Savannah this'd caused questions to be asked about Romano, who was being called the 'Dippy Don'. Behind his back, of course. Dale chortled.

'Romano's beginning to look like a dunce. He can't control a simple restaurant. I tell you he's looking God damn silly. I mean it's August and Spencer's is still there. The other dons will be taking a good look at all this.' Dale fished around for a cigarette. He lit up, pointing it at Spencer and Savannah. 'These guys are always looking for a weakness. I tell you the sharks will be circling the Romano syndicate, don't worry about that.'

Dale had made himself comfortable on one of the kitchen chairs, watching as Spencer prepared some salads. 'You're really getting into this cooking lark, aren't you Spencer? I didn't know this was one of your talents.' Before Spencer could answer Dale laughed, pointing a finger. 'I know, It's a long story, right?'

'Dale, for God's sake, my mother was Italian. Of course I can cook. I am in fact a man of many talents.' He grinned, while executing an extravagant bow.

Dale blew a smoke ring at the ceiling. 'I have to say, I'm very impressed with the both of you. So far this's been a textbook operation. In fact, I have to tell you, the word from above is the boss himself is taking notice.'

'You don't mean …' Savannah cut in.

Dale put a thumb in the air. 'Yes, Agent Steele, the man himself, J Edgar Hoover.' Dale threw down the latest New York Times. The headlines screamed "Judgement Day For Mobsters" superimposed over a photo of Spencer's.

Dale chuckled. 'Yeah, the boss just loves a good headline. In fact, he's so impressed, he's thinking of doing the same thing in other cities. Chicago, Los Angeles, maybe Miami. When this's over, how would you both feel about doing it all again?'

'Speaking for myself, I'd love to. Spencer?' Savannah's eyes gleamed.

Spencer found the conversation unnerving. The very idea of planning something that may take years to complete, hit him with a jolt. Would he be here for that long? *What about my life? What about Michiyo?* 'I guess so,' he mumbled.

Savannah dropped her whisk into the bowl of cream she was beating. 'Hell, Spencer, you'd want to be a part of this, surely?' she said softly.

'You bet,' he declared. 'Why not eh?' Spencer figured he'd no control over his ultimate destiny and whether or not he was going to remain or be flung back to his old life. *You can only play with the cards you've been dealt.*

Dale rubbed his hands together. 'Great. But meanwhile, back in Greenwich Village, the God damn Indians are still circling the wagon train.' Dale took a couple of heavy drags on his Lucky Strike, then looked thoughtful. 'Romano's not going to give up. That's for sure.' Dale cautioned as he studied the faces of his two crime fighters.

Savannah was completely unfazed. 'We'll be waiting,' she said, and glanced at Spencer.

Spencer on the other hand was worried. He knew Romano would throw everything he had at the problem in Morton Street.

CHAPTER TWELVE

THE DESPERATE DON

'Hey Savannah, I've just created my masterpiece, come and taste this.' Spencer grabbed a large tray of ground beef and pasta casserole out of the oven. The tempting scent wafted through the kitchen.

'Shit, that's hot!' He plonked the heavy tray on to the bench. 'I tell you, girl, I reckon I've turned into a pretty good chef. This has some fresh basil as well. I tell you it's delish'

Savannah laughed. 'Yeah, well don't get to carried away. We'd have to be about due for a visit from Murder Incorporated.'

Right on cue, the peremptory jangle jangle of the payphone disturbed Spencer, dragging him reluctantly back into the world of Mafiosi and mayhem.

'Thank God, I've got you.' Dale's voice was filled with relief. 'Spencer, we've heard Romano talking to Gino and Louie. Those two thugs will be heading your way shortly. They're driving a grey Hudson Hornet. We couldn't get everything, but it sounds like they're going to throw a petrol bomb at the restaurant. Get everyone out. Lock the joint up. Leave now, that's an order.'

Spencer grabbed Rafael by the arm. 'You and Wayne leave now.'

Rafael's face paled. 'Trouble?' Spencer nodded.

Their only customer heard the exchange and scampered out the door, leaving two dollars for his lasagne and coffee.

Spencer raced into the kitchen. Savannah stirred a big pot of Minestrone soup. Spencer grabbed her by the hand and told her what Dale had said. 'C'mon, we gotta get out of here pronto.'

'No, no and no,' she snapped at Spencer, her eyes blazing. 'I'm not letting those bastards torch this joint, ok.'

Savannah stood, her hands on her hips, her white apron splashed with tomato puree and olive oil.

'And what exactly do you reckon you can do?'

Without answering his question, she checked her revolver. 'A Hudson Hornet?'

'Yes.'

Savannah ripped off the soiled apron and flung it on the floor, ran from the kitchen and planted herself on one of the outside chairs under the candy-striped umbrella. Her chest heaved as she scanned the street. 'Come on you bastards. Come and find out what Mama's got for you,' she muttered under her breath.

'What on Earth can you do with this woman?' Spencer was nonplussed.

Savannah held her revolver in her lap. The red checked tablecloth concealing the weapon. She surreptitiously checked the load.

Twenty minutes elapsed. Spencer was now sitting at the table with her, his 0.38 in his pocket.

'Look, a grey Hudson,' Savannah leaned forward, whispering as the car snaked quietly down the narrow street.

'Let's not get ahead of ourselves. It may not be them,' Spencer muttered.

An angry blast of horns erupted as an old Ford Coupe ground to a halt in front of the Hudson, steam billowing from its radiator.

'Hey, Savannah, this looks interesting.'

The driver's door of the Hudson flew open. A large Mediterranean man leapt out, screaming at the hapless coupe's driver. Then the Hudson's passenger door burst open and a familiar figure emerged.

'Shift this fucking heap, fella.' Spencer could just hear Gino's strident words.

Gino's red nose was the first distinguishing feature Spencer recognised on either of the two men. Spencer watched closely at the sight of Gino and Louie pushing the Ford into a driveway. Mission accomplished; the two men clambered back into the Hudson. The engine roared as the grey sedan resumed hurtling towards Spencer's.

Savannah waited. As the car drew nearer there was a burst of light. Louie had lit the cloth hanging out of a bottle, filled, Spencer imagined, with gasoline.

Still fifty yards away, a difficult shot, particularly with a moving target, Savannah aimed her pistol. It exploded twice, the noises reverberating like amplified cracks of thunder. The first round pierced the door. The second slug hit the bottle held in Louie's hand and whoosh, the petrol bomb exploded in a flash of yellow flame, engulfing the car. Momentarily Gino and Louie's terror-stricken faces were illuminated.

Spencer jumped to his feet. 'Oh my God.'

A woman shrieked, pointing at Savannah and Spencer. 'Why don't you just close your restaurant and just go? What's next? A bomb?'

An angry mob, full of fear, hormones and primitive impulses gesticulated and yelled, at whom, it was hard to tell. 'God damn police. Where in hell is the law?' One man pointed at Spencer, shouting, 'This is Mafia, isn't it? Just pay the bastards, like we all do.' Spencer ignored him, recognising the owner of the liquor shop further up Morton Street.

'Will you just look at that?' Gunter the manager of the Happy Heels shoe shop, stood transfixed, clutching a pair of red stilettos. A lone woman screamed. An elderly man removed his hat, acknowledging this impromptu funeral pyre, his walking stick lay beside him as he leant against a US mail post box.

Mostly it was a stunned silence as a crowd gathered, as the ghastly spectre of violent death imprinted itself indelibly on the canvas of their minds. Fodder for nightmares in the years to come.

He knew there was nothing he could do to help. The car was a fireball. Spencer heard the crack of exploding cartridges from the men's hand guns. Arms flailing, the two men struggled to get out of the flaming wreckage.

CHAPTER THIRTEEN

A JAPANESE PARTNERSHIP

Convinced the minor annoyance in Greenwich Village was now sorted, the Don was entertaining two Japanese guests in his sumptuous Manhattan apartment. The impressive high ceilings had wide oaken beams. Like a Monet painting, floor to ceiling picture windows afforded a view over Central Park. Wide polished timber floorboards were adorned with priceless Persian carpets. The apartment exuded class, taste, and above all wealth.

When Romano had purchased his apartment on West 57th Street, he really felt as if he'd made it. Everything about it breathed style. Not that Romano or his wife had particularly good taste; they didn't. But this was New York, you could hire people who did.

The apartment was strewn with paintings and *objet d'art* that neither nor he nor his Brooklyn raised wife understood, but his theory that if it cost a lot of money, it must be good, had overall worked quite well. Romano had even worked on his harsh Brooklyn accent, by and large he'd managed to avoid using double negatives. Secretly his loyal lieutenants, his close colleagues, thought that he'd become quite pretentious, not that they'd have used that particular word. 'Yeah Romano, he's become a real *cafone.*'

Every time Tony left the building, he was made aware of his place in the world. The smartly uniformed doorman in his military green uniform, and snowy white peaked cap would wish him a good day, enquiring if he wanted him to hail a cab or fetch a newspaper.

Tonight, there'd been much bowing and exchanging of pleasantries. One of the Japanese men was hard muscled, lean, watchful. He was yakuza, the Japanese equivalent of the New York Mafia.

The average New Yorker wouldn't understand the significance of the full body tattoos of this man, even the meaning of the missing little finger on his left hand. For those in the know, the yakuza were even scarier than the New York mob. Their level of violence and cruelty was on a completely different level.

This man was an important lieutenant in the Yamaguchi-gumi, the most feared criminal society in Japan. The other was soberly dressed, studious looking, with his conservative wire framed spectacles, he looked like the accountant he was.

Secretly the Don despised all Japanese. His favourite nephew had died on Iwo Jima at the hands of these sadistic bastards. But business was business. Romano smiled and offered more cognac.

CHAPTER FOURTEEN

LIGHT RELIEF

A week had passed and Spencer was still unnerved at the horrific death of Gino and Louie. Their screams as they died had given him nightmares. Also, the memory of Dutch Ambroos and Isaac the Jew the two hitmen who'd left a significant amount of their vital organs splashed liberally over *his* restaurant; the restaurant he'd become quite attached to. Savannah, on the other hand, was as bright as a button. *I guess when it's war it doesn't help to be squeamish.* He was determined to put it all out of his mind.

The phone rang.

'Hey, Spencer, how's tricks in the restaurant business? I gotta tell you, from where I sit, things aren't too bad at all. Good guys five. Bad guys none, but we do have a development you and Steele have to hear about. Can you leave Dwayne and Rafael to run the show and come round to the Brooklyn FBI office? I'll be waiting.'

'Well, I wonder what's up?' Savannah enthused. 'I'm so glad we have this assignment. I seriously thought my FBI career would continue on in the same vein forever. Thank God for Romano. What a darling! He's saved me from a fate worse than death.'

'What exactly was the fate worse than death?'

'The FBI didn't know what to do with me. You know, the little woman, that sort of thing.'

'So, what were they doing with you?'

'The most boring irrelevant paperwork imaginable. For Chrissake I was even lecturing God damn schoolchildren on the evils of crime.' She grinned. 'If you remember, that's why we met; babysitting Spencer Marlowe in hospital. I was only there because it wasn't considered an important assignment.'

Spencer laughed. 'Well, I'm glad they had a woman assigned to me.'

'Why exactly would you care?'

Spencer was still laughing as he pointed a finger at her. 'Don't you remember? Are my testicles black?'

Savannah blushed. 'Yeah, ok. I get it. That aside,' she rolled her eyes, 'this wasn't why I signed on. If this assignment is successful I reckon my career, my real career, will start happening. Who knows? I might be climbing the ladder, so to speak.'

They hailed a yellow cab, its New York Taxi medallion proudly riveted on the bonnet. The driver manually thrust down the mechanical flag fall sign; he was a typically garrulous native of New Jersey.

Spencer quickly got the impression the cab driver was using his customers for a sounding board for a comedy act, starting with "the one about the two Irishmen." Spencer grinned at Savannah as the cabdriver plied them with jokes about every known New York ethnicity.

Although more than two months had now passed since the restaurant had opened, Spencer still felt like a tourist. The yellow cab slithered and juddered over the pot-holed road on Canal Street. They passed the garish Canal Rubber sign before the cab driver finally ran out of gags.

'Spencer, do you know what they're calling this part of Canal Street now?' Savannah gazed out of the window, a scowl on her face.

'No idea.'

'Hell's Hundred Acres.'

'It looks peaceful enough,' said Spencer, looking around.

'Juvenile delinquents.'

'Come again?'

'Honestly sometimes I wonder where you've been. Teenage gangs … you know, like the Hawks. The Rebels. They organise these rumbles …'

'What's a rumble?'

'For God's sake, Spencer, seriously. A rumble, a rumble.' She shook her head in frustration.' A rumble is when these gangs organise a confrontation. There could be fifty or sixty of them. They come with baseball bats, knives and zip guns.'

'What's a zip gun?'

'Spencer, Spencer,' she murmured wearily. 'A zip gun is a home-made pistol that shoots real bullets.'

'Sounds terrible.' Spencer had no idea about such things, but it was clear crime fighter Savannah was concerned.

Savannah lowered her voice. 'Frankly I wouldn't mind, that is, I mean when all of the Romano business is done with. I wouldn't mind getting involved in sorting out these young thugs.'

'I assume you mean in your capacity as an FBI agent.'

'Well … I guess … Yeah, I suppose'

'Savannah?' I'm getting a horrible feeling. Tell me I'm imagining it.'

'Look, I guess I was thinking out loud. It's just that these gangs wouldn't exist without the God damned kingpins that organise them.'

'Let me guess. Savannah and her trusty bazooka take out the kingpins. Oh, and of course we don't bother with things like due process, a trial, or any of that stuff. Anyway, it sounds like a catch-22 situation.'

'What? Catch what?'

'Catch-22. You know, like the book. You would if you could, but your situation, which gives you the means and the expertise, also prevents you from …' Spencer's voice trailed off.

'Yeah, right, a God damn book no one's heard of. Where do you dig this stuff up from? Honestly, Spencer, you're … you're … I tell you what you are. You're a square.'

The Yellow Cab rumbled to a halt at FBI, Brooklyn, with Savannah still complaining about goody-two-shoes Spencer. 'I'll just bet you'd be like some of the Democrats wanting to get rid of the God damn death penalty. Kiss my go-to-hell! You're not a Democrat, are you?'

'How about we have this conversation another time another place? For all you know the joints probably bugged.'

The elevator whisked them to the fifth floor. A skeleton staff were still hard at work in FBI central. They were greeted by the sound of clacking typewriters, phones ringing and the subdued hum of office chatter.

Savannah whispered to Spencer as they made their way down the corridors towards Dale's office.

'This place makes me nervous. You don't suppose we're in trouble, do you? I mean I had to shoot those bastards … you were there. I mean it's not like we had a choice, I mean …'

Spencer held a finger up to his lips. 'Hey! A bit less of the we. You shot them remember? Anyway, I don't think Dale's going to be upset about two less mobsters to deal with.'

Spencer gazed around the general office where Dale worked, not sure what exactly he'd expected. It was almost too nice, too ordinary, bland even with its almost-new gunmetal grey linoleum, the off-white walls and photos of past US presidents. Surprisingly, there were no signs of cops and robbers. No pictures of America's most wanted. The Brooklyn Bridge dominated the view from the office windows.

Savannah jabbed Spencer in the ribs, whispering, 'I just wonder how many of these office warriors ever get behind the business end of a gun. just look at all these delicate little flowers and the women? For Chrissake they all look like vogue models.' Savannah spat. 'Do you reckon that anybody here's ever shot anyone?'

'Well, I'd certainly bet no one here has shot as many people as you have.' Spencer stifled a laugh.

'Really … do you think so?'

'Savannah. That wasn't meant as a compliment. As for the ladies looking like Vogue models, this is New York. It might surprise you to know most men actually don't mind if ladies look like Vogue Models.'

'Are you for real?' Savannah hissed.

'I really don't want to get personal. In any event I do think you look quite … quite …'

'Quite what?' Savannah barked. Spencer could see the startled faces of some office girls, craning their necks to hear the conversation.

'Quite … nice,' he said hesitantly. Spencer's fear index leapt into the red. *How do I get out of this?*

'You bastard,' Savannah hissed, her voice back to a whisper. 'You're just saying that.'

'Yeah. Possibly, but then I don't want you to shoot me.'

'Alright then, you tell me, smarty pants. What's wrong with this outfit?'

'Savannah, we're under attack by hired killers and you want to discuss fashion. Give me a break.'

'You started it.'

Oh, dear I'm really entering dangerous territory. 'All right then, let's start with the shoes … do you notice any difference between what you're wearing and say, what that lady over there's wearing?'

Savannah peered at the attractively dressed woman walking along the corridor in front of them, as if she had never noticed such things before. 'For Chrissake,' she gasped, they're not shoes, they're stilts. How on Earth could I chase the bad guys wearing those?'

'Well, just maybe she doesn't want to go chasing bad guys.'

'Alright, since you're on the subject, what else?'

'Right then, how about your dress?'

'What's wrong with my dress?'

'How old is it?'

'Let me see … My mother bought it for my graduation … that was … well, it was quite a while ago, I guess.'

'Mm! I rest my case.'

Savannah rather thoughtfully started examining her dress, looking at it, turning to gaze around at the female office staff still here at this hour.

Spencer said nothing. *I wonder if you'd call this a light bulb moment?*

Spencer rather timidly held up a hand. 'What now?'

'*See-ing* as we're on the subject …' He then pointed to his head.

'Hair? You bastard. Everyone says I have lovely hair.'

'That you do.'

'Well, what then?' My mother says I always had hair just like Mary Pickford.'

'Oh of course, Mary Pickford! Isn't she in that new movie … now what's it called … let me see, I think she's starring with Gary Cooper.'

'My God Spencer you really are an idiot. Mary Pickford hasn't been in a movie for thirty ye …'

Oops, I think we may have had another light bulb moment.

Savannah paused at a reflective window, squinting at the poor reflection, at the same time patting her hair into place.

Spencer knocked on Dale's door.

'Come in, come in,' Dale welcomed them both.

It was a pleasant office. In view was a photo of his two young sons in their little league outfits, another of what was presumably a photo of his wife, looking prim and proper as if she was off to church. Spencer smiled. there was even a framed award from the local Lions, the award emblazoned with their distinctive blue and gold logo. Spencer thought it actually looked like an FBI badge. There was a floor to ceiling window. A bookshelf bursting with books in the corner. On the desk was a philodendron in a garishly coloured heavy glass bowl, a notebook lying open, a stack of papers under a paperweight fashioned from a hand grenade cut in half. Spencer wondered about the grenade. Was Dale trying hard to project the macho image expected of a gung-ho crime fighter? Spencer felt like asking, 'Where exactly do the hardcore interrogations take place? Do you have a basement fitted with various instruments of coercion?'

Dale couldn't have looked more corporate if he'd tried, clad in a grey flannel suit, a sombre blue tie and a blindingly bright white shirt, looking like a soap powder commercial.

'First of all, I'd like to say ...' he then cleared his throat as if he was about to announce the grand opening of the Empire State Building, 'Agent Steele, your actions have been commendable, absolutely commendable. And, and of course, while we abhor unnecessary loss of life, you do know you'd no alternative but to take the steps you did. I well understand you'd now be going through a feeling of remorse and guilt ... While personally I've never killed anyone in the line of duty, I know others who have. I do know, by now you'll be going through a guilt phase.'

Savannah said nothing, keeping her eyes downcast.

'I admit, I can't imagine what you must be going through. Four men dead in such a short period of time.'

'Yes, sir, I have to say, it's been hard.'

Spencer watched in amazement as Savannah grabbed a handkerchief from her bag, dabbing imaginary tears.

'Well.' Dale stated earnestly, 'You simply have to get over it. Move on. After all,' he reassured her brightly, 'this's our job isn't it?'

'Yes,' sniffed Savannah, 'but it has kept me awake at night. Perhaps they had children.'

Spencer was doing his best to keep a straight face, all the time thinking *What a performance.*

Dale stood up, and taking a cigarette from an embossed silver cigarette case, carefully fitting it to an ivory cigarette holder. He lit it, turned away and gazed for a moment at the majesty of the bridge.

Spencer flashed a frown at Savannah, shaking his head. She gave him a wink.

'C'mon, c'mon agent Steele, cheer up. Get over it. They're dead and good riddance I say.' Having dispensed with his sage words of advice and wisdom with a clearly guilt-ridden agent Steele, Dale got down to business. 'What we have here is a recording of Romano talking business with some Japs.' The latest model Grundig was sitting on the desk. A truly powerful piece of modern spy catching technology.

Dale was like a child with the latest yoyo.

'I tell you this is really something. The voices are captured on this tape here. Um … now what do I do? I'm still getting used to all of … Ah yes … I press this button, I think.' Dale smiled, giving them a tentative thumbs up. The two reels started to turn. Spencer made appropriate noises. *Just what would you make of iPhone and laptops?*

Dale was obviously proud of this new science. 'I must admit I was a bit surprised when I first brought a tape recorder into the restaurant and, Spencer, you didn't seem at all surprised. I mean you wouldn't have

… I mean, would you've ever have seen one of these gizmos before?'

Spencer was momentarily lost for words. 'No … no, not at all. I think I read about them in a magazine somewhere. The thing is, Dale, science is making such huge advances, I wouldn't be surprised by anything. I mean, I wouldn't be at all surprised if one day they put a man on the moon.'

'Yeah … right. Spencer old chum. I think you've seen to many Flash Gordon movies. Now just gather round, listen up. Romano is talking to a couple of nips. One doesn't speak English, so he's translating. I think the other guy's the boss. Unfortunately, we don't have anyone handy that speaks the damn lingo but we can work out the gist of it.'

'I speak Japanese.'

'Come again?' Dale stared open-mouthed at Spencer

'I speak Japanese.'

'Where on God's Earth did you learn that? I mean, were you in the army? Stationed in Japan, after the war? It can't be that big a secret?'

'It's a long story.' Spencer shrugged.

'I imagine it is.' Dale gaped at Spencer, raising a finger. His mouth opened, then shut. He raised a finger again, his eyes flashing between Spencer and Savannah. He went to speak, then apparently thought better of it. He shook his head mumbling something incomprehensible.

'Yeah ok … ah … moving right along.'

They sat hunched over the recorder as it spilled out the conversation between the crime lord and yesterday's enemies of the land of the free. The coffee and cookies that had been brought in for the occasion sat untouched like unwanted Christmas presents.

Even without Spencer's translation it was possible to grasp the scope of the extraordinary plans being hatched.

The Japanese men had access to a virtual mountain of heroin and morphine. Pharmaceutical quality, apparently a residue of the Imperial Army, stockpiled during the Second World War, in anticipation of an American invasion, which never eventuated. The yakuza had acquired this from the now disbanded military.

The scheme, while certainly bold, was quite simple. The yakuza wanted to sell this white powder for an unbelievable number of US dollars. Of course, the Mafia had the dollars and a market for the product. The booming United States economy had an unquenchable thirst for hard drugs.

At one stage Romano asked the two men idly what they were planning to do with the ill-gotten gains, if the plan could be brought to fruition.

The yakuza, unlike their American counterparts, occupied a curious position in Japan, while they were undeniably a criminal organisation they were also involved in legitimate business.

Listening in on the conversation, it sounded like the alcohol had been free flowing. The accountant was a little unguarded with his comments.

It was like listening to a radio play. Spencer could visualise the scene. Intuitively he understood Romano would have loathed the Japanese, but of course business was business. As the tape rolled Spencer mentally filled in the gaps of the unfolding conference, imagining Romano's thoughts.

'We have big plans,' the accountant boasted. 'Japan is going to rise from the ashes and be greater than ever.' Romano would have nodded politely, his distaste for the Japanese exceeded by the thought of the wealth that would roll in with the sale of the heroin and morphine. Spencer could imagine the don raising a glass. 'Here's to success.'

The Japanese accountant explained to Romano and by proxy the FBI that the plan was to pour money into the practically non-existent Japanese car industry.

'We're going to manufacture automobiles,' he said proudly. 'Furthermore, we'll export them to the US.'

Dale turned off the recorder, and chortled. 'Are these guys in cuckoo land or what? Can you imagine Americans buying Jap cars?'

Spencer smiled.

'Anyhow,' Dale continued, 'all we're interested in is stopping them. At the same time we bring down Romano. We're going to be here for a while, how about I order us some fresh coffee and sandwiches? Anyone hungry?' Spencer and Savannah shook their heads as Dale picked up the phone and ordered, agonizing over whether he should have pastrami on rye or a lobster roll. 'We get stuff sent up from the deli next door and oh boy, it's just great.'

They spent the next hour listening to the gangster's small talk with Spencer translating. Eventually the recording came to an end.

Dale was leaning forward listening intently, munching on his pastrami sandwich, slurping on his coffee, oblivious to the crumbs scattered haphazardly across his shirtfront.

'Ok,' declared Dale, 'Let's leave it there for the moment, I'm going to run it by the chief. We'll come up with a plan.'

CHAPTER FIFTEEN

DELIGHTFUL GREENWICH VILLAGE

'Looks as good as new. Awesome.' Spencer spoke out loud to nobody in particular. He leaned on his broom at the front of Spencer's, marvelling at how quickly the government clean up people had removed any sign of bloodshed and mayhem. Spencer's had hardly missed a beat.

The nights were cooler. Spencer reflected it was now five months since the that fateful day when he'd been stunned by the day bill telling of Einstein's death. Spencer was grateful for the life that had unfolded, giving him a sense of purpose. Always at the back of his mind however, was how long? Was it going to be forever?

Once again, the abyss of self-pity lay before him, a yawning chasm, threatening to swallow him whole. He stared at his reflection in the window. *Get a hold of yourself.* With a brutal determination he forced these maudlin thoughts out of his mind. *Focus on now. Focus on Romano, if he has his way, you're not going to have a bloody future.* Spencer wondered just what Tony Romano had in store for them. He knew vengeance would be uppermost in the don's mind. But for now, Spencer was a proud restaurateur, he enjoyed every aspect of the business. He had insisted on the restaurant having the latest espresso apparatus The imported Italian Faema machine was his pride and joy. it was certainly impressive, lashings of chrome, it sizzled and hummed, steam erupted like a mini-Vesuvius and the fragrant smell of espresso coffee wafted across the room. It had been a conversation piece.

Savannah stared at the new machine and shook her head, 'All that, just to make coffee, you're kidding?'

Rafael whooped with joy, 'Hey man, real coffee. Dwayne, check this out. I know you're a God damn heathen from Indiana but this is real cool.'

Dwayne rolled his eyes. 'Actually, compadre, I prefer Dr Pepper. Give me a hand with these dishes.' He threw a dishcloth at Rafael and sauntered back into the kitchen.

Spencer enjoyed the light-hearted banter, but these wanna be G-Men made him feel old.

He'd just made himself a double espresso, Savannah had quickly become a convert, insisting on starting every day with caffeine hit from the exotic Italian espresso equipment.

Spencer now sprawled on one of the outside chairs sipping his coffee and surveying the street, wondering just when Romano's thugs would reappear. He waved to O'Reilly the friendly beat cop, who yelled 'May the road rise to greet you, young fellow-me-lad.'

Spencer smiled at the burly figure of the cop as he made his way along Morton Street. *We still have some friends.*

He loved Greenwich Village and its bohemian residents, interesting shops and the gracious architecture. The vibrant music scene was so different from the brash commercialism of Times Square.

A pair of Red-Tailed hawks had taken up residence on the facade of the apartment block opposite Spencer's. Two babies had just hatched; they had the curious name 'eye asses'. Spencer had got into the habit of leaving a small bowl of leftovers under the silver maple. Spencer smiled now as the father hawk come swooping down, greedily grabbing every morsel then fly back to feed the ravenous chicks.

'Somebody should tell mummy and daddy hawks it's the wrong time of year to bring babies into the world.'

Greenwich Village abounded with curious and bizarre characters. It was a mecca for radicals, beatniks, artists and guitar playing folk musicians. Spencer usually enjoyed his walk to the Italian deli up the street to buy his precious coffee beans in bulk. The food delivery organised by Dale was efficient but a little unimaginative, certainly good quality coffee beans weren't on their menu. *Time to visit Alberto.*

Spencer sighed as he trudged passed the shoe shop and on to Alberto's Delicatessen

Alberto would normally greet Spencer. '*Buongiorno*, Spencer, *come sta appeso*?' (Good morning Spencer, how's it hanging?)

'I need coffee beans *tu ladro Italiano*.' Spencer would reply in Italian. ('I need coffee beans, you Italian thief.')

Alberto would laugh, they would chew the fat, the swarthy Alberto with a perpetual five o'clock shadow that extended to midnight, would usually thrust a golden delicious apple into Spencer's hand, '*Here chomp su questo paisan*.' (Here, eat this, friend.)

But today the normally ebullient Alberto handed over the jute sack of coffee beans. He seemed sullen.

'Hey man, cheer up, the Dodgers look like winning the World Series, why so *triste* eh?'

Alberto sighed as he took Spencer's five dollar note and handed back some quarters in change. '*Compagno*, I like you, we all like you.'

'I can feel a "but" coming Alberto. What's the problema, my friend?'

'Spencer, all of this *violenza*, it's too much. It's gone too far. You have to pay these people, we all do.'

'Alberto, these people are bad people; they need to be stopped.'

Spencer jumped as Alberto thumped a hairy fist on the counter. 'Who do you think you are? These people can't be stopped. I pay them in New York, my padre pay them in Naples and his father pay them in Milano. You are a nice guy, but you can't win this fight. This is now costing all of us.' Alberto pointed a finger. 'Look over there.' Spencer's head swivelled. 'That's Aristos the barber. How many customers do you see?'

Reading a newspaper, Aristos reclined in one of his leather and chrome steel barber chairs, not a customer in sight. 'He's a good barber, *paisano*. Just look, he has wife, kids.'

'Take your coffee and go. Don't come back.'

Deep in thought, coffee beans under his arm, Spencer strolled sadly back to the restaurant, pausing to glance in the window of the Curious Minds bookstore. Bernard, the scholarly proprietor, appeared to be struggling with a couple of heavy bound tomes while climbing a ladder. Spencer had been a frequent customer of this delightful establishment. He opened the glass and timber door. Bernard, jumped, nearly falling, as the brass bell tinkled.

'Hey, Bernard, can I give you a hand there?'

Bernard seemed to heave a sigh of relief, 'Oh, it's only you. Yes, please Spencer, my hand never really healed properly. Could you please place Ulysses and Finnegan's Wake up on the top shelf?'

Happy to oblige, Spencer grabbed the books and clambered up the ladder, 'Quiet day buddy?'

'Well, Spencer, every day is a quiet day now.'

There was no rancour or bitterness in the bookseller's voice, just tired resignation.

They nattered about books and authors for a few minutes. 'I'm waiting on the new Graham Greene novel, The Quiet American, I think you'd like it.' Bernard spoke as he arranged a display of paperbacks.

'When it comes in, put a copy aside for me please?' Spencer had heard of Greene but never read any of his works.

'You never did tell me, Bernie, what happened to your hand?'

'My hand? Bernard held up his right hand, his fingers bent and twisted. 'Your friend and mine,' he said cryptically.

'Fazio?'

'Have a good day, Spencer. I'll let you know when the book arrives.'

Spencer wended his way back to the restaurant gazing at the stores in Morton Street with a different perceptive. It hadn't occurred to him that there would be collateral damage in their crusade to destroy the Romano criminal empire. He noticed "For Sale" signs posted on a couple of stores. Passing the Morton

Street news stand, a New York Times day bill trumpeted: *Two mob killings in Queens—read all about it.* His resolve was invigorated. *We'll stop these bastards.* He quickened his pace as he approached the restaurant.

An itinerant African American flower seller had set up across the street from Spencer's. She had a stunning array of roses and assorted other blooms that Spencer couldn't identify. The scent wafted gently across the street. She called out to Spencer, 'Hey there. You Spencer?'

Spencer grinned and waved 'Yep that's me.'

'How 'bout you buy some of my roses for your restaurant?'

Spencer wasn't sure if buying roses was accepted in the FBI budget.

'Not today, love. Maybe tomorrow.'

Why must we have the Tony Romanos of the world destroying this delightful colour, harmony and tranquillity?

Spencer had accepted he was in 1955 and could be there for ever or just as before, unexpectedly wake up alongside Michiyo. He missed his wife terribly. His biggest problem, coping with the isolation and not being able to confide in anyone, was difficult as it had been on his two previous trips into the past. It didn't help matters to have Savannah probing and asking awkward questions. 'Do you ever hear from your wife?'

'Ah … not for a while … no.' A bit difficult, as *she hasn't been born yet.*

'Are you separated?'

'Well … we thought we would have some time apart.' *Yes, about sixty-five years in fact.*

'Tell me again, what exactly did you do in Australia, something to do with fishing Fletcher said?'

'Yes … we … umm … used nets, the company was called Internet.'

'And this lady Dorothy. What was it again? Dorothy Comopoulos, wasn't it?' Savannah looked a little smug. 'I'm guessing you and Dorothy might have had a thing going, and your wife, Michiyo, wasn't it?' Spencer nodded. 'And perhaps she found out about it. So, have I hit the nail on the head? You and Dorothy, good old Dot Com were having a bit of a fling, a bit of "making whoopee" perhaps?'

Savannah looked triumphant, 'And while we're on the subject. Michiyo, what sort of name is that? It sounds Jap to me.'

Spencer gazed, bemused at this lady who could simultaneously be a delight and an annoyance. There was something homespun and honest about her, with her nose and freckles. Her half-hearted attempts at fashion suggested she would've been more comfortable in blue jeans and sneakers as she frolicked through the woods and fields of South Dakota. *You can take the girl out of the country.*

'Yes, Savannah. My wife is Japanese. I might add, I love her dearly. And no, I didn't have an affair with Dot Com.' Spencer had decided to nip this conversation in the bud.

Spencer enjoyed Savannah's company and most importantly trusted her, even though her mission to rid the world of the bad guys without the annoyance of a judge and jury was not only confronting but decidedly messy. He'd tried to have a gentle chat about the wisdom of using hollow point rounds, 'Savannah, could we have a little chat?'

'Sure.'

'These cartridges you're using, do you think that sort of fire power is really necessary? Surely a conventional bullet will kill people just as dead?'

'Spencer, when I shoot someone, it's for keeps, ok?' Savannah gave him a withering stare.

I think that effectively ends the discussion.

The balmy morning with its silky sheen of cirrus clouds in a blue sky was about to be interrupted.

New York renowned for sudden changes in weather was now ominous and threatening, the sky was now dark, there was the odd flash of lightening and clap of thunder, then like a harbinger of doom the payphone rang. 'Spencer, glad I got you. I reckon Romano might be on his way. I've had a guy tailing him this last week, and he's just called, saying the Caddy is rolling in your direction.'

'Romano … on his own?'

'Well, he has his driver of course. But that's it. He's on his lonesome. This isn't his style he always has some of his goons with him, so frankly I'm not that concerned. There's simply no way he'd get his hands dirty. Well, certainly not in public. But … but, it's an interesting development. Keep me informed.'

Spencer was puzzled. He too, couldn't for one minute imagine Tony Romano would be planning anything violent on his own.

Savannah was sorting table napkins. Meanwhile, one of the trainees was serving ice cream to a group of college students, all wearing New York Yankees caps. Their raucous laughter carried across the room.

'Romano … on his own?' He's not going to try anything surely?'

'Well, I've got my 0.38 in my pocket.' Spencer shrugged.

Savannah laughed. 'I'd suggest if push comes to shove, hit him with it, don't try and shoot him.' Savannah had seen Spencer's attempts on the firing range. She'd made some very caustic comments.

Savannah froze in the middle of replacing napkins. 'He's here.'

CHAPTER SIXTEEN

ALL IS FORGIVEN

The big black Cadillac swept majestically up to the front of the restaurant; the driver jumped out and flung open the rear door. Romano climbed out, frowning at the light drizzle. Immaculate in a camel hair coat and black homburg he looked more like a captain of industry than the head of a crime empire.

He strode under the restaurant awning just as the rain unleashed itself, puddles started to form and roofs of cars danced with spray. Romano glanced upwards at the tar black sky as some fat drops descended on him, he grimaced, crossing himself. Spencer was amused to see the don's Catholicism on display.

'Spencer, Spencer, nice to see you.'

In spite of everything, Spencer had to smile; Romano's warm greeting extended to a hearty handshake. He almost expected the bear hug and the traditional mobster's kiss on both cheeks.

Meanwhile Savannah watched, gimlet eyes flitting between the Don, his driver and the street. Spencer knew at the first sign of trouble Savannah's heavy artillery would be out, blazing away. The thought occurred to him: Romano perhaps didn't know it was Savannah who'd despatched his lieutenants to mobster heaven.

Romano relaxed; legs crossed. Reclining on one of the rattan chairs at the front, protected from the now drizzling rain by the candy-striped canvas awning. 'I see you've a proper coffee machine, you sure you're not Italian?'

'Italian mother.' Spencer couldn't help but smile,

In spite of all that'd transpired, Spencer found it difficult to dislike the don. It was if Romano lived in a parallel universe, one where he was attempting to wipe Spencer off the face of the Earth, the other where they were old buddies.

'Please join me for coffee, my buy. We need to talk.'

Spencer cast a sideways glance at a scowling Savannah as he folded himself onto the other chair, signalling her for coffee.

They faced each other, there was an awkward silence. A sullen Savannah brought out two double espressos. She wore a hard artificial smile. 'Can I get you anything else, sir? Guns, knives a hand grenade perhaps?'

There was a flash of annoyance from the surprised crime lord, then he cackled. 'Yeah well, I guess I deserved that.'

'Savannah,' Spencer held up a warning finger. 'Just leave us be. Tony comes in peace.' Spencer then turned the finger on Romano. 'You do come in peace Tony?'

'Yeah, yeah, of course I come in peace.'

'Okay girl, get back to work. There's plenty to do in the kitchen.' Spencer winked at Savannah.

Spencer could see Savannah quivering with anger, her nostrils flared, her hands balled into fists. She abruptly turned, striding back into the restaurant.

Tony Romano shook his head, laughing at the exchange. 'Women, eh? Can't live with em, can't live without em.' He pointed at the retreating Savannah. 'Good worker?'

'Yep, good worker, but you know how it is. Thinks she's the boss. I just have to put her into her place sometimes.'

Romano laughed briefly as he gazed at the obviously unhappy serving girl. He was then silent for a minute, appearing to be gathering his thoughts. 'First of all, I'm sorry that Gino … or should I say the late Gino gave you such a working over. I told him to be gentle.'

Gentle, are you kidding me?

Tony sipped his double espresso appreciatively. 'Mmm, hey, that's good coffee. I suppose seeing as you made him look silly, he did use a bit of … poetic licence.'

Poetic licence, you're making it sound like a bible reading. Spencer stared at Tony in amazement.

'But I guess seeing as he's now departed, it sorta makes us even.'

Spencer was lost for words. It seemed as if Tony thought of the business of death destruction and mayhem was some sort of game. Clearly the demise of Gino and Louie hadn't caused the Don any particular distress. *Perhaps he hides his grief.*

Tony waved his hand like the Pope blessing the faithful. 'Spencer … Y'know really, I'm just a businessman. I don't want to hurt anyone. I admit, perhaps some of my methods are … well … perhaps a little unorthodox, but …' And he shrugged. 'You can't make an omelette without breaking eggs, now, can you?' Once again that warm, engaging smile.

So now we're discussing a cooking lesson? Spencer still had trouble reconciling the pleasant Tony Romano with the vicious gangster. 'You forgot to mention Angelo, and of course the two hit men.'

'Ah … yes … Angelo, I can see that was bit of a mistake. But the thing was, I didn't realise at the time it was your restaurant. Had I known, I'd have sent some backup.' Romano shrugged. 'That's really very good coffee.'

'And the would-be assassins?'

Tony pondered that one. 'Yes, they came highly recommended … expensive too, I might add …' He chuckled. 'Fortunately … they only got paid on results. But look, all of that's water under the bridge.'

It may well be water under your bridge, mate, but from where I sit it's a bloody tsunami over mine.

'Yes.' Tony looked pensive. 'I really haven't covered myself with glory. That's what I want to talk to you about. I really couldn't believe Dutch Ambroos and Isaac the Jew could have fucked up so badly.' Romano grimaced, clearly upset at the declining quality of hit men. 'Seriously … in the old days you were given a job … Y'know whack this guy, torch his business, blow up his car … and it was done. I dunno the modern generation …' Tony shook his head in disgust. 'You know what it is, don't you?' Tony pointed an aggrieved finger at Spencer.

Spencer shook his head.

'They get their money too damn easy. That's the problem. In my day if you fucked up there were consequences. Yes sir, consequences. I remember when me and Vinnie … oh my God, what was his last name?' Tony glanced at Spencer for inspiration. 'Yeah, I remember, Vinnie Rizzo. Nice young kid, a bit green but reliable. He ended up being whacked by mistake, someone in Giuseppe 'the Lips' crew mistook him for … oh God it was so long ago. In retrospect it was quite funny; you see poor Vinnie was the spitting image of, of … well it doesn't matter. Anyway, Vinnie and I had to whack some guy. It was winter. Absolutely freezing. The guy was meant to be home at ten and in the end, he didn't roll up until three in the morning. God knows what his wife thought.'

'Would have?' Spencer enquired.

'Well yeah, of course we whacked him as he got out of his car. So, I guess we'd never know what his wife thought about him getting home so late. Anyhow, the point I was making was the modern generation wouldn't sit in a car in the middle of winter. It was snowing. I tell you freezing, absolutely freezing.' Tony shook his head in disgust. 'Seriously, the up and coming wouldn't sit out there freezing their balls off, just so they could whack some guy.' Tony laughed. 'Yeah, they were the good old days. Anyway, that's all history.' Tony took another sip of his coffee, then removed his homburg, placing it carefully on the seat next to him. 'I have a proposition.' Romano drained his coffee. 'I gotta tell you Spencer, I like you. Seriously, from when I first met you at Antonio's and we each had a Reuben sandwich. God, it seems a lifetime ago, doesn't it?' For a moment it was as if Romano was reflecting on the past history of two buddies who had shared life's experiences.

'I'm flattered you like me, Tony, it just makes me wonder how things would have been if you actually disliked me. You sort of give a new meaning to that old saying, "with a friend like that, you don't need enemies".'

Tony waved his hand in a dismissive gesture. He then reached into his coat pocket. Spencer immediately tensed and looked askance at Savannah, whose hand was already snaking towards her shoulder holster. To his relief Tony retrieved a Cohiba and a gold cigarette lighter, proceeding with great care to unwrap the cigar and then light it. 'I woulda offered you one but I know you don't smoke. You really don't know what you're missing,' he added as he inhaled the pungent fumes.

And you my gangster buddy don't know just how close you came to having your brains spread all over Morton Street.

'Ok, Spencer, here's the thing. I gotta problem.' Romano leaned forward, glancing from side to side.

A conspirator about to reveal all. Spencer smiled to himself at the melodrama. 'Really?'

'Yeah, yeah, I'm starting to look silly. Not only in front of my own crew, but the other bosses even the other businesses around here. Once the word spreads that someone ain't paying … well …' He let the statement hang in the air.

'You want me to apologise for not letting your goons kill me?' Spencer stared at the don in open mouthed amazement.

'No, hardly … but here's the problem. it's now a matter of life and death for me. I've always got guys just waiting to take my place. Let me tell you it aint like General Motors where the CEO gets a gold watch and retires, see?' Tony laughed an easy laugh.

Spencer was nonplussed that Tony would discuss the career path of mobsters with him. 'I guess I can see your problem; would it help if I just went and committed suicide?'

'Yeah, that'd work. No, like I said, I gotta proposition, but it's gotta be confidential.' Tony patted Spencer on the shoulder.

'Go on.' In spite of everything, Spencer was intrigued.

'Well, you see, the fact is you've been breaking my balls, but I gotta say I respect you.'

Surprisingly Spencer believed what the Don was saying.

'But the sad fact is, it's now a matter of life and death.' Tony gazed impassively at Spencer, making sure he understood the gravity of the situation. 'I simply don't have a choice. I have to get rid of you. If I don't someone's gunna get rid of me, so I'm gunna have to throw everything at you. So far you been lucky. But remember I've only gotta get lucky once. I have to do whatever it takes. *And I will win.*'

'You said you have a proposition.'

Once again Romano reached into his coat pocket. Spencer could see out of the corner of his eye Savannah standing poised like a gunfighter in a cheap Western.

Romano drew a large brown envelope from his pocket, carelessly throwing it in front of Spencer.

'What's this?'

'Open it.'

Spencer eyed the Don and couldn't see an immediate threat. He opened the missive. Spencer gasped; it was stacked with $100 bills. 'I don't get it.'

'It's simple. There's ten large. I want you to just pack up and leave. There's enough there to go set up somewhere else. I don't care where, Brooklyn, Queens, the Bronx, anywhere you like. But not here.'

Spencer knew the average wage at that time was around $4,000 a year so $10,000 was a small fortune. Spencer gazed at the urbane don, sitting, expressionless, flicking the odd bit of ash off his fine tailoring. Spencer's first reaction was to slide the envelope back. Tony swiftly shoved it back into Spencer's hand.

'Spencer I really don't want to kill you. Ok?' His voice was stone. Tony abruptly stood up, pulling a pristine dollar note out of his billfold, placing it on the table. 'The coffee was my buy. You gotta week. Then I want an answer. All right?'

Spencer thought for a minute. 'I've got partners. I'll have to talk it over with them.' Spencer grabbed the cash, stashing it into his coat pocket.

Without so much as a backward glance the immaculately coiffed and suited crime lord strode to his awaiting limousine.

Spencer glanced at the vacated seat; Tony's homburg remained.

'Hey Tony,' Spencer called out to the disappearing Cadillac.

Savannah galloped to the table. 'What on Earth was that all about?' Her eyes were like saucers. Before Spencer could answer, her gaze fell on the hat. 'Oh, and look he left his stupid "look at me I'm a tough gangster, hat."' She sneered. 'I'll damn well chuck that in the bin. Now, also, what the hell was all that, "Savannah, get back to the God damn kitchen" bullshit? What's your game? Who do you think you are? Spencer the big boss. For Christ's sake, I'm the real deal. I'm Savannah Steele, FBI agent. Who are you? Just a blow in. A man of mystery. All of a sudden, you're the big boss. Geez, you've got some nerve.'

Spencer held up his hands. 'Whoa, hold it right there. It's a game, a bloody game. Romano thinks I'm the boss and you're the harmless serving girl. A serving girl, I might add, who has a big mouth. He sure as hell doesn't need to know you're Annie Oakley in disguise. He probably has no idea of who or what you are, and it's a lot better if it stays that way. You can see that, surely?'

Savannah scratched her head, frowning and staring at the tiled floor. She looked up; a smile wreathed her face. She held a hand out, Spencer shook it.

'Sorry Spencer, you're right. That was the best move by far.' She frowned again momentarily. 'I should've known better. I should've known *you* better. It's just that all along I've had this "She's just a woman" crap. For a silly moment I thought you were, well you know, just like the rest of them.' She grinned. 'I think Maggio's a lucky woman.'

Spencer rolled his eyes. 'Maggio indeed. Anyway, I'm glad that's all sorted. Now let's get back to the man in question. I could easily get the impression you don't like the dapper don?'

Savannah 's eyes narrowed. 'He's well presented. He has superficial charm. But don't for one minute forget the man is a psychopath. He's a big boss in an organisation that murders and extorts money, he's simply evil, and … If ever I get him in my sights, he's dead. I promise you that.'

Spencer shook his head in thought. *You look and act like an innocent country girl that wouldn't hurt fly, but in your own way you're as frightening as Romano.*

Spencer picked up the offending hat. 'I'm going to put it in the office with the things people have left behind … oh look, he's even got his name stitched on the inside band. There's no point upsetting him over something as inconsequential as a hat. If he come back for it, or sends someone for it, I'm giving it back to him, ok?

Spencer placed the homburg on his head at a rakish angle, smiling at his reflection in the office mirror. Without another thought, he placed the hat on a shelf. He had no idea that in just a week's time this very same hat would alter lives.

CHAPTER SEVENTEEN

THE CUSTOMER ISN'T ALWAYS RIGHT

'For Chrissake woman you really are a pain in the ass. All you do is whinge and whine. Keep it up and I'll give you something to complain about.'

The big man in his fashionable double-breasted suit was large with a five o'clock shadow. His olive complexion hinted at his Mediterranean ancestry. The lady was wasp waisted, with rapture blue eyes. Impeccably dressed in a sapphire and white polka dot skirt and a soft grey twinset. The cashmere sweater adorned with a string of pearls. Perched daintily on her head was a dark blue pillbox hat. Altogether an expensive and pleasing combination, spoilt by her subdued and hangdog expression, like a puppy waiting for its owner to give it another kick.

'Here, gimme that menu. You want something to eat?'

'Just coffee please.' She replied, in a voice little more than a whisper.

'Hey, how about some service here? I ain't got all day.' The big man clicked his fingers. Savannah approached the table.

'Yes sir, what would you like?'

'Got any strawberry shortcake?'

'We sure do, and it's the best in Manhattan.'

'Yeah, well spare me the commercial, girlie. A large piece of cake and two coffees. And make it quick. Things to do, places to go. You follow? Where's the John?'

Spencer couldn't help but overhear, smiling as Savannah put on her best subservient 'I'm just a country bumpkin' act. At the same time thinking, *just keep pushing her buttons, pal, and you might live to regret it.*

'Through the main doors, sir. Over to the right you can see the signs.' Savannah smiled sweetly.

The big man laboriously climbed to his feet, waddling off to the Gents.

The lady turned her face to Savannah and smiled. Savannah gasped. One eye was black. Her arm bruised. Savannah spoke quietly. 'Did he do this to you?'

'Yes, but please, please don't say anything. I'll just cop some more when we get home.'

'You must go to the police. They'll charge him.'

The lady sobbed. 'You don't understand. Nick's a lawyer. A lawyer with very, and I mean very, powerful clients. If I went to the cops, I'd be dead. And then there's the kids.' She wrung her hands, her gaze focussed on the retreating figure of her husband.

CHAPTER EIGHTEEN

THE WHITE HORSE

'Get out ya bum, and stay out.' The beefy bartender who clearly doubled as bouncer was in the middle of throwing out a troublesome drunk from the White Horse Tavern in Hudson Street, Greenwich Village. The bartender's massive arms, with faded sailor tattoos and his weightlifter's chest, should have been enough to deter even the most obnoxious of drunks.

Dale, Spencer and Savannah watched in awe as the barman so adroitly dealt with the troublemaker. He'd picked the man up effortlessly, throwing him into the gutter, wiping his hands as if to say, 'Well, that's the trash sorted out.'

The bartender's snarling features quickly morphed into a dazzling smile of welcome. 'Come in, folks. Take the load off. I'll show you to a booth. We're pretty darn busy.' He shoved the brass handled swing doors open for them.

Three business-suited guys breasted the bar. One pointed, yelling across the crowded room. 'Yo, Spencer Marlowe. You're a God damn hero. We heard what you did to the Romano outfit. Keep it up, boy.' Spencer smiled and waved.

The ragtag collection of drinkers stared at the newcomers with interest. A burly, bearded man in a longshoreman's khaki bib and brace overalls slurred, 'Hey tootsie, let a real man buy you a drink.'

The barman watched, a gleam in his eye as he picked up the phone.

'Remind me not to get drunk here,' Savannah whispered.

'You could always shoot him.'

Savannah poked him painfully in the ribs. 'I'll damn well shoot you, if you keep this up.'

'Now, now, children,' Dale said mildly. 'No squabbling.'

Spencer glanced sideways at Savannah, who laughed. 'Yeah ok. I guess I asked for that.'

Spencer turned his attention to this New York watering hole. *Well, it certainly has atmosphere.* A hubbub of voices. A hundred conversations told in loud voices. Tantalising scents as waiters scurried, juggling multiple plates of food creating a warm friendly environment. Fine dining it wasn't, but heaped plates of meatloaf, fried chicken, spaghetti and pizzas were wolfed down. Froth-topped tankards of ale appeared with lightning speed. No one was kept waiting. *Yep, atmosphere plus.*

There were white horses everywhere. Crammed on shelves were countless white horse figurines. There was a large statue over the entrance. Even the circular light fittings had miniature white horses on them. Exotic spirits were jam-packed onto the shelves behind the bar.

Dale led the way to a private booth. They crammed into a tiny cubby hole next to an illuminated mirror advertising 'White Horse Tavern' in bold blinking technicolour lighting. Spencer had told him about the don's offer and the $10,000.

As always, Dale reminded Spencer of a schoolboy planning mischief with his buddies. Dale rubbed his hands together and his face broke into a wide smile as Spencer handed over the cash-filled envelope. Dale weighed it in his hand. 'Oh boy, this is great, isn't it? Here we have Tony Romano's hard earned. If he only knew the Feds had its hands on his moolah, he would …' Dale left the sentence hang as he slid the envelope into his coat pocket. 'It's not every day that things go to plan. But so far, we've been having a dream run. Here's to crime.' He raised his glass in a toast.

Given that the White Horse was a known hangout of villains and sinners, Spencer wasn't sure if he was referring to the bar or the development with Romano. They perched on the worn oak bench with their Budweisers, waiting to hear the plan.

'Who would've thought, eh? The don gets his wish and the government gets the ten gs.' Dale grinned, a rakish exposure of immaculate dentistry.

Savannah immediately exploded. 'Romano gets his wish? 'We're going to let that creep win?' She shook her head with disgust. Spencer kicked her under the table. With difficulty she held her tongue, knowing, in the FBI you didn't want to antagonise your superiors. Spencer on the other hand didn't see himself as being on a career path.

'Dale, honestly, I'm with Savannah. We're on the cusp of destroying Romano. If we can stay in business the mob is going to get rid of him. I don't get it. We've got him on the ropes. Another few weeks of this and he's going to be kaput. He's said as much himself. Dale, I tell you, Romano wasn't joking, he's scared. He knows he's in big trouble.'

Dale held his hands up. 'Believe me we're not backing off. Oh no!,' He wagged a finger. 'We're going to cause a load of grief for the whole five families and I'm sure we'll be getting rid of Romano in the process.' Dale leaned forward, lowering his voice. 'Sure, the mob will get rid of Romano, if he doesn't get rid of you two first. But … what happens then, eh? I'll tell you what happens. All of a sudden there's a new godfather. A new *capo dei capi* and then the whole God damned thing starts again. Oh no, boys and girls, we have bigger fish to fry. You're gunna love this.' He leaned back in his chair. Spencer and Savannah waited expectantly. Dale was clearly relishing the moment. He then leaned forward, placing his hands on the table.

'Romano's given you a week to get out? So, you have another six days, right? I don't think he'll try anything in that time. After that, pack up and leave, ok? Disappear. Skedaddle. Vamoose.'

Spencer and Savannah were silent, knowing there was more to come. 'And then …' Dale flashed a reassuring smile, 'you're both going to Japan.' He leant back; hands clasped behind his head.

Spencer and Savannah were momentarily speechless. She found her voice first.

'Japan? Are you serious?'

'Serious? Of course, I'm serious. October in Japan they tell me is perfect. I've checked it out. The occasional rainy day, 65 degrees. Cherry blossoms, Mount Fuji. Hell, why am I telling you, Spencer?' Dale grinned.

Spencer focussed on Dale starting to wonder if there was perhaps some sort of undiagnosed mental illness lurking. *Perhaps he's bipolar?*

'I know it sounds crazy. But just listen. Romano has had a meeting with all the families. We've got it recorded. We can recognise Mario the Impaler. Luca Russo. In fact, the whole darn gang. Honestly this's classic. They're coughing up one mill between them. It's all being handled by their mouthpiece, Nick Genovese. Genovese is going to fly to Tokyo along with one of their made men, a vicious rat-faced little punk, Carmine Ferrera. They're going to inspect the smack, make sure it's top quality, then oversee its shipping to New York. They'll wire Tony Romano, who'll transfer the cabbage.' Dale sat back again, his hands folded behind his head, a smirk on his face.

'So where exactly do we fit in?' Spencer was puzzled, glancing at Savannah, who shrugged.

'Thought you'd never ask. Oh boy, you're gonna just love this. We're going to grab Genovese and Ferrera at the airport, tell them what we've got, and this's the best bit, we're gonna get them to rat on the others. But in any event, you two,' he waved a finger at Spencer and Savannah, 'are going to take the place of their guys, Ferrara and Genovese. The nips wouldn't know 'em from Adam.'

Spencer's mind was in a whirl. *This could work.* 'Dale, how can you be sure these two will rat out their buddies?'

'Spencer, we know all about this bullshit code of silence the Mafia are so proud of. This … what's it called? Yeah, *omerta*, that's it. Ferrara on his own probably wouldn't squeal, but the mouthpiece wouldn't have too many loyalties. So … my man, we can virtually guarantee the lawyer will roll over. Once we confront the unlovable Carmine with that bit of info, he really won't have a choice. Anyway, you let us worry about that.'

Spencer was speechless. Predictably Savannah's first question was, 'Can I carry?'

'I had an idea that'd be your first question, Agent Steele. As of April, '52, Japan became a sovereign country again. But they give us and our agencies almost unlimited leeway. Yes, you can carry, ok?'

'I imagine we'd have to liaise with their police?' Spencer queried, scratching his head.

'This is where your language skills will be important, Spencer. By the way, you never explained how come you speak the lingo?'

'It's a long story.'

'That's what you said last time,' Dale said drily. 'Perhaps one day you might fill me in with the missing pieces. I don't know anyone who speaks Japanese. Why is it I get the feeling there's so much I don't know about you?'

Spencer decided this was an ideal time to change the subject. 'What about back up from any of our guys who are still stationed in Japan?' Spencer had a better idea than most just how ruthless the yakuza were. He could imagine just how quickly things could get out of hand.

'I'll give you the contact details of a battalion of Rangers who are currently stationed in Tokyo. I can't imagine you'll need their help, but let me tell you, they're a bunch of tough guys. They don't have a lot to do now days. I imagine they'd be pretty keen to get involved if there was any trouble,' Dale said with a grin. 'Oh, and nice one.'

'Nice one, what?'

'Nice one, changing the subject. You're very good at that I've noticed.' He shook out a cigarette from a soft pack, lighting it with a practised motion. Dale sucked greedily on his cigarette as he continued to stare at Spencer as if he was waiting for a detailed explanation. Dale winked at Savannah. 'Somehow, I don't think I'm about to be enlightened, what do you reckon, Agent Steele?'

Spencer shrugged, not knowing what to say. Savannah merely glanced between them for a few seconds before shrugging it off with a bemused smile.

'Oh well, let's stick with the business at hand.'

'Dale, I don't know why you should think I have secrets. I mean seriously, lots of people speak several languages, I think I've told you all there is to know.'

'Yeah, well as John Wayne said, "That'll be the day".' Dale sat back in his chair; his mouth curved upwards in a cynical smile.

Spencer was feeling decidedly uncomfortable. This type of scrutiny made him feel very vulnerable. *Time to move this along.*

'Who's the commander of the Rangers and where exactly are they stationed?' Spencer had a feeling that in spite of Dale's optimism the yakuza were not to be underestimated.

'Let me see, oh yeah … their commander is Colonel Buck Randall. They're situated at Hardy Barracks at—'

'I know the barracks,' Spencer interrupted. 'That's in central Tokyo.'

'How the hell could you possibly know that?'

I've really got to learn to keep my trap shut.

'Um … my company Internet Fishing, did a lot of trade with Japan. Dot Com and I had quite a few trips to Tokyo, and ah … of course we got to know Tokyo pretty well. And … well the Japanese, just um … I mean, they love their fish, don't they?' Spencer smiled half-heartedly.

'Did you sell them fish? Did you buy fish? What exactly?' Dale stared at Spencer, his eyes narrowing.

'Ah … yes, they particularly liked a fish found only in Australian waters.'

'And what sort would they be?'

Spencer realised that Dale hadn't completely swallowed the story of his somewhat vague history. 'Oh um, that would be micro fish. They just loved micro fish. They were also known locally as gigs. There was always a lot of excitement when there were giga bites.'

'Enough already about fish. This calls for a celebration.' Savannah grabbed a passing waiter.

'Yes, ma'am.'

'I'll have a vodka martini, easy on the vermouth.'

'Will that be all?'

'No, hang on, make it a double. What about you Spencer? You going to join me? Let's make a little whoopee, hey?'

'No, not right now, and you've already had two Buds.'

'Two Buds. Listen here. I'm a country girl. Drink you under the table any day, Jeez, what a square. I seem to remember you saying, "Remind me not to get drunk in this place" so I'll just watch. What about you, Dale, you going to join the party?'

Dale hastily swallowed the last of his Budweiser.

'Love to, but I'm actually still working and I've just seen a guy I know go into the other bar. So,

Savannah, Spencer, great deeds are going to be done. You'll be fighting the good fight. See you both soon.'

Spencer waited for Dale to add the Superman slogan, 'Truth, justice and the American Way.'

'Hey, go easy on that.' Half of Savannah's martini had disappeared, the olive now delicately gripped between her teeth.

'Did anybody ever tell you Spence baby, you're a bit of a square? Waiter!'

Another double martini appeared. *What the hell? She's been a bit tense lately and I'm sure that dickhead boyfriend wouldn't be a barrel of laughs.*

And then, as if Savannah could read his mind, 'Y'know Spence, Sesh, I mean Seth, he's a good man, isn't he? He's dedicated, I mean, like, hell I'm a bit squiffy, aren't I?'

'Yes, and yes. You are a little tiddly. And yes, I agree Seth's dedicated and I'm sure he's a good man.'

Savannah's eyes narrowed, 'You don't like him, do you?'

'I like him fine, Savannah,' Spencer lied.

'S'good. I think we better go.' She rose unsteadily to her feet.

Savannah swayed out of the White Horse with Spencer holding her arm. Night was beginning to creep over Manhattan and Hudson Street.

'Whoa, the ground keeps moving. Whassup Spence, why's the ground moving?'

'C'mon girl, you have to walk this off.'

'Hey Spence, did I ever tell you about good old downtown Pierre?

'Yeah, well you told me a little.'

'I tell you, it was ordinary, I mean real ordinary. It was like a Rickey Mooney, shucks, Rooney, Mickey,

Beautiful summers, swimming in the Oahe Reservoir on the Missouri River. Wintertime, oh boy, skiing on Deer Mountain. No kidding, we had it all until that bastard ...' Savannah started to cry.

'Yeah, I know. C'mon, Savannah.'

Spencer pointed Savannah in the direction of James J Walker Park. He figured there would be a bench. Savannah could sit until she sobered up a little.

He scanned the area for a coffee shop. Nothing. Just as they entered the confines of the park, Spencer noticed a red Cadillac pull into a vacant car space. *Surely not?* Spencer's stomach lurched as he recognised the beefy frame of Angelo Fazio climbing out of the Caddy, scanning the area. An oily smirk spread across Fazio's face. Angelo leaned into the car, probably speaking to his passengers. Three others clambered out, two clad in typical Mafioso loud tailoring and a fit young guy shaped like an isosceles triangle; broad at the top, narrow at the hip. Spencer thought he knew the face but couldn't put a name to him.

Spencer spied a bench and hustled Savannah onto the seat. 'Hey, slow down. Where's the fire?' Savannah slurred.

The four men strode grim-faced in the direction of the park, Angelo at the front, three behind they stood braced for action. Spencer felt puzzled by the odd man out. An athlete, surely. Tall, not an ounce of fat but ginger hair? Certainly not Mafiosi. The others looked like they had the same tailor, right down to the two-tone Oxfords and the black and white fedoras.

'Angelo, how's it hanging, sport?' Spencer smiled.

'You got lucky last time, Marlowe. But not today,' Angelo sniggered.

'Dear me, Angelo, you really are slow on the uptake. Just look at what we have. It's not exactly a fair fight, now, is it? Seriously, only four. You're going to need more than that. If you want to send out for more backup, I can wait. I'm a bit curious, however; what the hell is the carrot-top doing here? How old is he, sixteen? He doesn't look like one of your usual Mediterranean morons.'

'You sure got a mouth on you, Marlowe. We don't need no more help. This is Terry the Terror, from Toronto.'

It was all Spencer could do to hold back laughter. He remembered now, seeing day bills advertising a prize fight at Gleason's Gym on the Brooklyn waterfront, and he'd shaken his head at the ridiculous name of the contender.

'Angelo, you're kidding. *Terry the Terror?*'

The redhead broke his silence. In a nasal Brooklyn accent, he whined, 'I told you, Mr Fazio, I didn't like that name.'

'Toronto?' Spencer laughed, 'The kid's never been on the other side of the lake. Where are you from, sonny?'

'I'm from Brooklyn Heights, Mr Marlowe. Mr Fazio reckoned, "Terry" rhymed with "terror," which rhymed with "Toronto".'

'It's a good thing your name wasn't Buck,' Spencer guffawed.

One of the Mafiosi chipped in, 'Hey Fazio, stop the gab. Let's just take this shmuck apart. Some of us have things to do.'

'You asked for it, Marlowe, say your fucking prayers.'

'Well boys, it's time for something different.'
There was still a good six feet between Spencer and
Angelo when Spencer launched the *mae geri* jumping
kick. It was lightning fast and caught Angelo
diagonally across his face. The heavy welted sole of
Spencer's shoe was like a baseball bat. Fazio's nose
broke with a loud crack. He dropped. Lights out,
nobody home.

Terry the Terror watched in horror. Spencer
winked at him and with two hands grabbed another
stunned Mafiosi by the collar, wrecking his carefully
shaved face with a powerful headbutt. He threw the
semi-conscious thug into the arms of his comrade. As
the thug unwittingly wrapped his arms around him,
Spencer drove his fist into the side of his head. The
side of the skull is the thinnest bone and potentially
the most lethal. The second hoodlum folded on top
of the first, in a neat, bloody pile.

Terry the Terror had adopted a boxing stance.
Spencer cast a critical eye over him.

'That's not too bad, Terry. You're protecting your
face which is good, but elbows, man, elbows?'

'What do you mean?'

Spencer moved in close, punching him, not too
hard in the solar plexus. 'See what I mean? Keep those
elbows in.'

Terry gasped, trying to suck in air. 'Thanks, Mr
Marlowe. I'll watch that.'

'Remember, Terry, this isn't Marquis of
Queensbury here, so anything goes.'

'Who?'

'Marquis … It doesn't matter.' Spencer darted in
close, easily avoiding a roundhouse swing. 'Now

watch.' Spencer feinted with a right, then kicked Terry firmly in the right shin.

'Shit,' the boy screamed, 'that fucking hurt!' He sat down, rubbing his aching limb.

'See what I mean, Terry? It's not lethal, but there aren't too many guys who have a lot of fight left in them after that happens.' Spencer spun around at the sound of running feet.

'Freeze, hands in the air, FBI.'

'Here comes the cavalry,' Spencer muttered.

A panting Dale Fletcher, gun and badge in hand, raced up. 'Ok you, hands against the wall …'

Spencer grinned. 'Dale, we don't have a wall.'

'Oh, right. Blast. I don't get to do this sorta stuff very often. Yeah, of course. Hands above your head.'

A stricken Terry the Terror from Brooklyn Heights placed his hands on his head.

'Actually, Dale, young Terrance here isn't one of the mob. There's a bit of a story. Can we just send him on his way? He's got a lot of training to do. Isn't that right, Terry?'

'Yes, sir, Mr Marlowe.'

Spencer placed a fatherly hand on his shoulder. 'Now Terry, I suggest you find yourself another backer. These guys,' Spencer pointed at the untidy heap of unconscious wise guys, 'they're nothing but trouble.'

'Yes, sir, Mr Marlowe.' Terry nodded vigorously.

'One more thing.'

'Yes sir?'

'Don't tell Angelo about this gentleman here.' Spencer pointed at Dale.

'No, sir. Anyway, I'm done with these guys. Angelo wanted me to take a dive in the fifth. All for a lousy C-note.'

Dale holstered his gun, casting a doubtful glance at the retreating Terry the Terror.

'What in hell happened? And is Agent Steele ok? Did someone hit her? She's unconscious.'

Agent Steele now lay peacefully on the park bench, emitting unladylike snores.

Spencer recounted the story to the incredulous Dale Fletcher. 'No kidding? Four of them? Amazing.'

'Well, three really. Young Terrence was a reluctant draftee. He's a good lad.'

Dale scowled at the unconscious villains. 'I'll get NYPD to pick them up. I reckon we could get then to do some time, for sure.'

'Don't do that, Dale, please.'

Dale's eyes narrowed. 'You trying to tell me my job, Marlowe?'

'Dale, all I'm saying is, right at this moment, let's not rock the boat. You can bet your bottom dollar Fazio won't tell Romano about this. He'll be too embarrassed, and the last thing we need is for Tony to get a whiff of the Feds.'

CHAPTER NINETEEN

THE FAT MAN

'Have your bags packed and, be ready to go at a moment's notice.'

Spencer and Savannah had to wait until Dale gave them the go-ahead for Japan.

Savannah whistled a tune from a Broadway musical as she wiped down tables. She seemed to have forgotten about her drunken escapade. Her eyes narrowed when she spotted the fat lawyer from the previous week, alighting from a cab, then entering Spencer's.

Apparently in a better frame of mind, he smiled at Savannah. 'You were right, sweetie; you do have the best strawberry shortcake in Manhattan. I'll have a large slice and a coffee.' He sat down heavily on the chair, seeming to fall into it, his chins wobbling in unison with a stomach that rose in a wave and settled like ripples on a pond.

'Certainly, sir.' Spencer noticed a resolute glint in her eye.

Savannah brought out the cake and coffee, then putting on a voice, suggesting she was in awe of this important man. 'Excuse me, sir, I believe you're a lawyer.'

'Yep, sure am.'

'Well, sir,' Savannah whispered in a timid voice, 'I need the services of a lawyer, could you help me?'

'What's it about?'

'I want to see about a divorce.'

Spencer was moving in and out of earshot. He had grasped the gist of the conversation. *What on Earth are you playing at? Divorce? And what in hell is this 'I'm just a simple serving girl' bullshit?*

The lawyer looked her up and down, Spencer thought like the spider and the fly.

He handed Savannah a card. 'I've gotta fairly full day tomorrow, come to my office at 42 Commerce Street at five pm. You'll be my last client for the day.' He gave her a wink. 'We might have a drink afterwards.'

Savannah glanced at the card. 'Thank you, Mr Genovese, that'd be nice.'

CHAPTER TWENTY

LOOSE ENDS

'**G**'night Spencer I'm off.'

'Savannah, you're up to something. I know it.'

'Who me? Just some shopping … you know?'

'Actually, I don't know. I do know you of all people don't just go shopping. Would you like some company?'

'No, no, it's just, you know, ladies' stuff,' she said airily. She had her handbag and a large paper shopping bag emblazoned with the bold red Macy's star.

Savannah entered the plush office of Nick Genovese, Attorney at law. Everything about the office reeked of money and bad taste. Savannah grimaced at the garish carpet, the smoothly nasty wallpaper. Prominently on the desk was a coffee mug with the words 'Biggest Dick in Manhattan' in black lettering. *Well Nick you certainly lift bad taste to a whole new level. This looks like a Kansas City brothel.*

'Come in, gorgeous, make yourself at home. All the staff have gone for the day. Would you like a drink?' Genovese was slumped in his chair, in shirtsleeves, the two lower buttons undone exposing a fat hairy stomach, reminding Savannah of the overlapping rings of the Michelin Man. His braces strained to hold his trousers up over his distended belly.

Savannah shook her head, sitting primly on a brocade chair. The lawyer hauled his bulk to the drinks trolley before plonking himself heavily behind his ostentatious teak desk. He laced his hands behind his head, revealing dark sweat stains under his arms.

He poured himself a whisky and soda, belching loudly into his hand. 'Now sugar, tell me all about it. I warn you I don't come cheap, but … we might be able to work something out.'

'Well actually, Mr Genovese, I've come to talk about you using your wife as a punching bag.'

'Did that bitch of a wife of mine put you up to this … did she? Well, she's gonna suffer. I'll tell you that for nothing. Now you can just fuck off out of my office. Go on, fuck off out of here, *now*.' He started to raise himself out of his chair. His meaty hands grasped the wooden arms, trying to propel his considerable mass upwards, his face red and sweaty.

'Sit down.' Savannah delved into her handbag, fishing out the 0.32 revolver that had once been the property of the late, colourfully named Isaac the Jew.

'Now, just you wait a minute. Do you know who you're dealing with?'

'Oh yeah. I know alright. A fat pig who beats his wife.'

Sweat beaded on his brow as he unsuccessfully tried to adopt his best courtroom persona. Managing a weak smile, he pleaded, 'I've got money here. Lots of money.'

'You have lived too long, Nick Genovese.' Savannah smiled, a dreamy contented smile.

Crack, crack. One shot, centre mass. The other, a head shot. The small calibre handgun's noise didn't carry outside of the office.

Savannah glanced briefly at her handiwork. She opened the bag with the bold Macy's logo 'Way to Go', carefully removing Tony Romano's homburg, placing it on a chair. The well-used 0.32 Smith and Wesson revolver she threw carelessly into the wastepaper basket. Her white gloved hands were stained with powder burns.

With a spring in her step the lady from Pierre, South Dakota headed in the direction of Morton Street. A country girl. Country clothes, country hairstyle, clutching her Macy's shopping bag.

CHAPTER TWENTY-ONE

PLANS CHANGE

*I*s this the calm before the storm, no bad guys, *just regular customers?* Spencer was afraid they were being lulled into a false sense of security. There was no intelligence from Dale.

'I don't get it, Savannah. Dale and his boys would still be listening in on the ungodly, I can't imagine we haven't been featured in the mob's comedy hour.'

Spencer noticed Savannah seemed to be quite upbeat, happily serving customers, working in the kitchen and joking with their FBI staff. 'Hey, Dwayne if you change your mind about the FBI, you could always become a chef. Those pork tenderloin sandwiches you whipped up were the bee's knees.'

Dwayne grinned and continued wiping a table.

Spencer gazed grim-faced out of the window, scanning Morton Street for hoodlums.

'Stop worrying Spencer, I reckon they're on the ropes. Hell, they're probably thinking it's all got to be just a little too hard.' She punched him playfully on the arm.

'Yeah maybe, but it could be the calm before the storm.' *I could get used to this: nice people, serving them coffee and sandwiches. Time flies, how long have I been here? It's been, my God, it's been six months.*

The FBI waiters and kitchen hands had adapted to their new environment, appearing to be enjoying their roles.

He knew it couldn't last. Once again the phone rang, Spencer glared at the annoying instrument. *It's never good news.*

'As soon as you close, catch a cab to the Brooklyn office, you and Agent Steele.' Dale was terse and to the point.

The Yellow Cab sped across Manhattan and over the Brooklyn Bridge, a wall of summer rain descended, hammering the cab. The driver cursed as the wipers fought a losing battle. Savannah and Spencer were lost in their own private world. Savannah was uncharacteristically withdrawn. The upbeat Agent Steele had disappeared. 'Well Savannah, what surprises do you think Dale has for us today?'

'How the hell would I know? I'm not a fortune teller.' She snapped.

What the hell's the matter with her?

Savannah continued to peer morosely out of the window. 'Look, I'm sorry Spencer, I guess thing are getting to me, I didn't mean to bite your head off.' She managed a weak smile. 'I guess just knowing these gangsters are trying to come up with inventive ways to kill us, well … it gets to me a bit. I think it's damn unfair they have plenty of money and no rules and we are the reverse. Precious little money and all the rules.' Savannah sat with her legs crossed fidgeting with her hair and avoiding eye contact.

Something's got you worried girl. What have you been up to?

'I suppose you'd be happy to hunt them down and shoot them?'

'Oh … no … That would never do, would it? Imagine if I went and ambushed Romano or any other of those Mafia bastards and shot them in cold blood. That wouldn't be proper, now, would it?' Savannah lapsed into a surly silence until they arrived at Dale's office.

'Make a run for it.' Spencer handed the driver a five, for a three sixty fare and they made a mad dash for the grey concrete façade of FBI Brooklyn. Savannah held her handbag over her head. Spencer was grateful for his smart fedora, now sodden with the relentless downpour.

They flashed their ID's at the unsmiling security guard who looked at them enquiringly as he slid the window back on his steel cage. The foyer was steel and polished concrete, institutional and brutal.

'Marlowe and Steele to see Special Agent Fletcher.' Spencer tried a smile, to no effect.

'Fifth floor' The steel gate swung open and they stepped into the elevator vestibule.

'Customer relations don't seem to be a part of FBI training.' Spencer observed drily.

'Poor darling,' Savannah muttered.

Once again, they strode along the now familiar grey and off-white corridors of power to hear the latest.

'Come in, come in. Gee whiz, you look like drowned rats. Have a seat. We got news.'

Spencer and Savannah waited expectantly. He got straight to the point. 'The mob lawyer's been shot.'

'How does this affect us?' Spencer glanced at Savannah, who sat there, grim-faced.

Dale appeared pensive, selecting a Lucky Strike from his silver cigarette case he fitted it to his holder.

Searching through his pockets, eventually locating a worn Zippo. He drew back on the cigarette, immediately breaking into a paroxysm of hacking coughs. 'I should really switch to Camels. I believe that's what the doctors recommend. You don't smoke, do you Spencer?' Spencer shook his head. 'I tell you there's nothing better to settle your nerves. Anyhow, back to the business at hand, I'm not entirely sure how it affects us. Frankly it's all a bit mysterious.'

Agent Steele leaned forward. 'Surely mob people get killed all the time for all sorts of reasons. How can this possibly affect us?'

Spencer glanced again at Savannah. Somethings not right. She's edgy. She's sweating. None of the smart comments you'd expect.

Dale scratched his head, shuffling through some black and white photos of the dead lawyer. 'This was Nick Genovese, a nasty, greedy, grasping creep; someone went to his office and executed him.'

'One in the head and one in the chest.' Spencer winced as he flicked through the photos. The man's face was unrecognisable.

'The classic professional hit, the double tap.' Dale nodded.

Spencer was curious, so again he asked, 'So how does this affect us?'

'I'm not entirely sure. Genovese was going to be the guy who was going to Japan to inspect the merchandise and authorise the money transfer to the Japs, when the heroin and morphine was on its way.' He held both hands up. 'I'm sure they'll have someone else quick smart. But here's the rub … the police found the murder weapon thrown into a wastepaper basket in his office and … wait for it … Tony Romano's hat was left on an office chair.'

Spencer's head jerked around like a marionette doll, he glared at Savannah, who sat silently.

'Romano has been picked up by the NYPD, but they know it's a very thin rap, his new lawyer will have him out in no time.' Dale looked grim.

'Surely that sort of evidence would be fairly damning?' Spencer stammered, his mind in a whirl.

'Even the cops don't think he did it. I mean … come on … top crime lord goes to his lawyer's office … shoots him … leaves the murder weapon where it's certainly going to be found and then conveniently leaves a hat with his name stitched on the band, yeah … really?'

Spencer sneaked a surreptitious glance at Savannah, whose gaze seemed to be steadfastly fixed on the Brooklyn Bridge.

I can't believe this. She couldn't have, could she?

Spencer forced himself to focus, he felt like a heavyweight boxer had driven a pile driver blow into his stomach. *I have to say something.* The ghastly word *murder* kept running rampant through his mind, over and over *murder, cold blooded murder. My God this is nightmare stuff. Can I in all conscience do nothing?* He forced himself to play the part of an interested observer. As he tried to speak, he felt his mouth drying up, he swallowed, managing to mumble. 'So, who do you reckon did it?'

'The ballistics from the weapon that was retrieved from the wastepaper basket is linked to a number of homicides involving the criminal fraternity, so there's little doubt that it's a mob hit, but to try and link it to Romano just doesn't make sense.'

Spencer and Savannah spilled onto the street. The meeting with Dale had finally wound up.

'Well,' said Savannah gaily, 'I'm off to see Seth.' She seemed to have mysteriously regained her normal good humour.

'Just hold it right there. You and I need to talk.'

'Sure, what about?'

'Not out here. I'll buy you a drink, ok?' Spencer took her by the hand.

They were facing the historic Brooklyn Inn on Hoyt Street with its unique triangular façade, and grey stippled paintwork. The bar was dark and furtive, which to Spencer seemed fitting. The rough finished ruby red walls and subdued lead lights added an air of subtle menace. He ordered two Knickerbocker beers; they went to a secluded booth. 'Sit,' he ordered.

Savannah perched meekly on the hard oak plank.

'Why … why did you do it?'

'Do what?'

'You know bloody well what I'm talking about. I really don't want to yell it out.'

They were both silent as the waiter placed the drinks before them.

Savannah took a long pull of her beer. 'Boy oh boy, that's good. Just what I needed.'

Spencer was drumming his fingers on the tabletop. Savannah sighed. 'Ok, let's talk.'

Spencer glanced around, making sure nobody was in immediate earshot. 'I can't believe it; you murdered that guy.'

'Executed, Spencer, executed.'

'I've a good mind to tell Dale. And then there was the hitman, Isaac. You set him up. You knew he was going to go for his gun.'

'It really was his choice, wasn't it?' Savannah smiled sweetly. 'Now. How about you listen to me for a change?' Savannah daggered her finger, her face flushed. 'The hitman, Isaac the Jew? Sure. I knew he was going to go for his gun. For chrissake Spencer, he was a cold-blooded murderer. He killed people for money. He didn't care who, or what they were. It was just about the *dinero*. Now you tell me, is the world a better place without him or what?'

'And what about the lawyer? I bet he didn't go for a gun?'

'Oh yes the lawyer,' Savannah said with a sneer. 'He was a wife beater and a lap dog for the Mafia. He was a piece of human excrement.'

'You can't just go round shooting people.' Spencer had a horrible feeling he was losing the argument.

'Really, why on Earth not? I'm good at it. And please, you tell me … why not get rid of these people? Time and time again they get off. Or they serve a few years and they're out again. Do they go straight?' She laughed cynically.

'I really don't know what to do with you.'

'Do you really want to tell Dale?' Savannah placed her hand on his.

'I suppose if I said yes, you'd shoot me?'

Savannah smiled. 'Spencer, you really are a man of mystery, quite frankly your story about Michiyo and Dorothy, what was it?'

'Oh … ah … Comopolous.'

'No … I remember now, Comopolous. You don't even remember her name. Nothing about your story makes sense. You say you love your wife, Michiyo, wasn't it?'

Spencer nodded.

'You don't talk about her; you don't seem to want to make contact with her. I wonder whether you haven't got some deep dark criminal past you don't let on about.'

Spencer wanted more than anything to pour his story out to Savannah, and in spite of the fact she'd confessed to wilful murder, he really couldn't find it in his heart to tell Dale.

'To answer your question, I'm very fond of you and there's no way I could shoot you. That'd be an act of pure evil. And that's what I'm fighting against, but,' she said with a twinkle in her eye, 'I would be very disappointed.' Savannah drained the last of her beer.

CHAPTER TWENTY-TWO

THE LAWYER

Lorenzo Moretti strode purposefully up to the jury box. Tall and distinguished, his aquiline features, grey hair and olive complexion often had female jurors swooning. He stood tall, hands clasped firmly on the balustrade. It was a warm afternoon and Lorenzo had discarded his coat, but he still had the theatrical glamour of a movie star, resplendent in his fine wool charcoal trousers, outlandish red braces, white shirt and scarlet bow tie.

Lorenzo's client, a wealthy councillor, had been charged with the violent rape of a fifteen-year-old girl. The drunken politician had driven her home after a political rally.

Lorenzo, of course, was supremely confident as he had been instrumental in coercing and bribing the parents of the unfortunate young lady, who had in turn, pressured their daughter to modify the evidence when called to the witness stand. The guilty politician smiled his oily smile as the verdict was handed down.

Lorenzo Moretti was about to make the leap into the big time.

At that precise time a glum Antonio Alphonse Romano cast sad eyes over what he prayed was temporary accommodation. Reclining unhappily in a squalid holding cell in the 9th Precinct Station House, 321 East Fifth Street.

He waited impatiently for his new lawyer, Lorenzo Moretti, to bail him out. This wasn't the first time Romano had seen the inside of a police cell. As a youngster coming up through the ranks of the Mafia corporate world, he'd been a reluctant guest of several juvenile detention centres. As a young adult he'd done his obligatory jail terms for felony car theft and criminal assault. However, since becoming a don, he'd hoped he'd finished with penal servitude forever.

He wondered if Spencer Marlowe knew of his arrest. *If the sonofabitch thinks this alters anything he's dead fucking wrong.*

He gazed forlornly at the charmless square box covered in mindless graffiti. Its institutional-grey painted walls seemed to be closing in on him. The harsh concrete floor with a steel bed bolted to the wall mocked the now impotent crime lord. Instead of the gracious picture windows of his apartment there was a narrow, barred opening with no glass. The stench of festering sewage assaulted his nostrils. In the corner was a putrid toilet with absolutely no privacy. The mattress was foul; he shuddered at the sight and smell of the stains left by years of unknown and unwashed thugs.

There was a constant cacophony of sound from aggrieved inmates, their screams and yells layered on top of each other. Tony Romano was well and truly used to the good life, an immaculate home, tastefully furnished with clean linen, cutlery and crockery. 'Jesus fucking Christ, I'm too fucking old for this,' he mumbled dispiritedly. Romano put his head in his hands. *Where, where did I leave that damn hat?*

The prison door clanged. 'Good morning, Mr Romano. You have a visitor.'

Tony awoke from his daydream with a start. 'What? Oh yeah. That'll be him.' Romano glanced at his wrist now unadorned by his usual expensive watch.

'Thanks, Ralph. How's the wife and kids?'

Ralph's head swivelled as he nervously checked the corridor 'All good, Mr Romano, and Betty just loves the new Chevy.'

Romano tried to remember just how long Ralph, *My God, what's his last name?* had been on the payroll. *Must be God damn years.'* A friendly prison officer was an essential cog in the Tony Romano machine. His business was all about knowledge. Knowledge was power. Ralph could always be relied upon to supply him with just what was happening in the dark dangerous prison world.

'I'm sorry, Mr Romano, I gotta do this. You understand?'

'Don't worry about it, Ralph.'

Tony held his hands, palms together, in a practiced motion. A sweating Ralph clicked on the steel bracelets.

'This way, Mr Romano.'

Like there's a choice.

Ralph the guard appeared uncomfortable as they walked down the long cellblock passing the motley collection of mainly remand prisoners. The jailhouse telegraph appeared to be in good order. Prisoners stood at their cell doors waiting for the celebrity guest to pass by. A barrage of assorted chatter erupted.

'Give 'em hell, Romano. You'll sort these pricks out.'

'Hey, Ralph, you gonna suck the man's dick?'

Ralph blushed and in a hoarse voice. 'Keep it down, mother fuckers.'

As they passed the last cell before entering the visitors area, the last celly, a heavily tattooed prisoner sneered. 'Big time mob boss Tony Romano. Not so tough now, *paisano*. Eh?'

'Wait up, Ralph.' Romano stopped at the front of the cell, and with a stare that would have nailed a sign to a post. 'Do I know you?'

'No, you fuck. But I know you.' The man grinned, showing a big smile with an assortment of stained teeth.

Romano turned to the guard, 'Who is this piece of shit?'

'That's Augustine Rivera.'

'What's he in for?'

'Grand theft auto and aggravated sexual assault.'

'On remand?'

'Oh yeah, but he's going down. I guess with his prior, ten to fifteen unless he cops a plea.'

Romano stepped forward, invading Augustine's personal space, save for the bars separating them. 'I got good news and bad news for you, *paisano*. What do you want first?' Romano flashed a beaming smile, that didn't reach his eyes.

The convict let go of the bars and seemed to shrink.

'Not talking? I'll give you the good news. You'll be outta here within a month. Now about the bad news. Actually, you're obviously a bright boy, I'll let you figure that out.'

The prisoners face drained of colour. 'It was just a joke, Tony, a joke.'

Romano shook his head. 'Tony?'

'Mr Romano, I didn't mean nothin.'

Romano chuckled. 'Ok, Ralph. Lead on.'

Ralph leaned forward whispering, 'Mr Romano, you didn't oughtta threaten these pricks. There are witnesses.'

'Threat, Ralph? I just implied his sentence would be a short one.'

A large, bright room with high ceilings, along with clamour and noise. Distraught prisoners and equally distraught family members. Hard-eyed guards making sure there was no physical contact. A room of misery, hope and desperation in equal measures. A large clock that always said 12:30. This was the visitation area.

'Over there, Mr Romano?'

Ralph pointed to a distinguished grey-haired guy, scrambling to his feet with a smile worthy of a southern evangelist.

As Tony and Ralph made their way through the crowded room, some stared. Tony Romano was a public figure.

'Lorenzo Moretti held out his hand 'It's a …'

'No touching,' Ralph the guard barked.

Romano slid the steel chair out from the small childlike desk and sat down. Fixing his new attorney, Lorenzo Moretti, with a hard stare.

Moretti nervously cleared his throat. 'First of all, Mr Romano, I'd like to say how grateful I am that you've retained me as your lawyer.' He cleared his throat again. 'Of course, I was saddened and shocked that your previous attorney, Nick Genovese, was so brutally murdered. A fine counsellor and a—'

'Cut the crap, Moretti. He was a fat pig who beat up his wife. The son of a bitch was no loss. The reality is, I don't know you, but we need someone and you were recommended. Do the right thing and we'll all be friends, ok? Now let's get down to brass tacks. How bad is it?'

'Well, Tony, may I call you Tony?'

'No.'

'Yes, of course. Let's keep it professional. Mr Romano, I'm obliged to inform you the DA has offered a plea deal.'

'Ok, and?'

'Well, it's … well …'

'For fuck sake, Moretti, get on with it.'

'They've offered you a five stretch, for a plea of involuntary manslaughter. Out on parole in three.'

'Sounds not too bad. What if I don't take the plea?'

Lorenzo Moretti shuffled some papers on the desk in front of him and pushed his spectacle high up the bridge of his nose. 'Um … it's the chair. That's if you're found guilty,' he added hastily.

Tony felt his heart hammering his rib cage. 'Well, out in three isn't so bad.'

'Mr Romano, it's a fit up. Honest, I'd stake my life on it. They don't have a case.'

'Did I hear right, Moretti? You'd stake your life on it?'

Lorenzo Moretti gulped. 'Yes, yes, I would Mr Romano. I'm not kidding. Like I said, they don't have a case. They desperately want you to take the plea. They don't have a hope and they know it. I've seen the discovery. It's bullshit. Unless they come up with something at the last moment and you must tell me Mr Romano, is that possible?'

'What do you mean?'

'Is there anything, anything at all you haven't told me.?'

'Like what?'

Moretti sat motionless for a few seconds, then leaned forward. 'Mr Romano, I'm sorry but I have to ask you. Did you kill Nick Genovese?'

Romano rose to his feet. 'Listen you son of a bitch, I'm fucking innocent.'

'Yeah, yeah, I know. Of course, I know. But I gotta ask.'

'So, tell me what you got?'

'Mr Romano, first of all if they were sure of a conviction, they'd never have offered that plea. It might have been twenty to life with a possible parole of ten. You understand what I'm saying?'

'I gotcha. But the circumstantial is pretty damning, I would have thought?'

Moretti smiled, looking like the cat who'd wandered into a cream factory. 'If this goes to trial, and I reckon I can quash that. The jury knows you're a pretty smart guy. A guy who's that smart isn't going to leave a monogrammed hat and the murder weapon right where the cops are going to find it. The cops didn't have a choice. The DA didn't have a choice. They simply had to charge you. The shmucks thought you might just accept a plea. The DA gets his picture on the TV. He looks like a fucking hero. Crime lord gets sent down. A home run as they say.'

Romano was silent. *This guy is on the ball.*

'Mr Romano, with your permission, I'm going to speak to the DA. I'm going to tell the son of a bitch no deal. We're pleading not guilty and I'm going to demand your immediate release. And ...'

Romano's eyes twinkled. *I like this guy.* 'Yep. And?'

'We want an apology. But right now, I'm going to get you bailed and I guarantee you won't be back here.'

Romano beamed from ear to ear. 'Mr Moretti … Lorenzo. You do that and this could be the start of a beautiful friendship.'

Moretti grinned and saluted. 'Call me Loz.'

CHAPTER TWENTY-THREE

FAMILY NIGHT

Like medieval emperors of old, these well-groomed men, either Italian or second generation, were gathered in the Staten Island mansion of Giuseppe 'The Lip' Bianchi. These men had discarded the remnants of their poverty-stricken early years. They had mansions, holiday homes in the Hamptons, the Catskills; they drove Cadillac's, Lincolns, Luca Russo who some thought was pretentious; drove a British Jaguar.

They'd been allocated their own fiefdoms. They had a corporate structure. Their underlings were known as 'made men,' who were the equivalent of company directors. They weren't as important as the boss, but they were always treated respectfully. Under them, were the warriors, the foot soldiers.

The fabric holding this unlovable bunch together was thin and worn; periodically the fabric would tear and war would break out.

Giuseppe, known as Joe Luca 'The Removalist' Russo, had a little too much to drink and was annoying his colleagues. Luca Russo, resplendent in a high-end tailored three-piece suit, waved a finger at the bunch, his voice thickened with years of imbibing red wine and Cuban Cigars.

Mario 'The Impaler' Esposito sat quietly, sipping on a malt scotch.

His brother, Roberto 'The Wheel' Esposito, loved nice cars. What wasn't known by the group about the affable Roberto was, he also enjoyed the company of young boys. While the mafia was an acknowledged organisation of criminal brutality, they did have the code they lived by. They were all church going Catholics. They were believers in family. Having a mistress was acceptable, even necessary to uphold the image of heterosexual virility. But homosexuality or an unnatural interest in children was enough to bring about a swift end.

Mario was quite the opposite of Roberto. Mario had an unhealthy interest in underage girls.

Serious business was being discussed.

The crime lords naturally enough were a little upset about the death of their lawyer Nick Genovese.

Collectively along with Romano they'd chipped in one million dollars to purchase the heroin and morphine from the yakuza. While their money wasn't at immediate risk, as Genovese had put it into an account only, they could jointly access, they were still concerned. The police, of course, had to deal with the handicap of proving guilt beyond a reasonable doubt. The Mafia didn't have to deal with such annoyances. They too had reasoned Tony Romano wouldn't have been stupid enough to leave evidence of a hat and a pistol behind, and why would he have wanted to kill Genovese anyway?

But ... there was doubt.

'I tell you; the sonofabitch has to go.'

Giuseppe the Lip held up a placatory hand. '*Attenzione ... attenzione.*' The Mafia chieftains fell silent. Guiseppe Bianchi was respected as a serious man, a man who thought things through. Giuseppe looked like everyone's Italian grandfather, a kindly man, originally the epitome of a gladiator. He was tall with surprisingly blonde hair. With advancing age, the gladiator had turned into a plumper version of a Roman warrior, sadly also a balder version.

Giuseppe held up a hand for silence. '*Silenzio.*' The three elder statesmen fell silent, disrespecting a man of The Lip's stature was unwise. 'Like the rest of you, I have wondered if Romano still has what it takes … this debacle with the restaurant, what's it called?'

'Spencer's,' Roberto snarled.

'I can't believe it can be so difficult to collect a legitimate payment?' There were mutterings of agreement. 'I mean, who is this guy, Spencer? He's a nobody, right? I've half a mind to send some of my crew around to sort things out, but …' He shook his head in disgust. 'If this bullshit isn't nipped in the bud, we're going to have other businesses questioning whether they have to pay. How many dead so far?' Joe gazed quizzically at his colleagues.

'Five if you count the lawyer.' Luca Russo piped up.

'Luca.' Giuseppe shook his head as if he were dealing with the village idiot. 'There's hardly likely to be a connection between Spencer and the death of the lawyer. The two wouldn't even have known each other.' Giuseppe fixed Luca with a contemptuous stare.

'Just sayin is all,' muttered the chastened removalist.

'Who is this guy, Spencer? 'Roberto asked again. 'Something about him don't smell right. Are we absolutely sure he aint FBI?'

Guiseppe raised a hand. 'All we know is he's an Australian. We know for sure he gave Gino Petrelli and Lou Palazzo one hell of a beating.' There was much shaking of heads, for one man to take down two of Romano's bodyguards was unthinkable.

'And what about the hit men, Dutch Ambroos and what's the other guy's name?' Roberto added.

'That would be that slimy bastard, Isaac the Jew, grubby little kike. I never liked him anyway.' Luca shook his head.

'Sure,' Giuseppe interjected, 'we don't care whether you liked him or not. He knew his job and he's dead.'

Luca stood up, waving an arm at the group. 'Not only did this prick give Gino and Lou a hiding, he shot them, a moving target in their car. Come on!' He threw his hands in the air. 'As well as shooting the two hitmen, for Chrissake, he takes out Gino and Lou, what is he, God damn Superman?'

Giuseppe took the floor. 'Look, we don't know absolutely for sure he did all the shooting. It hasn't been confirmed. We have a shortage of reliable witnesses.'

'Well,' spat Luca sarcastically. 'Who the fuck else do you think did it? There was only a serving girl there at the time, I think her name's Savannah. There were some kids working there, waiters, busboys, something like that. We can count them out. So, it's either this … what's her name? Savannah or this guy Spencer. I hardly think a … God damn serving bimbo took out two of the best hitmen in the business, plus Gino …

and Lou … come on, do you seriously think a broad could do that?'

The rest nodded in agreement.

Mario Esposito held a hand up. 'Look Joe, I agree it'd be real nice to send in some competent people to sort out this nonsense. Like you say, if word gets around about the trouble Romano is having the other businesses will say, why should we pay protection money when you can't even protect yourselves?'

There were murmurs of assent from the others.

'But.' He held up a hand. 'If we send soldiers into someone else's territory, it could be seen as an act of war.'

'What do you suggest, Mario?' Giuseppe looked thoughtful.

'Well … we've got this deal going down with the nips, we've got a lot of dough tied up in it. We have the new mouthpiece, what's his name?'

'Lorenzo Moretti. He's pretty sharp. We can count on him. He's a greedy son of a bitch.'

Mario continued. 'I suggest we bide our time with Romano. Right at the moment, speaking for myself, I don't wanna rock the boat until the deal goes down. Romano's been dealing with the Japs. It wouldn't do to spook 'em. Our problems ain't their problems. Also, we may have ongoing business with our slant-eyed friends. If they can guarantee high quality smack at a good price, I'd sooner deal with them than the wetbacks.'

The others murmured their approval.

CHAPTER TWENTY-FOUR

MT FUJI HERE WE COME

'Ok!' Dale's excited voice practically exploded out of the phone. 'You're both off to Tokyo. Get over to my office as soon as you can.'

Savannah punched the air. 'Yes! I don't believe it. *Tokyo*. And you speak the language. Oh my God, they have a different currency, don't they? How the hell does that work? What about the food? I don't fancy rice for breakfast. What about the hotel? Dammit, they'll speak American there, won't they? Can you believe it October already. It'll be warm in Japan, right?'

Spencer held his hands up, laughing. 'Savannah, don't worry about it. You'll be able to change your US currency at the hotel. I can assure you they'll have an American breakfast. You'll find the people very helpful and obliging. It's coming up to Autumn in Japan, but not too cold. However, if we're dealing with the yakuza, just watch yourself. Keep a low profile. Their attitude to women is … well let's just say, women aren't exactly treated as equals.'

Spencer was a little concerned; he had visions of Savannah instigating a reign of terror against the yakuza.

Savannah was beside herself as the lift sped to Dale's floor. 'My God, I've never been out of the country before. I've never flown in an airplane. What's Seth going to say? He probably won't be happy about me travelling alone with you,' she giggled. 'Well, he'll just have to get over it, won't he?'

'Spencer, Savannah, come in. Coffee?'

Dale sprang up from his desk to busy himself with the coffee. 'Ok,' he beamed, 'we've got the go ahead.' He strode to the window before flopping onto on his chair, appearing a little flustered, Spencer thought. 'Now, wait just a minute I've got all sorts of stuff here for you. Let's see now. Travel brochures. What to expect in Japan?' He paused, glaring at Spencer. 'Bit of a waste of time, Spencer mystery man, you probably know it all, right?'

Spencer shrugged.

'Anyway, moving right along. The lawyer Lorenzo Moretti and that little weasel, Carmine are due to fly out tomorrow. They'll be arrested at the airport. I'm absolutely confident they'll rat out their buddies. Wow, this's just great.' Dale was like a big kid on Christmas morning. He sprang up from his chair again, pacing restlessly to the window with its view of the bridge. 'Oh, and by the way, the FBI have called this operation the 'Manhattan Sting'. Sounds great, don't you reckon?'

Spencer smiled at Dale and his infectious enthusiasm. It was difficult not to get caught up in the moment, but Spencer had a healthy respect for the yakuza. He didn't share the prevailing view that Japan was a defeated nation inhabited by morons.

'So, what exactly is the plan?' queried Spencer.

'You'll adopt the identity of the lawyer, Lorenzo. Savannah can be either your wife or a gangster's moll.' He grinned. 'As far as we can tell, the yakuza know nothing about Lorenzo's travelling companion.' Dale hesitated for a moment. 'Oh yeah, one more thing, the yakuza are expecting a slightly older man, they've been given a description of someone with Mediterranean features, but with greying hair, so I'm sending one of our makeup specialists to put colour in your hair. She'll also give you some tablets to make your skin look a little older.'

Spencer grimaced. 'I'm not keen on that idea.'

'Spencer, Spencer, it's temporary. But you simply have to look about fifteen years older. Authenticity, ok? I mean for Chrissake, you don't want the whole plan to derail because of your own personal vanity, now do you, huh?'

'Well doll, I guess ya gotta sugar daddy,' Spencer chortled, affecting his interpretation of a Brooklyn accent.

'Yeah, yeah. Let's get on with the plot, ok? You'll be contacted at your hotel by the nips. You'll go and inspect the heroin and morphine. We'll show you how to test it for quality. You'll oversee its delivery back to the states. Then you'll wire the mob in New York with the details of the Swiss bank account the yakuza have set up, and then.' Dale rubbed his hands together. 'And then, of course the yakuza will be arrested, because you're going to be in touch with an inspector Yamamoto of the Tokyo National Police Agency, who'll turn up as you're inspecting the merchandise. Duck soup really. Naturally the details of the Swiss bank account will be our account.' Dale jabbed a thumb towards his chest. 'Well, whadya reckon about that?'

Off the top of his head Spencer thought the plan sounded simple, but simple didn't necessarily mean easy.

Savannah had said little. She sat wide-eyed like a schoolkid at her first concert.

Spencer thought for a moment. 'When do we leave?'

'Two days' time. Tuesday, ten in the morning.'

Without thinking Spencer chipped in. 'So, we leave at ten in the morning from JFK. We'll be in Tokyo the next morning.'

Savannah cocked an eyebrow, glancing sideways at Dale.

Dale sat back in his chair, studying Spencer as if he was an exotic specimen. He shook his head. 'What do you think this is … time travel? I know modern airplanes are fast, but come on Spencer, we're talking Tokyo, not LA. And what the hell is JFK, for Chrissake?'

'Sorry,' mumbled Spencer, 'I really don't know what I was thinking.'

CHAPTER TWENTY-FIVE

GOODBYE COUNTRY CLUB. HELLO SING SING.

The Checker cab swung into the drop off zone at Idlewild Airport. The noise and clamour assaulted the ears. Car doors were slamming, porters were hustling to grab luggage. A sea of Yellow Cabs as cheerful as a field of marigolds jockeyed for a position. A popular TV actor gabbled a fifteen second sound grab to WNBT News. The pungent odour of av gas hung in the air.

'Pay the driver,' Lorenzo, the newly appointed lawyer for the mob, instructed his travelling companion, Carmine.

With his thin pinched features and prominent gold front tooth, Carmine was truly an unattractive individual. 'You listen to me, Shylock. I ain't your fucking servant. Keep it up and you'll be wearing the Chicago overcoat.'

Lorenzo wasn't entirely sure what a Chicago overcoat was, but he had a fairly good idea he didn't want to wear one. 'Sorry, Carmine,' Loz soothed in his best courtroom manner, 'I guess I'm a little stressed.'

Carmine and Lorenzo presented themselves at the check-in desk. The ever-so-attractive lady in her smart military style navy blue jacket with matching pleated navy-blue skirt perused both passports. With a warm smile she handed them back. 'Have a nice flight, gentleman. Just go through that door on my right.'

Lorenzo winked at his companion as they picked up their bags and headed to the doorway Carmine walked through first, followed by Lorenzo.

'What the fuck?'

As the doors shut behind them, they found themselves in a room with three suited men, holding 0.38 revolvers.

'My name is Agent Fletcher of the FBI. You're both under arrest.'

CHAPTER TWENTY-SIX

HOLIDAY TIME

'God damnit, Spencer. How long is this going to take? I mean the airplane isn't going to wait while those two jerks make a God damn decision. What if they don't squeal on the mob? And what about Carmine? What if he pulls a gun? Perhaps we ought to step in. What do you reckon?'

Spencer sighed, glancing at the door. Right on cue, a grinning Dale Fletcher burst into the room. 'Those bozos never saw it coming. And Carmine is now officially a rat. Boy oh boy, we couldn't shut him up. You should have heard Moretti; he couldn't help himself. Always the lawyer. There he is telling Carmine to take the fifth. Did I jump on him? Anyway, they both rolled. You're on your way.'

Dale held a manila folder, bulging with documents. 'Listen up. We don't have a lot of time. We have here your new passports, your travel itinerary and as much background info on good ole Loz Moretti as we could dig up.'

'Just a mo, Dale?' Savannah held up her hand, 'What about rat-face? I'm sure as hell not going to pass for that little creep?'

'Sure, no plan is ever perfect, but remember Carmine's role was to keep an eye on Moretti and be some muscle if it was needed. The yakuza have absolutely no interest in that little creep.'

Spencer wasn't entirely convinced 'So if the yakuza ask, why the switch? What do we say?'

Dale rolled his eyes. 'Man of the world "it's a long story Spencer Marlowe." For God's sake, Marlowe, you decided to travel with your mistress instead of Carmine. Give me a break. You're a womanising attorney for the mob. Surely that stacks up? Happy now?'

'Actually, no, Dale. There're some bloody loose ends.'

Dale rolled his eyes, and sighed. 'Hit me. What's the problem? Everything's sorted, God dammit.'

'It's not your life on the line. What about Carmine and Moretti— they will be expected to get in touch––wives, girlfriends, the mob, their bookies?'

'Yeah, Dale. Spencer's right.' Savannah frowned.

'We're not amateurs, you two. Everyone knows that phoning from Japan has problems. If you feel the need to contact Romano, do it by telegram. Just, you know … send a message, "Everything ok," whatever you like. There's no reason for him to expect you to phone.'

'Ok, is there a Mrs Moretti, a girlfriend? Someone? She or they might expect a call.'

'Like I said, we're not God damn amateurs. We have spoken to Moretti's wife, Maria. Lovely lady. We've told her if everything works out, her husband may get off with probation. She's been sworn to silence. Believe me she's gonna cooperate. She's scared stiff. To be on the safe side we've tapped her phone. But honestly, she's not going to squeal.

'What about rat face?' Savannah asked.

Dale laughed. 'You wouldn't believe it. The little creep doesn't seem to have a friend in the world. Lives alone in an apartment in Jersey. Not even a cat.'

Two hours later Savannah and Spencer crossed the runway to board the TWA Lockheed Super Constellation bound for Tokyo. Savannah as eager as a little girl off to her first birthday party. They had said their goodbyes to Rafael and Dwayne, at the final closing of Spencer's, promising to look them up on their return to New York.

'Hey, slow down woman, the plane won't take off without us, I promise.'

Savannah's eyes were agog as she bounced up the gangway and into the plush aircraft. Their itinerary included a two-day stopover in Los Angeles, then on to Honolulu for a fuel stop. And then, the land of the Rising Sun.

They were shown to their seats by the TWA hostess, immaculate in her sky blue military style uniform. Spencer reached into his pocket, making sure the cornicello was there. Pulling it out, he kissed it. 'Just for luck.'

'What exactly is that? Oh of course, let me guess, it's a long story, right?' Savannah cast a sceptical gaze over the *cornicello*.

'Honestly, Savannah, you're looking for a mystery that isn't there. It's just a lucky charm. People have lucky charms, don't they?'

'I'd just like to know the truth about you. Why is it I've this feeling that you've a deep dark secret?' Savannah grunted.

Spencer shrugged, changing the subject. 'I think you're going to enjoy Japan. It really is a land of mystery.'

'Oh really! Mystery, eh? Well, ring-a-ding-ding, you'll certainly feel right at home.' Then her eyes widened in panic. 'Whoa, hell in a basket, we're moving.'

Savannah grasped her armrest her knuckles white; her face drained of colour. The Super Constellation smoothly took to the air.

Finally letting go of the armrest, Savannah smiled. 'Well, that wasn't so bad. What were we talking about? I remember, da da da dah. *Man of mystery Spencer Marlowe*, is it a bird, is it a plane …'

'Hang on just a minute smarty pants, you reckon I'm a mystery? Here you are, a female FBI agent with a very big gun. There's still a lot I don't know about you. How about you fill me in on things?'

'Like what?'

'About your training? I'll just bet you raised a few eyebrows when you entered the FBI men's club?'

Savannah laughed. 'I'll tell you a little story, this is classic. I was this green kid from Pierre, South Dakota. Boy oh boy was I a fish out of water. This was the first day on the range—'

'Range?'

'Firing range, dummy. Stop interrupting. There were nine of us, I was the only girl of course, and the attitude towards women was … it's hard to explain.'

'In Australia, the word we use is sexist.' Spencer was reasonably sure the word hadn't seen the light of day in 1955.

'Hey, what a great word. Yeah, that's very descriptive. Anyway, this first day we were allowed to bring our own weapons. There they were all of these nervous Nellies with their mostly brand-new handguns in their nifty plush-lined wooden cases.

Mainly 0.38 s, a few Colt semi-automatics, and there's me with my Magnum. Anyway, this jerk with size fourteen shoes and a comb-over, just about wet himself when he picked up mine. I can still hear him today "Well little lady," little lady, for Christ's sake. Can you believe it? "And what do you plan to do with this?" he says.'

'And what did you say?'

'Embarrassing! I mumbled something about upholding the FBI Motto of Fidelity, Bravery and Integrity. Then he tells me I wouldn't be able to hit anything. The recoil would knock me over. And that I'd be better off with a God damn 0.22. That was the last straw. I reckon the whole God damn class was laughing at me.'

'And then?'

'After this jerk actually called me sweetheart and rolled the target out fifty yards, I blasted out six shots. Centre mass, every God damn one of them. It was priceless. He rolled the target in and just stared, saying over and over "It's not possible."'

She smiled indulgently at her past before returning her attention to Spencer. 'Now, how about your story?'

'Of course, but we really need to acquaint ourselves with our new IDs.

Savannah rolled her eyes. 'One day, Superman, one day, so help me …'

Spencer was perusing his new identity documents, in particular a passport in the name of Lorenzo Moretti. 'Hey Savannah, cast your peepers on this.' He flashed the document in front of her.

Savannah was excited at the view from her window, and nudged Spencer. 'Just look, I can see the

Statue of Liberty, the Brooklyn Bridge … oh my God … this's just amazing.'

I'd probably do the same if it was my first time in a plane.

'When I was a little girl, I went up for a short spin in a crop duster, I just loved it … but it was nothing like this, this is … just … I think the best word is … wow.'

Once again Spencer was struck with the enigma of Savannah, with her childlike enthusiasm on the one hand, and her casual brutality when it came to the bad guys.

Spencer was pleasantly surprised at the spaciousness of the Lockheed Constellation. The aircraft was far smaller than he was used to, but for the average passenger it was faultless. There was no such thing as business or economy class, every passenger travelled in the lap of luxury.

It had wide brocade seats facing each other with a table in between. Egyptian cotton antimacassars and drapes over the portholes to blot out the light if required. Already Spencer had been offered French Champagne or in fact just about any tipple he wanted.

Savannah screwed her nose up at Spencer's champagne. 'I don't want any of that foreign muck. Would you happen to have a Budweiser?'

'Certainly, madam.'

They settled into the flight. Savannah had well and truly recovered from the take-off but was still wide-eyed at the sights the smells, in fact everything. She cast surreptitious glances at the other passengers.

'Spencer, just look, they're serving lunch already. See that well-dressed lady over there? She's got frogs' legs.'

'Yes, and her friends aren't much better.'

Savannah was momentarily mystified, she then broke into peals of laughter, causing others to stare. 'Honestly Spencer that razzes my berries. You're a funny guy when you want to be.'

Quiet reigned, as lunch was served. All the meals were individual, with exquisite cutlery and crockery.

'Spencer, what in hell is steak au poivre? For Christ sake why isn't it in English?'

'That's steak in a creamy peppercorn sauce. Try it, you'll love it.'

'I don't reckon we'll be seeing this in good old Pierre any time soon.' Savannah mumbled. 'Hey, how come you know all of this gourmet stuff anyway?'

'Just another aspect to add to the mystery of Spencer Marlowe.' Spencer grinned.

Savannah wolfed down her steak. The menu informed her It was from Wyoming. 'Spencer, that had to be the best steak ever.'

Spencer had baked catfish with a superb glass of French chablis. He sat back appreciating the excellent wine, reflecting again on the twists and turns of his life. *You can only play the cards you've been dealt.*

'Spencer, can you believe it, we've got forty-eight hours in Los Angeles and just look at this brochure. Walt Disney has opened a fun park called Disneyland; this's so exciting! I've just got to go there. Will you come with me, please?'

Spencer scanned the brochure; he couldn't believe they'd just had the grand opening. He'd no idea Disneyland had been an institution for so long. 'I'd love to.'

'Just look at our accommodation. We're staying at the Roosevelt Hotel on Hollywood Boulevard, and all at the mob's expense. Mister Moretti indeed? We'll be able to see the Hollywood Walk of Fame. Maybe we'll see some real-life movie stars.'

Spencer sneaked a glance at Savannah, who was avidly poring over brochures. 'I imagine you'd like to be sharing all of this with Seth?' Was it his imagination, or did her face cloud over?

'Yes …yes of course. I guess that'd be nice? I suppose you'd like to be here with Maggio?'

'Savannah,' he said sternly, 'You know bloody well it's Michiyo, don't you?'

'Sorry, Spencer, I always get her name mixed up with the baseball player. She doesn't look like Joe Di Maggio, does she?'

'No,' he growled, 'she doesn't look like Joltin Joe. She's beautiful. I miss her terribly.'

'Sorry, Spencer, I didn't mean to poke fun, it's just that … I don't understand. Why don't you have contact? How can it be in these modern times when we have telephones, telegrams, even letters? As far as I can tell, you just don't seem to have any contact at all. I don't doubt your feelings for her, but I wonder, are they reciprocated? Does she not want to keep in touch with you?'

Spencer could see nothing but concern in Savannah's expression. He desperately wanted to confide in her, but he knew it was impossible.

Savannah touched his hand and then suggested sadly, 'Sometimes I think it's Michiyo who doesn't want to be in touch with you. And just maybe you're fooling yourself, clinging to an impossible dream.'

'Please, let's just change the subject? We're going to enjoy our time in LA and that's that.' Spencer could feel himself sinking into an abyss of self-pity.

The seven-hour flight seemed to pass quickly. The Super Constellation impressed Spencer, riding the sky as if it was on sleek and perfect tracks, landing on the tarmac in LA, its wheels kissing the earth with a tiny cheerful bounce. There were no customs, bag checks or surprisingly for Spencer, any obvious signs of security. Air travel in the 1950s was a very casual affair.

The taxi rank had a seemingly endless line of Chevs, Fords and Chryslers. Spencer still hadn't got used to the size of everyday automobiles in America.

Bags in hand, they made their way to the head of the taxi line.

'We're in luck.' Spencer tapped on the window of a grimy cab. The driver slouched out and jerked the trunk open, watching as Spencer loaded the cases.

'Sorry, Mac, bad back.'

The driver's body odour combined with the less than fragrant aroma of the years of ingrained dirt made the journey from the airport a dismal introduction to the City of Angels.

Obviously a country music fan, the radio blared all the way with songs about, trucks, unfaithful women and gambling. The chain-smoking driver lit each cigarette from the stub of his last one. It seemed as if one cigarette at a time couldn't satisfy his nicotine craving. The smoking was only interrupted by the occasional hacking cough; his spittle spraying over the window.

Spencer was having difficulty dealing with the cigarette smoke that seemed to be everywhere. When he turned to Savannah and grimaced, she simply smiled, her eyes crinkling as she mouthed, 'Oh, you poor darling.'

The beaten up big-finned Rambler with its taciturn driver jerked to a halt outside of the Roosevelt Hotel on Hollywood Boulevard. The driver hawked, spitting noisily out of his window. 'Seven dollars, ninety plus tip, bud.'

'Seven dollars, ninety?' Savannah peered at the driver. 'Listen, buddy, we're from New York, not Hicksville, Arkansas.'

The driver stared hard at Savannah, sneering. 'Well, you sure coulda fooled me.'

Spencer handed over eight dollars. 'Keep the change.'

'Tightwad country bumpkins,' the driver mumbled.

Spencer and Savannah checked in with adjoining rooms. Savannah suggested they meet downstairs after they'd freshened up.

CHAPTER TWENTY-SEVEN

STAR STRUCK

'Spencer, we're not that far from the Brown Derby.' Savannah was waiting in the lobby, champing at the bit, ready to go.

'We're not far from what … a hat?'

'Truly Spencer, sometimes I think you're from another century. The Brown Derby is where the movie stars eat. It's not far away. It's on Wilshire Boulevard.'

The very smart Chevrolet Bel Air cab whisked them swiftly and efficiently to the restaurant, the immaculately turned-out driver with his grey uniform and peaked cap, a stark contrast to the surly brute who'd picked them up from the airport.

'Spencer, cast your peepers. It actually looks like a hat.'

Only in America. The Brown Derby looked exactly like a huge hat.

The waiter in black trousers with his tight button up white vest, complete with gold buttons and matching gold bow tie, escorted them ostentatiously to their table and stood waiting for his tip. Spencer handed him a dollar note and was met with what he thought was a sarcastic, 'Oh, thank you, sir.'

'My God, Spencer,' Savannah whispered, 'six bucks for a steak. You're kidding me?'

Spencer laughed. 'I know Dale has given us a pretty generous expense account. In fact, you might remember he said don't worry about the cost. We have to play the part of rich gangsters. So, eat up.'

The dishes arrived slowly, a good indicator that Spencer's tip wasn't up to expectations. The food, however, was excellent.

Spencer and Savannah reclined in the comfortable brocade chairs enjoying their coffee. Considering the FBI had a huge windfall in receiving Tony Romano's ten thousand dollars Spencer had spoiled himself, ordering an expensive Remy Martin Louis X111 Cognac. Savannah peered suspiciously at the brandy balloon as the waiter with great flair carefully warmed the glass over a small brass gas burner.

'What on Earth is that rotgut you're about to drink?'

'That my girl, is just about the finest cognac on the planet.'

'Really? Dare I ask? How much?'

'Ah yes … I thought you might ask. Just think expense account, ok.'

'How much?'

'Ten dollars.'

Savannah's jaw clenched. She whispered, 'Holy cow. Ten dollars. Back home we could buy a quart of old Ben's white lightening for fifty cents. Fifty cents for Chrissake.' Jabbing a finger at Spencer like a dagger, she growled, 'Listen daddy-o, I'm responsible for the God damn expense account. How the hell do I justify this expensive crap you're swilling? It's ok for Dale to say don't worry, but I reckon the bean counters at head office will have a God damn heart attack. Great horn spoon, this'll be coming out of my pay for years.' She shook her head in wonderment, mumbling something unintelligible at this extraordinary extravagance.

'All of this,' Savannah waved her hand around. 'Is just so different from good old Pierre, South Dakota. We could just as easily be in another country. Or even another century.'

Yeah well, I certainly can relate to the other century bit. Spencer was relieved Savannah had recovered from her angst over the expensive cognac.

Her eyes now darted around the room like a rabbit caught in headlights. Starstruck, she was desperate to see someone famous. 'Spencer, Spencer,' she hissed, 'is that Jimmy Cagney?' Savannah's gaze was fixed on an older couple that to Spencer looked like retirees on a once in a lifetime trip to LA.

'They,' Spencer declared patiently, 'were very probably an old married couple celebrating a wedding anniversary. Looking at their clothes, I'd suggest probably from the backwoods of Tennessee.'

'Yeah, I guess they do look a bit countrified.'

Clearly Savannah was on a mission to find at least one famous person. 'What about that couple hiding in the corner? I'm sure that lady was in a movie recently, what do you reckon Spencer?'

Before he could answer Savannah was at it again. 'Spencer look, just look I know for sure who that is. Oh my God, I don't believe it.'

Spencer gazed across at a dimly lit table where two unusually handsome men sat, with eyes only for each other. 'I give up, who is it?'

'Spencer you really are hopeless. That's Rock Hudson.' Savannah kicked him under the table.

Being so close to one of the major film stars of the day and such a handsome one as well, had temporarily transformed her from FBI agent to lovelorn schoolgirl.

Spencer of course had heard of him, remembering how he'd come out as gay before his death of aids in the 1980s.

'I know I'm engaged to Seth, but confidentially…' Savannah blushed.

'I don't think Seth would have a lot to worry about.'

'What on Earth are you talking about?'

'Do you remember in your FBI training, the segment on body language?'

'Yes … so?'

'Well, put your training to use. Study them. Their body language. What does it tell you?'

Savannah stared hard. Her eyes fixed on the two men as if they were on the FBI'S most wanted list. 'No, no. I don't believe it. You're not suggesting? No, it's not possible. He's gorgeous. They're both gorgeous. Oh my God, what a waste. Half the women in America are in love with this guy. Son of a bitch. Hollywood has a lot to answer for. Do you know what?' Savannah scowled.

'I give up. What?'

'That's gosh darn false pretences, that is. They've got no right to flaunt this guy. Just about every woman in America is in love with him and he's a friend of Dorothy. I can't believe it. Do you know what?'

Spencer shook his head.

'I reckon all of this … this …'

'All of what?'

'All of this, you know … Hollywood heartthrobs that are actually nancy boys. I reckon this could be a case for the FBI. We could have a big sting operation; I mean, I wonder who else may be one of *them*?'

'One of *them*?'

'Fruitcakes, pansies for God's sake. I mean, who knows? I mean, what if John Wayne was one? Maybe some men are actually women and vice versa.'

He leaned in conspiratorially. 'By God, you're right. I think you're on to something. I reckon when we get back to the States you contact J Edgar himself and see if the FBI can't start arresting and charging people. Perhaps even send them to the electric chair. I mean, this is crime of the highest order. Gee whiz, what if we find out Lassie is really a boy doggie and Rin Tin Tin is a girl? Savannah, I can see a big future for you here in tinsel town.'

'Shut up, Spencer.'

Spencer was still chuckling as they left the restaurant.

The bell boy hailed a cab for them. Spencer had learned his lesson, tipping him two dollars.

'Oh, thank you, sir,' was the grateful response.

Arriving back at the Roosevelt Spencer collected their room keys from reception.

'Mr Marlowe, you have a telegram.'

With some trepidation Spencer ripped open the envelope. SPENCER'S FIREBOMBED THIS MORNING. — TOTALLY DESTROYED. GOOD LUCK, -DALE.

Spencer gazed at the telegram for several minutes. He felt a sense of sadness. Curiously, he realised Spencer's had meant quite a lot to him. He wondered why. Was it a symbol of permanence, of not being a stateless hobo? He reflected on the business, how proud he was when he saw happy customers, the enjoyment as he learned new cooking techniques, the camaraderie that existed between him and Savannah. Once again, he had that fleeting feeling of being homeless, a solitary man being despatched through time at the whim of unseen forces.

Savannah was standing by as Spencer read the telegram. 'What is it?' she demanded.

Spencer held up the telegram, his eyes glistened. 'The restaurant's been destroyed.'

'Bastards.'

Paradoxically, he couldn't help but feel relieved that in all probability the destruction of the restaurant meant Tony Romano would live to fight another day. He smiled to himself remembering Romano sliding over the $10,000 like a street tout handing over dirty photos. *I hope you got your ten grand's worth Tony.*

Spencer awoke with the California sun streaming through the window. He could see the branches of a Eucalypt waving in the light breeze, his heart leapt. Was he back in Australia? Was it all over? 'Michiyo?'

Spencer had cried out as he woke with a jolt realising he'd been dreaming. Eucalypts grew in abundance in California, having been introduced by Australians in the gold rush of 1848.

For a moment despair washed over him. Spencer mentally ticked off the months since he'd arrived back in April 1955. So much time. *I have to keep telling myself, one morning I will awake. I will go back, it has to happen, but … not today. Just remember, you can only play with the cards you've been dealt.*

He fumbled for the phone and rang Savannah. 'How about if I see you down by the pool in, say twenty minutes?'

'They have a pool?' Savannah exclaimed. 'And I didn't pack my swimming outfit.'

Spencer was sprawled at the poolside bar nursing a coffee when Savannah appeared. Spencer thought she looked unusually stylish in white three-quarter length trousers, a bright multicoloured blouse that tied in a vibrant knot under the bust. Spencer immediately thought: *All of a sudden Savannah 's become fashion conscious.*

The pool area had been transformed into a bustling film set; cameras, stage lights and people running around like frenzied ants. A red-headed woman with dark glasses, a head scarf, black trousers and shirt was registering her displeasure. 'For Chrissake, the pool scene should have been shot an hour ago, what's the problem?' she shrieked at her hapless assistant who looked like he was on the verge of a breakdown.

'Oh my God, Spencer … do you realise who that is?' Savannah's eyes were out on stalks as she grabbed Spencer's arm.

Spencer of course, didn't have a clue.

'That's Lucille Ball.'

'Who?'

'Spencer, don't tell me you haven't heard of Lucille Ball? They're shooting an episode of I Love Lucy.' Spencer vaguely remembered seeing reruns on cable television.

'I'm going to ask for an autograph.' Savannah jumped to her feet.

Spencer gazed at the redhead who by now was apoplectic, he grabbed Savannah's arm and jerked her back on to her seat. 'I think if you try to talk to the lady, you're going to have to draw your gun. She'd eat you for breakfast.'

Savannah looked askance at Spencer. 'Yeah, you may be right, she sure is different from the Lucy I've seen on TV. Let's get out of here.'

'What? Where? 'Spencer drained his coffee and ran after Savannah.

'Disneyland. Where else?' Savannah bounded out to a waiting cab.

The cab drove past orchard after orchard, soaking in sunshine under a sky made even more pretty by the scattered clouds.

Spencer was amazed at just how similar the land was to Western Australia. The California sunshine was like a balm to his mood. The gas stations and farms were neat and orderly, a giant jig-saw of food production. The laid-back lifestyle looked appealing. Men were driving tractors in the bountiful fields. The Mexican labourers, with their colourful bandanas, Stetsons and sombreros, toiled in the hot sun. The gas guzzling Chevrolets, Fords and Chryslers with their ostentatious big fins seemed to make a statement about America's wealth. The taxi ride was over thirty miles. Spencer shuddered as he saw the old mechanical meter relentlessly clocking up the dollars and cents. He hoped Dale wasn't going to have a heart attack at the ever-burgeoning expense account.

CHAPTER TWENTY-EIGHT

DISNEYLAND

'Spencer, there it is. Disney Land.' Savannah's eyes were like saucers.

The green and gold Desoto taxi rattled up to the Disneyland entrance. 'That'll be twelve dollars ninety-six cents, bud.'

'Kiss my go-to-hell. Dale's going to have a pink fit,' Savannah whispered, rolling her eyes.

Spencer was amazed at the sheer size of Disneyland, with its acres of car parking, and the sprawling Disneyland sign proclaiming it 'The Happiest Place on Earth'.

'Spencer, just look, a castle and mountains. Can you believe it? Over there, it looks like a haunted house. Wow.'

Spencer and Savannah strolled along Disney Land's main street. Savannah's eyes shone like a ten-year-old. 'Look, old man, cotton candy and popcorn.'

'Old man?'

'Have you looked in the mirror lately?' Savannah laughed.

They passed a funny hat stall with a mirror out the front; Spencer gazed mournfully at his reflection. *Those tablets Dale gave me and the grey in my hair, oh my God, I look at least fifteen years older.*

'That's ok, everyone will think you're my dad.'

'No, they won't.' Spencer nudged Savannah. 'They're going to think I'm the older man out with his mistress for a bit of fun and hanky-panky.'

The Disneyland band marched past, resplendent in outlandish blue costumes. This was followed by a float with Sleeping Beauty, and of course Prince Charming. Mickey Mouse and Donald Duck pranced in front, to the delight of the children and Agent Steele.

'I didn't know being an FBI agent could be so much fun. This is like Coney Island, but, wow, bigger, better, more modern. It's just like we've seen it on TV. Don't you reckon?'

'Yep,' Spencer agreed, although he couldn't actually remember seeing it on television.

But Spencer's thoughts now flashed to the Land of the Rising Sun. He shuddered at what he knew about the yakuza's cruelty.

CHAPTER TWENTY-NINE

TOKYO

The day was sharp and clear as Savannah and Spencer flew in to Tokyo. Spencer gazed out of the Super Constellation window, not recognising anything. He'd been a frequent visitor to this great city, but in a different century. Nothing looked the same.

Clutching their complimentary maroon viny TWA flight bags, they strode into the terminal. Savannah's eyes widened as she gazed around at the unfamiliar sights and sounds.

'Everything is in Japanese! How in hell are you supposed to know what anything is?'

'What exactly did you expect? This is Japan. They speak Japanese. The advertising is in Japanese. Get used to it.' Spencer chuckled.

Savannah rolled her eyes and grunted, 'Alright smart ass. But look, there's something in God damn English. The handheld sign in the arrival hall was emblazoned WELCOME MR MORETTI.

'Don't I exist?' she grumbled, pointing at the man and the sign.

'Remember, you're just the gangster's moll.' It occurred to Spencer that the Japanese very probably didn't know what the gender of his travelling companion was.

The gleaming black Toyota Crown whisked them through the dense Tokyo traffic to the stately Imperial Hotel.

Savannah was agog. 'Spencer, can you believe it? They drive on the wrong side of the road. No wonder they lost the war.' She sniffed contemptuously.

Spencer wondered exactly how Savannah managed to make the connection between driving rules and losing wars, but he decided not to pursue that particular line of discussion.

Neither Spencer nor Savannah knew what to expect. The doorman resplendent in his uniform opened the door of their taxi. '*Konnichiwa.*'

Spencer thanked him in Japanese, giving him a tip. The porter appeared surprised to hear this tall Caucasian effortlessly speaking the language.

Savannah nudged Spencer. 'Just check out the uniform, I mean seriously.'

The porters' uniforms seemed to be an odd potpourri of flamboyant military, looking like leftovers from a Broadway production of *The Student Prince*. The jacket was a vivid blue double-breasted satin number with gold buttons and outlandish tasselled gold epaulettes. This was exceeded in garishness by a large matching blue satin top hat, looking as grotesque as a cartoon character's ensemble.

'Sort of "Saville Row meets Disneyland",' Spencer whispered to Savannah.

The Imperial was one of the oldest hotels in Tokyo, renowned for its service and discretion.

'Spencer, get a load of this. I mean ... wow.'

They were greeted by the sight of a foyer that appeared to go on forever. Breathtakingly high ceilings were supported by stunning glass and marble columns. A ruby red carpet stretched ahead of them, disappearing up a broad marble staircase.

Savannah was speechless, grabbing Spencer's arm and pointing at the black and white marble ceiling. The centrepiece was a chandelier, a million sparkling pieces of crystal, shimmering like the silver scales of fish. Spencer had stayed in some fancy hotels but this, he thought, was unusually spectacular.

Spencer was not entirely sure what arrangements had been made as far as who slept where. He needn't have worried; the porter escorted them to the executive suite. With a flourish he opened the double doors. Savannah gasped. The suite was truly magnificent, consisting of a large lounge, sitting area with a picture window overlooking the stately Imperial Gardens.

Not one, but three bedrooms and two bathrooms. Spencer's room was like a guest suite in an Italian palace. The bed was king size with pure white Egyptian cotton sheets. A sprawling beige leather lounge took up one entire wall. On the other side of the floor-to-ceiling windows was his own private terrace. The bathroom had a bath big enough to accommodate a football team with everything fitted out in marble and handcrafted tiles.

Savannah stood transfixed, reverently holding a carved ivory ornament of a sumo wrestler in her hand. 'If only my girlfriends from Pierre could see this.'

On the coffee table was an extravagant, dancing rainbow of flowers wrapped in cellophane with a large red bow, with a bottle of Dom Perignon and a note. Spencer examined the champagne. 'Wow, vintage 1926.' He whistled. 'These guys are seriously out to impress.' Spencer knew little about champagne, but he recognised the famous name.

Savannah sniffed. 'A cold Budweiser would suit me. Bloody foreign rubbish,' she muttered.

Spencer opened the envelope. 'Can you believe this?' He showed the letter to Savannah,

'What am I looking at?'

'Well, the letter says they're sending a car for us at seven to take us to dinner. But can you believe, they actually have their own letterhead?' In embossed gold lettering it proudly proclaimed *Yamaguchi-gumi*.

'The Yamaguchi-gumi is like the Mafia back home, right?' Savannah looked puzzled.

'Pretty much.'

She examined the letter closely. 'This is a bit like Tony Romano having a letterhead stating "Mafia, all types of criminal activities at your service. Contract killings, best price guaranteed." At least the Mafia try and pretend they don't exist. What sort of country is this, for Pete's sake, and how come the US has allowed these mobsters to operate so blatantly? They'd better not get in my way, I'll tell you that,' Savannah said darkly, reaching into her luggage, taking out her Magnum and shoulder holster and strapping it on.

Spencer laughed. 'I know you've been given permission to carry your Howitzer, but whatever you do, don't let anyone see it. Under the terms of the rules set up by the US after the war, guns are virtually banned, so people are going to be a little alarmed to see a woman carrying a weapon.'

'So, does that mean that the Yama goolie-goolie won't have any firepower?' Savannah looked thoughtful.

'That's Yamaguchi-gumi, and in the main they probably won't have guns. Japan has the strictest gun rules on the planet. But they'll have knives and they do know how to use them. They'll also have a vicious piece of equipment called a *sai*, a three-pronged instrument. A bit like a gardening fork, but razor sharp.'

'That's ok, they're welcome to use their knives. And what did you call it?' Savannah pulled out her revolver, checking the load.

'*Sai*.'

'Ok, *sai*, say what?' Savannah smiled at her play on words. 'I think the knives and the *sai* will meet their match with a .357 Magnum, what do you reckon?'

'Savannah please try and avoid killing people. Japan is now a sovereign country, it's likely to cause a diplomatic incident if you go round shooting yakuza.'

'You know me, Spencer. Generally, I only shoot bad guys in self-defence.' Savannah batted her eyes.

'Yes,' Spencer said drily, 'it's the word "generally" that causes me some concern.'

Spencer had no way of knowing just how prophetic his words would be.

CHAPTER THIRTY

JOHN WAYNE

'Mr Moretti,' the soft melodic voice of the receptionist said when Spencer picked up the phone. 'There is a Mr John Wayne requesting your presence in our coffee shop. If you're free?'

'Did you say John Wayne?'

'Yes, sir.'

'Tell him we will be there in ten minutes.'

'Did I hear right, John Wayne?' Savannah asked.

Spencer held up the fake antique ivory and brass handset, staring at it thoughtfully as he hung up. 'You did … whoever it is, it sure doesn't sound like our generous hosts.'

'What do you want to do?' Savannah was puzzled.

'Let's go see. I've always wanted to meet a movie star.'

'Ok, I'm sure John … Wayne wouldn't object to a lady coming armed.'

They travelled in the elevator to the lobby. Savannah was eying off the other passengers, her eyes narrowed as she appeared to focus her attention on a nattily attired man who had the temerity to smile at her. Nudging Spencer, she scowled as she mouthed 'yakuza?'

They stepped into the lobby, Spencer whispering to Savannah, 'Not everyone's going to be yakuza. Try very hard to behave. Just smile and bow and leave that bloody gun in its holster. It's going to be a bit of an issue if you go round shooting waiters and taxi drivers because they smile at you.'

'For God's sake, Spencer, I wasn't going to shoot the creep because he smiled at me, he just looked … you know, he sorta looked …?'

'Yeah, I know, he sorta looked Japanese. You're going to find a lot of that in Tokyo. Just try and … What can I say? Just try and go with the flow. As it happens the yakuza aren't our enemy; remember we're here on business. They want to sell drugs and we want to buy. Everyone's happy, so for Pete's sake just be nice, ok?'

Savannah grunted

Savannah grunted 'Yeah, got it. Be nice. I'll damn well show them "nice" if one of the little bastards puts a hand on me, I'll tell you that for nothing.'

Spencer planted himself in front of Savannah. 'Now look here, if you don't behave, I'll carry on without you. I need your word that you're going to behave and not let your prejudice against the Japanese derail the whole operation.'

'Prejudice!' Savannah snarled. 'I love the little yellow creeps.' In a stage whisper she muttered. 'Just remember Pearl Harbor. Nasty little worms, ugh.'

'*Konnichiwa*, could you direct us to the coffee shop?' Spencer shook his head as he spoke to the concierge.

Spencer and Savannah stood gazing at what appeared to be a convention of American businessmen and a sprinkling of Asian customers. The coffee shop was as plush as the rest of the hotel with tasteful patterned carpet and stunning brass and teak furniture. The decor and ambience trying to create the ambience of a Parisienne cafe with modern oil paintings of Paris, Montmartre, Place Pigalle, the Eiffel Tower and the Arc De Triumphe. As they stood at the entrance, a tall Caucasian stood up, smiled and waved, beckoning them to his table.

'Mr Moretti.'

Spencer nodded. 'John Wayne?'

The big man laughed. He resembled the movie star, perhaps a little tougher. Spencer immediately sized him up as military, a man of action, but certainly not one of their hosts.

'Please have a seat. I've ordered a dry martini, would you both care to join me?'

'Coffee for me. Savannah?'

'Coffee, please.' She studied the tall man, her eyes narrowing.

'Sorry for the subterfuge. Obviously as you can see, I'm not actually *the* John Wayne. I'm Colonel Buck Randall, Sixth Ranger Battalion. I didn't want to announce myself, so I decided on a name that would get your attention,' he said with a chuckle. 'Please call me Buck.'

Spencer felt immediately at ease with the big man, thinking. Very *handy in case of trouble.* 'Lorenzo Moretti, and this is Savannah.' Spencer held out his hand.

'Yeah, well I know that's not your real name, but it doesn't matter. Delighted to meet you … nice to have a bit of western glamour.' Buck held out a huge paw towards Savannah.

'Delighted to make your acquaintance, Colonel.' Savannah melted.

'Buck, Buck … please call me Buck'.

There was a silence as the coffee and martini was served.

'You're FBI?' Buck addressed Spencer.

'Yes, and so's Savannah.'

'What exactly is your role? Typing, shorthand … taking notes?' Buck frowned.

Savannah stared at him coldly. 'I shoot people.'

Buck first glanced at Spencer, then Savannah, both of whom were unsmiling. He was silent for a moment, then abruptly slapping his leg, he laughed uproariously. 'Good for you.'

There was a little small talk. 'How was your trip? How's the hotel?' Buck paused to scan the room. 'I really don't imagine that the yakuza would be spying on you. But you never know.' Buck leaned forward; his eyes darted around the room. 'I'm sure you know what you're doing. But I still feel that I need to impress upon you, these people aren't dummies and their level of violence is …' He seemed to ponder the right choice of words.

'I guess a good description would be medieval.'

Spencer raised an eyebrow.

Buck laughed. 'When I say medieval, I mean most of us have read about the Middle Ages when bizarre torture methods were used, well let me tell you these people have never moved on. Seriously, some of the stories I could tell you.'

Spencer eyed the big man. If you're trying to put the fear of God into me, it's sure working.

Spencer scanned the room. Most of the customers appeared to be American businessmen. Spencer observed a loud New Yorker and his companion noisily berating two harassed Japanese company men. Spencer could overhear the conversation; the

Americans were addressing their Japanese counterparts with ill-disguised contempt.

Buck leaned forward, lowering his voice. 'I tell you; the smart money is on Japan becoming a powerhouse economy. Those fellas should be a little more respectful. I think the worlds on the cusp of being flooded with all manner of goods, all stamped "Made in Japan".'

'Seriously Colonel, I mean Buck, do you really think Americans will ever buy Japanese rubbish?' Savannah snorted.

'Well, Savannah, I tell you, their car industry is gearing up, also cameras, televisions, the list goes on and on.'

Savannah laughed out loud. 'C'mon Buck can you really imagine we're going to see, what's that brand of Jap car?'

'Toyota.'

'Yeah, Toyota. Can you imagine we'll see God damn Toyotas motoring down Broadway anytime soon?'

Buck smiled, tapping the side of his nose. 'Just watch out America. That's about all I'll say on that subject. Now,' Buck banged his fist on the table, 'let's get down to business.'

For the next half hour Buck told them all he knew or suspected about the yakuza and the nationalists who could be a problem.

Buck had successfully rammed home the message that although their plan seemed foolproof, you just never know.

Spencer glanced sideways at the now fashion plate Savannah Steele, right at that moment he thought. *Just maybe your pop gun and your extraordinary ability to use it may come in handy.*

Simultaneously he wondered what the customers of the coffee shop would think if they knew that the homespun young lady who exuded all the innocence of a housewife in a Norman Rockwell painting packed a lethal handgun and the ability to use it with deadly accuracy.

It occurred to Spencer that he and his two companions looked just like any American tourists, here to see the sights.

With his powerful physique, Buck looked like a football coach on holiday, with his polo shirt, chinos and New York Yankees cap.

Spencer decided that he should go for the executive look, something befitting an upmarket mob lawyer. Dale had been happy to fund Spencer's sartorial splendour so a trip to Saks in Fifth Avenue had seen Spencer kitted out in the latest New York finery.

Spencer reclined, legs crossed, his immaculate deep blue double-breasted suit enhanced by a snowy white shirt and burgundy tie. His Florsheim Oxford shoes were polished to a deep glossy black. His iron-grey Bailey's fedora hat with its subtle black band added to the picture of a wealthy executive.

Savannah, it seemed, had a new appreciation of haute couture. The diminutive concierge of the Roosevelt hotel had been an enthusiastic participant in Savanah's transformation. The five-dollar tip pressed into his manicured hand had helped. Cecil had told her all the places to go for a complete makeover: hair, shoes, clothes, the whole lot.

'Ooo Dear,' he'd answered with a conspiratorial wink. 'You've come to the right man. The stars ask me this all the time. Hepburn, Bacall, Monroe ... well ...' and he stamped his foot. 'Well perhaps not Monroe.' He glanced around the room, hands on hips 'No class dear ... really ...?'

'Some men find her attractive. Personally, I don't know what they see in her.' He sniffed.

But it did seem as if Cecil was keen to help further. 'The gentlemen you're with ... your uncle perhaps?' Savannah smiled to herself.

Well Dale, your aging strategy seemed to work.

Savannah winked at Cecil. 'Yes ... he's my ... Uncle.'

'Well ... if your uncle ... would perhaps like some personal ... assistance ... in any way?'

It was as if Savannah had arrived from another planet. Quickly absorbing the nuances of Earthlings feminine style and fashion, the metamorphosis now complete. Poised on the black lacquered cocktail chair, a fine bone China coffee cup in hand she was a picture of cool sophistication, in her blue and white patterned swing dress. The stunning dark blue Peter Pan collar blouse completed the ensemble.

When Savannah met Spencer for lunch at the Roosevelt, having arrived from the hairdresser, her unruly field of corn hair was miraculously transformed. Spencer had never thought about women's hair particularly, but he had new respect for women's hair stylists.

'My God.' His jaw had dropped. 'You look just like Doris Day. Seth isn't going to recognise you.'

'When do you meet up with the yakuza?' Buck leaned forward on his chair, lowering his voice.

'They're picking us up at seven this evening. Apparently, they're putting on some shindig in our honour.'

Buck drained the last of his martini. 'I can't imagine you'll have any problems. But by Jiminy, be on your guard. In spite of what some Americans think, these people aren't dummies. If for one minute they don't trust you …'

Spencer laughed lightly. 'There's simply no way that they can have any inkling of who we are. They're going to be well and truly focussed on the million dollars. I imagine you know the broad outline of what the plan is?'

Buck nodded. 'Fletcher explained to me about the heroin … frankly that's your business. What we're concerned with is a nationalist group, a group of fanatics who simply can't accept that Japan lost the war.' Buck gave a derisory laugh. 'You would have thought a couple of atom bombs would have done the trick … No apparently. There's a group called,' Buck stumbled over the words '*kokumin ikare no koe.*'

Spencer immediately cut in. 'Voice of the people.'

'Hey, how in the Sam Hill did you know that?'

Savannah leaned back, putting her hands behind her head. 'Can you believe it, Buck, he speaks Jap? Oh, and before you ask Spencer, he'll tell you, "It's a long story." Isn't that right, *Uncle?*'

Buck looked on at the interaction, laughing. 'Look I really don't need to know any family secrets. But this is where we come in. We believe this Voice of the People is somehow managing to stockpile some arms, they're also running paramilitary training camps, somewhere away from prying eyes. What we want, is for you to lead us to where this so-called army is. The

Yamaguchi-gumi is not a nationalist group: they're simply criminals. But we believe there are many in that group have nationalist sympathies, certainly some of their senior members do.

'Who's their leader?'

Buck consulted a small blue spiral notebook. 'We're not entirely sure who the absolute boss is. The name that crops up frequently is a thug named Riko Takahashi. I don't think he's the boss of bosses, but he's pretty high up in the organisation. He spent some years in an American POW camp and is no lover of truth, justice and the American way.'

Buck consulted his notes again. 'I've never met this bozo, apparently, he can be quite charming. Speaks fluent English with an American accent. By all accounts he's the perfect figurehead to put a civilised face on what is a very nasty outfit. I've heard rumours about this guy.' Buck cleared his throat, gazing again around the room. 'One thing I do know, that's not a rumour. He came very close to being shot as a spy in the last little shindig. At the time he was in fact a US citizen. Anyway, that's history. He served his time then obviously decided that Japan was going to be his land of opportunity. So, what I'm saying is, tread carefully, my friends. If you can get the yakuza to take you to where the main camp of this God damned militia is, we'll be able to follow and hopefully sort them out. We don't believe at this stage they'll have enough weapons to start an uprising or any such nonsense.

'Now, let me see … Yep, here it is. The guy you'll be dealing with at the camp, if you can get there, is a Major Watanabe. We don't know a lot about him. But once again, tread warily. But certainly, Riko's the one handling the heroin. I imagine you'll probably meet him when you inspect the drug shipment.'

'Where do we come in?' Savannah looked thoughtful.

'Ok,' Buck rubbed his hands together, reminding Spencer of Dale Fletcher's boyish enthusiasm. 'What we want, is for you to cosy up to the yakuza and when they've had a few *sakes* suggest to them the Mafia has stuff to sell.'

'*Stuff?*' Spencer enquired, with a raised eyebrow.

Buck chuckled; he seemed to be enjoying himself. 'Guns, chum, guns. Tell 'em you can get Thompsons, handguns, grenades … I mean let's not go over the top, but certainly pretty much offer them unlimited small arms.'

CHAPTER THIRTY-ONE
YAKUZA PARTY NIGHT

Spencer and Savannah returned to their suite with Buck Randall's words of good cheer ringing in their ears.

'What a lovely man.' Savannah sighed.

Maybe Spencer had it wrong, but he'd the distinct impression Savannah was quite taken with the handsome colonel. *Well as far as I'm concerned, he's a better choice than that creep Seth.* Spencer immediately castigated himself for his thoughts. *For Christ's sake give the guy a break, Savannah loves him, he works with kids. What more could you want?*

'Hey, Savannah,' Spencer yelled, his voice carrying across their suite. Savannah was busy preparing for the night ahead. 'Feel like a beer? The fridge is stacked.'

'No thanks. I'm not drinking that foreign rubbish. What's it called? Ashi, or something like that. I want a nice cold Budweiser.'

'That's Asahi,' Spencer yelled back, 'and let me tell you it's a bloody nice drop.'

'Oh sure,' she yelled her sarcasm dripping like molten cheese. 'It's probably made from God damn rice.'

Spencer was reclining on the exquisite chaise longue; he couldn't figure out was it antique or a remarkably good copy. He was focussed on the black and white television and laughing uproariously. The incredibly bad acting featured ninja warriors fighting overwhelming odds was so bad it was entertaining. The dialogue and the fight scenes he found hilarious. Savannah was now in her bathroom going to a lot of trouble preparing herself for whatever the night had in store. The phone rang.

'Mr Moretti?' A lilting slightly accented female voice spoke, 'I do hope you are well and the accommodation is satisfactory? The limousine is waiting downstairs for you.'

Spencer's hand felt for the reassuring outline of the *cornicello* nestled in his pocket.

He paced nervously in the stunning lounge room, oblivious to the lights of Tokyo twinkling through the picture window. 'Where in hell is she?' This wasn't like Savannah; she was never late. The last thing Spencer wanted was to keep the yakuza waiting.

Finally, the door to the suite swung open.

Spencer was stunned at the new Savannah. *I think I might have created a monster.* She looked absolutely beautiful, no longer the girl from hayride and square dance country.

She wore a stunning black dress with a nipped-in waist accentuating her slim figure, a full skirt swirling about her legs, revealing slim, shapely ankles and the lower curves of her calf muscles. The material had a fine sheen that was quite striking, and the white elbow-length gloves were a final elegant touch.

Spencer had only just got over the shock of the new hair and her other new outfit. 'My God.' Spencer gasped, 'I'm speechless.'

'Does that mean you approve?' Savannah was biting her lip and fiddling with her hair.

'You look lovely. It's a shame Seth can't see you now.'

'Umm yes … of course.'

Spencer, grinned and bowed. 'Madame, our chariot awaits. Let's go and find out what the ungodly have in store for us.'

Waiting in the foyer was a short squat Japanese man, who appeared to know who they were, he smiled, bowing. '*Konbanwa, Moretti san.*'

Spencer acknowledged him, bowing and answering in Japanese.

They were escorted to an immaculate pre-war Rolls Royce, stunning in its black livery. The headlights the size of dinner plates, its distinctive grill with its silver goddess emblem, saying to the world, 'This is a Rolls, the world's finest.'

'How about that?' Spencer nodded at Savannah.

They were whisked silently through busy Tokyo streets.

Savannah leaned over, whispering, 'I'm unarmed. There was nowhere to hide my piece. This stupid bag is too small and the shoulder holster … well.'

'What a shame,' Spencer murmured, smiling. 'You won't get to shoot anybody tonight. Maybe you could make up for it and shoot two people tomorrow?'

Savannah's lips puckered into a scowl as she poked her tongue at him.

They arrived at the restaurant. Spencer explained to Savannah, 'This's a famous Tokyo eatery. it's been an institution for years. The food should be terrific.'

The Rolls swept up to the entrance of the restaurant. A kimono-clad staff member with a samurai bun hairstyle bowed low and opened their door before escorting them inside. Savannah giggled, whispering to Spencer, 'Get a load of the hair, and he's wearing a God damn dress. Who on Earth is this freak, a Japanese fairy?'

The restaurant had been cleared of all the regulars. Spencer glanced around the room realising it was full of hard-faced, serious-looking tattooed yakuza. Most of those who he could see had one finger missing. He shuddered. *I sure hope the natives are friendly.*

One of the yakuza with a body builder's physique, high cheekbones and shaved head bowed to Savannah, smiling and saying something in Japanese that Spencer couldn't quite hear. *Well, this particular native seems to be friendly.*

The room was both magnificent yet understated: dark timber flooring with tatami mats and shoji screens. Stout aged oaken beams supported the ceiling. Subtle miniature globes suffused the room with a soft light.

An older yakuza came up to them clad in traditional robes, he bowed. 'So glad you could join us, Moretti san, my name is Akihito Tsukushi.'

Spencer guessed Akihito was probably in his sixties. There was nothing about him to suggest yakuza. Average height and a muscular build, but it was the eyes, Spencer concluded, keen and watchful. *Not a lot would get past this guy.* It was clear Akihito wielded power; the deference displayed by the wait staff and the other yakuza was to Spencer both subtle and obvious in equal measure.

Spencer expected some questions about the nonappearance of Carmine Ferrera but Akihito said nothing. He breathed a sigh of relief.

A waiter stepped forward offering them small bowls of *sake*. Savannah glanced questioningly at Spencer, who sipped the sake. 'Perfect, Akihito *san*, sixty degrees centigrade.'

Akihito smiled approvingly. 'Excuse me, Moretti *san*, I must have a word with some of my guests.'

Akihito nodded at Savannah without asking her name. Savannah scowled, nudging Spencer. 'Who do they think I am, the hired help?'

'You're my mistress, remember.'

Spencer gazed at the retreating form of Akihito as he approached another group of hard-eyed men who'd entered the restaurant. Akihito, Spencer decided, was relaxed and not at all suspicious. *What's the old saying 'In like Flynn'. This's a doddle; everything so far is going like clockwork.* As Spencer sipped his *sake*, he cast a surreptitious glance around at the small groups of men chatting animatedly, some bowing in his direction and smiling.

Savannah tapped him on the shoulder. 'You could at least introduce me. Sonofabitch, don't just leave me stranded with these God damn monkeys.'

'Just try and behave,' Spencer whispered angrily.

They were escorted to a long low table.

'Remove your shoes,' Spencer whispered to Savannah, who rolled her eyes, but complied.

'What is it with the nips; they keep on staring?' Savannah whispered.

The same man appeared again, hard muscled, lean, his shaved head and high cheekbones giving him a slightly exotic movie star appearance. He bowed low, once again smiling and nodding at Savannah.

This guy is just a little too keen. I'll just bet he fancies himself as a tough nut. Spencer glared at him. 'Somebody likes you,' Spencer whispered.

'Not even on your birthday, slant eye,' Savannah glowered and mumbled.

'Don't knock it. Unless I miss my guess, you're getting a lot of admiring glances.'

'Ugh,' Savannah shuddered, 'Nasty little creeps, all of them.'

Spencer nudged Savannah. 'Just humour them, ok? The thing to remember above all else.' He shot her a warning glance.

'Oh yes, master, please enlighten me with your words of wisdom?'

'I'm not joking, Savannah. Now for pity's sake, pay attention. This is serious.'

Savannah rolled her eyes.

'Above all else, remember whatever transpires, and I don't think there's going to be a problem, but above all, they can't be seen to lose face. So, if any of these guys gets a little amorous, try and be gentle. My God, you don't even know the meaning of the bloody word.'

Savannah rolled her eyes again.

'Be diplomatic, if anyone gets too close, go to the bathroom, powder your nose, do any bloody thing, but don't bloody well antagonise them. I'm serious. Once you upset one of these guys anything could happen.'

'Yeah, alright, I get it. Anyhow look out, here comes Hiro Hito.'

Akihito appeared to be quite jovial as he smiled and nodded to Spencer. 'You are in for a treat, Moretti *san*. This is the finest food in the whole of Tokyo.'

Akihito nodded to the head waiter and immediately a host of waitstaff appeared.

Savannah screwed up her face. 'I guess a hamburger and a Bud would be out of the question? Why in hell don't these people eat regular food? Ugh … you just don't know what in tarnation they're likely to dish up. It seems as if it swims, crawls or flies you eat it. I'm surprised they don't all die of God damn food poisoning.'

Dish after dish was reverently placed before them.

Savannah was desperate. 'What on Earth is it? If I had my gun, I'd shoot it. What, is this?' She pointed at one of the dishes.

'That's sashimi and next to it is a bowl of soy sauce. Pour a little soy on the sashimi and eat,' Spencer commanded.

Savannah looked horrified but followed Spencer's instructions. 'Hey, that's actually not bad. What is it?'

'Raw fish.'

Savannah's face paled 'This isn't happening … for Pete's sake, who eats raw fish?'

The meal was a banquet, with one superb dish after another. Savannah was a little happier when she was offered a cold beer. 'Hey, guess what, this Jap beer isn't half bad.'

'Almost as good as a Bud?'

'Let's not get too carried away,' Savannah smiled, raising her glass, 'Cheers Spencer!' she leaned close, whispering, 'These slant eyed creeps aren't so scary.'

Spencer returned her smile and raised his glass. Don't fool yourself kid. Every man in this room could be a killer.

Dinner completed; a lady dressed in elegant geisha attire slid open the bamboo lattice divide. This was the signal for the guests to stroll through to the adjoining room where Spencer was formally introduced to the yakuza. They all smiled and bowed, which left Spencer a little less concerned.

This room's decor continued in the same vein, with the dark wood flooring, with the addition of magnificent watercolours adorning the walls. The wide oak timber beams had colourful Japanese lanterns suspended from them. Smiling geishas fawned over the guests.

This room opened up to a spectacular garden. They could see a stream with a traditional wooden bridge and a mini waterfall. The earth had been excavated and the grounds landscaped to form valleys, gullies and flagstone walkways. The combination of stone, water, bonsai, rhododendrons and cherry trees all lit by Japanese lanterns was as spectacular as it was soothing.

Savannah stood stock still. She whispered to Spencer. 'I've never seen anything like this. My God, it's stunning.'

Spencer of course had seen many such gardens, but he too was impressed. *Apart from the fact that this looks like a tattooist convention and just about everyone here has a finger missing this could easily be a corporate night out.*

After some more pleasantries, Akihito got down to business. 'Tomorrow you'll be taken to where the merchandise is. You can test the quality. It will be obvious it's all pharmaceutical grade. It was all the property of the Imperial Army.'

Spencer noticed Akihito referred to the Imperial Army with reverence. *Here's somebody who's not happy with the outcome of the war.*

'We'll show you how we plan to export it to New York,' he reassured confidently. 'The plan is foolproof. Hopefully this will be the first of many such transactions.'

Spencer bowed and clearing his throat. 'My colleagues and I certainly hope so and … we may be able to do some reciprocal business.'

Akihito had a sip of his *sake*, fixing Spencer with his inscrutable gaze.

This guy would have killed his fair share of enemies.

'Really?' Akihito raised an eye. 'What do you have that we might want?' he inquired cautiously.

They were both speaking Japanese. Close by, Savannah was being besieged by amorous yakuza who seemed to be captivated by this American beauty. Unfortunately, they only spoke a smattering of English, but it was clear this wasn't going to stop them from trying to impress her with their wealth and position.

Spencer glanced in her direction; she smiled and shrugged, as if to say, 'Well, what'd you expect?' To Spencer they appeared like callow schoolboys, completely out of their depth.

'Weapons, Akihito *san*.'

'What sort of weapons?'

'Small arms, pistols, rifles, shotguns, grenades.'

'And your famous Thompson that created such havoc against our Imperial Army?'

'Yes,' Spencer said, 'Thompsons.'

'How many?'

Spencer stood close and stared straight into his hard black eyes. 'As many … as … you … want.'

Akihito's eyes gleamed. 'I know someone … a patriot who would be very interested. Of course, I realise this is short notice, but then your time in Tokyo is limited. I'm sure I could organise a meeting tomorrow if that's not inconvenient?'

'I'm at your service, Akihito *san*. My clients in New York have made it quite clear they're very keen to establish reciprocal trade. I would certainly appreciate a meeting as soon as possible, as my time in Japan is indeed limited.'

'Of course, Moretti *san*, we can take you to where this … patriot is. I can get a message to him tonight, so that he'll be expecting you. He's situated about an hour out of Tokyo. I will arrange for my men to pick you up at your hotel and take you to his … to his camp. You can discuss with him exactly what he wants and see if you can work a deal. After that we'll take you to where our merchandise is. You can inspect it. If you wish, you may go with it and see it loaded onto the *Kyushu Maru*. Then, once you're satisfied, you can organise the transfer of the money with your colleagues in New York.'

'I understand you want the money transferred into a Swiss bank account.'

'Very unimaginative people the Swiss, but their banking system is faultless.' Akihito laughed.

Akihito and Spencer were toasting their business deal when they heard raised voices. One of the yakuza was clearly drunk and getting rather too close to Savannah, Spencer heard Savannah speak loudly. 'Just back off, you little creep.'

I had a feeling he was going to be a problem. Spencer grimaced.

It was the same man who'd been smiling and nodding at Savannah when they arrived. He didn't seem to be getting the message, then abruptly, leering at Savannah, he placed his hand on her breast. *Thank God she doesn't have her gun,* was Spencer's first thought.

And then a resounding noise echoed across the now silent room. Savannah had slapped him across his face with all her might. It wasn't the slap of a delicate young lady, this was the slap of a powerful, fit woman with years of martial arts experience.

The man howled in anger and pain, yelling, '*Umazume!*' which Spencer knew meant stone woman or a woman who has no desire.

The yakuza, whose name was Akio, then made a very bad decision. Knowing he'd lost face, he reacted violently, punching Savannah in the jaw and knocking her sprawling onto the floor. Spencer yelled at Savannah as he raced to her aid.

'Are you ok?'

Savannah grinned, giving him the thumbs up. She rubbed her jaw. Fortunately, the punch to her face, while painful had been a glancing blow. 'Go get the sonofabitch, Tiger.'

Spencer immediately grabbed Akio, spinning him around. 'Try it out on a man, *chin chin!*' he said in Japanese, referring to the yakuza's pre-pubescent penis.

Spencer was a true master of Karate and it was a fair bet, he thought, this tough, if slightly drunk Akio was no slouch either.

Akio howled, throwing a clenched fist at Spencer's face. Spencer grabbed the fist, pulling it to one side, at the same time administering a vicious elbow strike onto Akio's nose. The cartilage broke and blood gushed in a torrent onto Akio's finely tailored suit.

Spencer thought the surprised look on the man's features was priceless. Spencer's elbow to the face appeared to have the effect of sobering the yakuza, whose face now showed a mixture of emotions. He was clearly puzzled, Spencer thought, also a little afraid that the tall *baka gaijin* seemed to have a mastery of this ancient Japanese discipline.

Akio again came forward, this time a little warily. Spencer took Akio by surprise with the *ashi bari*, also known as a foot sweep, Akio fell heavily, but with a roar he bounded up to try for a groin kick, which if it had connected would have done serious damage.

'I think you've had a little too much *sake, chin chin.*' Spencer's taunt further enraged Akio, which is exactly what Spencer wanted. An angry fighter makes bad decisions.

Akio advanced on Spencer. Around the room the onlookers held their breath, willing Akio to defeat the tall foreigner. He shook his head as if trying to dispel the effects of the alcohol. He obviously knew he was in the fight of his life. It appeared as if he was still trying to compute that this foreigner, this *gaijin* seemed to have his measure. The two men circled each other warily. With a roar, Akio attempted a head strike with a closed fist.

Spencer laughed as he dodged the blow. 'You'll have to try a little harder, *chin chin.*'

Akio had a fine sheen of sweat on his brow as he advanced then retreated, then bounded forward, attempting a knee strike. Spencer easily avoided it, retaliating with a vicious kick to the stomach. Akio was momentarily winded, but recovered quickly.

Once again, the two men circled each other seeking an opening. Akio now appeared to have sobered up.

Akio was tiring, his eyes flashed around the room. All he would have seen was the stony glances of yakuza, who weren't happy. One of their own looking foolish, which was the ultimate disgrace. Spencer well knew that the collective yakuza would be irreconcilable.

Akio tried for a head shot, which failed to connect.

Spencer waved a finger at him. 'Oh, dear *chin chin*, you're really going to have to do better than that.' Spencer then kicked Akio's legs out from under him.

Akio once again fell to the floor. Grunting in pain, he jumped up. There was an ominous rumble from the spectators who were now talking amongst themselves, gesturing angrily. Spencer was aware of the vibe, a room full of unhappy gangsters wasn't what he wanted. *Too late to back out now.*

Spencer decided to bring the contest to its finale. *What the hell, I've probably done my dash with these kind folks anyway.* He was filled with regret that Savannah was mixed up in this. He just hoped the yakuza would be lenient with her. He knew what damage his next move was going to do. There was no hesitation on Spencer's part, knowing this could only be a duel to the death. There couldn't be any other outcome. *You won't be molesting defenceless women again.*

Spencer exploded onto the stunned Akio with the deadly *mae tobi geri*, the jumping front kick to the head. He didn't hold back, but gave it all he had.

There was an audible snap as Akio's head flopped like a child's rag doll, his neck broken. He fell in a heap. Spencer stood motionless. *What in hell happens now?* He expected instant retribution of some sort.

A stunned silence would probably be an understatement. Yakuza stared at yakuza; Spencer felt as if he could read their collective mind. *What on Earth's happened? How can this be?*

Spencer stood motionless. Savannah was still sprawled across the floor gazing fearfully around the room. It seemed as if no one was prepared to break the silence, to take the next step. Spencer eyes flashed around the room. *Whatever happens now won't be nice.*

Akihito stepped forward facing Spencer, he bowed. Spencer understood the complexities of the Japanese culture and the significance of the bow. This was a deep bow, bending at the waist, a bow that signified respect. This was gobsmacking, a high-ranking yakuza acknowledging, acknowledging what? *What on Earth is going on?*

'My most sincere apologies, Moretti *san*. I do hope you can forgive this unseemly behaviour, this dog … this …' Akihito shook his head in disgust. 'This … vermin insulting your friend was completely and utterly unforgivable. It is indeed lucky for him that you killed him. Because what I had in store for him tomorrow …'

'Moretti *san*, the yakuza are not animals. And I do hope that this … unfortunate incident doesn't affect our future dealings. Once again, my most profound apologies.'

Akihito turned to the still speechless yakuza. '*Hai*.' Once again, he bowed a deep bow to Spencer, immediately all the yakuza in the room did the same, they then raised their sake bowls and toasted.

'Moretti *san*.'

CHAPTER THIRTY-TWO

MAKING PLANS

Spencer rose early, going to the lobby to call Buck Randall. Akihito had been as good as his word. With typical Japanese efficiency the meeting had been organised.

'Yeah Buck, they're picking me up at eight tomorrow morning and taking me out to the militia's training camp. I don't know where it is but, get this, I've been told to take stout walking shoes. What do you make of this?'

'We have a pretty good idea of the general location of the camp. As far as we know, it's a regular little army. We think they're probably reasonably well armed. Our informants have been a bit vague, but whatever they are, we're going in hard. We have to nip this in the bud. We don't know exactly where they are. We think it's somewhere near Mount Takoa, that's about an hour from Tokyo. So, this fits in with what we suspected.'

'What are your guys going to do?'

Buck's enthusiasm radiated through the phone. 'This's just great. We'll follow your car at a safe distance. I don't think they'll be keeping close watch. You better remember to duck when we show up, there's bound to be a firefight.'

'Whoa, hang on a minute, Buck. I have to meet with the head of the militia. Then they're taking me to meet this guy Riko Takahashi in downtown Tokyo to inspect the heroin. So, you'll have to wait until I have the drug situation sorted out. After all, the militia aren't going anywhere. Don't forget the heroin is the whole purpose of my trip? You sorting out the militia is a bonus. I just hope they don't join the dots and link my visit to your attack.'

There was a prolonged silence.

'You there, Buck?'

'Yeah yeah, a bit disappointing but I suppose you're right. I guess my guys are going to have a night out in the woods.' There was a chuckle. 'Well the Rangers are sort of boy scouts for grownups, I guess we can wait. And yes I understand your concern, but their intel must have told them the Rangers were on their tail.'

'Ok, good luck, Buck.'

'Yeah, you too Kangaroo man. Be careful. I've heard Riko is a tough customer and no fool.'

Well, thought Spencer, *now all I have to do is sort out Savannah.*

'What the fuck do you mean, I can't come?'

Savannah's eyes flashed in anger as she paced the floor, heels click-clacking as they hit the tiles hard with a staccato beat. She eagerly fingered the shoulder holster, itching for the first opportunity to unleash the magnum. All dressed up and nowhere to go.

Spencer had never seen her so angry. Swearing like a longshoreman was something new. 'Savannah, Savannah,' he pleaded. 'Be reasonable, what possible reason can I offer to say I want to take my mistress on men's business … c'mon?'

'What happens if things get iffy?' Savannah snarled. 'I've seen your shooting skills. You couldn't hit the Empire State building if you were standing out the front. Jesus ... I don't believe this. I'm not happy, not happy at all, Moretti *san*. God damn *Moretti* san. For crying out loud it sounds like an advertisement for rice.' She shook her head in disgust. 'You need me. We're a God damn team, aren't we?'

'We know you can shoot, but come on, your handgun against probably a hundred-armed militia? The odds don't really work, do they? Look Savannah, I'm sorry there hasn't been more for you to do, but you knew all along you were playing the part of the lawyer's girlfriend. You're here, just in case.'

'Just in case what?'

Spencer sighed. 'Just in case. Just in case, that's all. If something went wrong. Nothing has gone wrong. Dammit, it's as if you want something to go wrong so you can shoot someone. So far, it's all been as smooth as silk.' Spencer laughed. "Well except when you attacked that bloody yakuza'

'Don't damn well start on that. You ended up killing the son of a bitch, remember?'

Savannah stood with her hands on her hips sulking like a little girl being told she couldn't go to the circus. 'I think I'll have one of those Jap beers.' Savannah stormed over to the bar fridge. 'Wouldn't you know it; the slant eyes even make whisky. Suntory Whisky. Probably doubles as paint remover.'

'Actually, it's an excellent spirit. Pour yourself a decent measure. It might just calm you down.'

The ice cubes clinked as Savannah splashed three inches of the copper-coloured liquor into the fine crystal tumbler. As she topped up the glass with a dash of water, the amber liquid swirled around enticingly. Savannah lowered herself onto a waiting *chaise longue*. She certainly appeared to be a touch more relaxed as she sank into the plush velvet. She took a sip, stretching out like a lazy cat. 'Hey … kiss my go-to-hell. That's not bad, not bad at all.'

Savannah appeared to calm down, she smiled a half smile, running fingers through her hair. 'Ok killer, after you've visited the slant-eyed army. What then?'

Spencer smiled at the killer jibe. *Thank God for that, I think she's seeing some reason.*

'Then they're taking me to meet the big chief Riko to inspect the merchandise and for me to then organise the transfer of the cash from New York.'

'And I suppose I'm not welcome at that meeting either? She jabbed a finger at Spencer. 'God dammit Spencer, you do need me you know. What happens if there's gun play? I mean, seriously, you have improved; I'll give you that … But let's face it, you're not exactly Olympic material.'

Spencer shrugged. "What do I say, "Hey Riko this is my mistress she wanted to come and have gander at a million dollars' worth of smack".'

'What in hell was the point of me even being on this trip?' Savannah's anger boiled over. 'Where are you meeting this jerk Riko?'

'There's a warehouse next to the Takashimaya Department store in downtown Tokyo. Apparently, it's going to be a quick meet-and-greet with the militia. They're about an hour out of town. Then we go to the warehouse, I inspect the gear and supposedly arrange the transfer of the cash and Bob's your uncle.'

Savannah studied him thoughtfully. 'Ok I agree, perhaps I wouldn't serve any purpose when you meet this pretend Army, but when you meet this, what's his name?'

'Riko.'

'Yeah, Riko. There's only going to be a couple of people there. Is that right?'

'I'm guessing, but I imagine so.'

'Spencer, you're dealing with the Japanese mafia. I agree on the surface there shouldn't be a problem, but how do you know once they're convinced the money is transferred, they won't kill you?'

'For God's sake, why would they?'

'Well for starters, as we just mentioned, you killed one of their own, or are you such a hardened killer you've forgotten already?' Savannah smirked.

Spencer retrieved an envelope from his pocket, handing it to Savannah, 'What's this?' she demanded, as she examined the missive.

'Relax, it's just a collection of telephone numbers. And I've written instructions as to how you use the pay phone in the lobby.'

'Whose numbers?'

'I've written Inspector Yamamoto's number, oh, and he speaks English. And of course, there's Buck Randall's number.'

'What do I need these for?'

'Just in case,' cautioned Spencer.

'In case?'

'In case I disappear,' Spencer replied testily. 'Also, I've written the address of where I'm going to meet this guy Riko to inspect the heroin. Just in case I don't come back. But there isn't going to be a problem. If there was likely to be a problem they wouldn't have given me the address. They love me. We're practically home and hosed. After I've inspected the drugs, I'm going to call Yamamoto, he's going to arrive with other cops to arrest this guy Riko and whoever else happens to be there. Nothing will go wrong. So, you can go shopping in the Ginza or watch Japanese Westerns on the TV.'

Their conversation was interrupted by the doorbell chiming, 'I'm dreaming of a white Christmas.'

Savannah shook her head. 'What is it with these people, are they trying to be funny or what?'

'Who the hell could that be?' Spencer was immediately alarmed.

'Oh … oh … I guess that would be for me … um… room service. How do you say enter in Japanese?'

'*Hiragana*,' Spencer called out.

The white-suited waiter pushed in a trolley covered with a white cloth and proceeded to produce a plate, placing it on the coffee table.

'Do I tip him or not?'

Spencer shook his head.

After placing some exquisite silver cutlery and a crystal decanter with chilled water on the table, the waiter bowed and left.

'Hang on?' Spencer stared at Savannah mystified. 'That's bloody *sushi!* What's going on?'

'Well actually … I discovered the other night at the restaurant, I like Jap food, so there.'

CHAPTER THIRTY-THREE

A NICE DRIVE IN THE COUNTRY

After a restless night's sleep, Spencer didn't enjoy being squeezed uncomfortably in the back of a tired Toyota Crown and wedged between two unsmiling yakuza. The driver turned, nodding to the man next to Spencer. The starter motor whirred noisily; the engine sputtered to life; a horrible rasping sound like that of a dying man. With a loud bang, a cloud of smoke erupted out of the exhaust. The Crown rumbled as it struggled to pick up speed, then came the knock knock of the big end bearings, clattering and banging in a strangely musical rhythm. Spencer was aghast when he first saw the car with its scratched and damaged panels. *Is the best the yakuza can afford? This car's had more hits than the Beatles.*

Spencer glanced sideways at his two surly companions. Bloody hell, did they have to pick two guys built like sumo wrestlers? This one next to me has more chins than Chinatown.

Speaking in Japanese he tried unsuccessfully to make conversation. 'Nice day for a drive. How far are we going?'

'Not far.'

'How long's it going to take?'

'Not long.'

At this point Spencer realised the futility of trying to converse, so he settled back to enjoy the scenery.

As they rattled and clunked through the Tokyo streets Spencer was surprised there was simply nothing he recognised. He knew the United States had virtually reduced Tokyo to rubble in the bombing of World War Two, but this remarkably industrious and innovative race had rebuilt at extraordinary speed.

Spencer observed there was no particular evidence of poverty, there were plenty of cars on the road, public transport was everywhere, with smart modern multi-coloured buses. All in all, it was as if the war was just a momentary blip on proceedings.

The tired old Toyota Crown continued to creak and whine as it went up hills. The clamour of the city was now slipping away. Spencer noticed peasant clothes and conical straw hats, the occasional horse pulling an ancient wooden cart loaded with produce. Nineteenth-century Japan with the occasional TV antenna.

A colourful scarecrow stood sentinel along a verdant green rice paddy; the raw earthy smell of wet mud Spencer found strangely comforting. Then the forest, the smell of pine trees mixed with the distinct aroma of fetid earth. Damp from a late rainfall, the ground was dark and moist, there was a carpet of curled brown leaves embedded in the rich soil.

Spencer knew that Japan consisted of about 70 percent forest. For a highly urbanised country there was quite a lot of semi wilderness. Spencer recognised the famous Japanese cedars and the beautiful red foliage of the exquisite maples.

Abruptly, the Toyota swung onto a rutted gravel track, lurching to a halt in a clearing. Dark gloomy gnarled trees blotting out the sun. For a brief moment, Spencer's heart raced. Was this to be an execution in the wilderness? Were his surly travelling companions going to put a bullet in the back of his head?

'Now we walk. Please follow, Moretti *san*.'

Spencer breathed a sigh of relief; he'd been casting surreptitious glances from the back window hoping to catch a glimpse of Buck's Rangers, but had seen nobody at all who looked like the American. Just at that moment, the thump thump of the rotors of an unmarked helicopter passing overhead disturbed the tranquillity. A flock of brightly plumaged birds screamed as they rose from the treetop canopy like a technicolour cloud. Spencer strained to see the helicopter, but it was too high and the foliage too dense. The yakuza didn't give it a passing glance.

They set off in silence through the thickly wooded forest. Spencer had forgotten just how beautiful the Japanese countryside could be. They passed hordes of chattering families of macaque monkeys, their pale brown fur standing out against the soft greens of the broad-leaved trees. As they marched into a clearing, they surprised an animal that Spencer was not familiar with. 'Tell me, friend, what's that?'

'It's a *serow*, a sort of goat.'

Doesn't look like a bloody goat. Spencer felt a little more comfortable. He figured if they were going to kill him, they would have done it by now. The trek through the dense forest had actually been a liniment for his soul; getting back to nature had settled his nerves.

They headed up a sharp incline. Spencer noticed the sumo wrestlers were starting to flag. As they came down the other side, they'd waded through a jewel blue stream, splashing as it moved through the trees. It hopped happily over rocks as it curved gently through the forest.

Then, passing through some particularly dense scrub, they came into another clearing. In front of them was a barbed wire compound with watchtowers on each corner. Watchful uniformed guards carrying rifles stared.

The two rough-hewn bamboo gates were dragged open, a boy wearing remnants of an army uniform gave a half-hearted salute as he strained to pull the heavy barriers across the muddy ground. They marched through. Spencer was amazed to see a row of wooden huts, and armed and unarmed men engaged in marching and drilling exercises. Non-commissioned officers barked orders. A Rising Sun flag hung limp from a crude flagpole.

My God, this is a small army. No wonder Buck's concerned.

The only sumo to have spoken to Spencer pointed to an office building. 'Follow me, Moretti *san*. You'll meet the Major.'

Spencer was escorted by his two taciturn companions to a spacious cabin fashioned from cedar logs with a neat garden of chrysanthemums at the front, bordered by white painted rocks. Momentarily Spencer was reminded of the office at the Northam Army camp when he was interrogated by Don Bidstrup prior to going on Operation DNA.

Spencer entered the small office. Sitting behind a neat well-ordered desk was an unsmiling, muscular older man attired in the uniform of the Japanese Imperial Army, with the insignia of a major. Around the room were framed black and white photos of historical military events. Prominent were photos of Japan's devastating attack on Pearl Harbor. Spencer was surprised to see a lot of photos were of Singapore while under Japanese rule. *Unbelievable, a photo of the Raffles.* Amongst the photos was a picture of the Japanese Singapore Headquarters, the old YMCA building.

Spencer was unnerved. It was as if the war had never ended. *My my, what a small world and here I am in a very similar situation.*

After a moment's silence, which felt to Spencer as if the major was trying to determine was he friend or foe, Watanabe abruptly stood and bowed. 'Welcome, Moretti *san*.'

Spencer bowed in accordance with custom. 'Thank you for seeing me, Major ...?'

'Major Watanabe. Now ... a welcoming *sake*?'

Spencer bowed, his mind whirling.

'You seem to be interested in my collection?' Watanabe smiled, handing Spencer a bowl of *sake* and pointing at the photos.

'Yes indeed, Major, quite fascinating. Singapore?'

The Major seemed to be quite relaxed. Spencer sat on a comfortable padded armchair in front of the Major's desk. 'Your health, Major,' he said as he raised his bowl.

'Yes, indeed Singapore. I was stationed there during the war. I was on the staff of our commander, Colonel Harada.'

Spencer almost choked on his sake. *This is getting a little close for comfort. Of all the people I could run into!* 'Difficult days I imagine?' Spencer smiled.

The major laughed. 'Far from it. Conquering Singapore was a glorious and swift event … and the occupation … well.' The major leaned back in his chair momentarily lost in the past. He laughed again. 'I tell you, Moretti *san*, they say war is hell; not so. Not when you were the occupying Army in Singapore.'

'Really?'

The major shook his head and was silent for a moment. It seemed to Spencer he was momentarily dwelling on past glories.

'I was billeted at the famous Raffles Hotel. Have you ever stayed there, Moretti san?'

'No no. I've never been to Singapore.'

I don't believe this. Could he be one of the officers having drinks at the Raffles when I ran into Harada and the Spanish Arms dealer, Cortez?

'Yes … indeed good days, glorious days. Unfortunately, it didn't end well for us.'

Spencer wasn't quite sure what to say as the major believed him to be American and on the other side. All Spencer could do was nod politely and hope they could start talking guns.

The major slurped another gulp of sake, spilling some on his desk. 'Let's get down to business, the business of guns. My army is prepared to buy all the weapons your associates can supply.'

The major by this time was obviously well into his cups. Burping loudly into his hand he smiled quickly in embarrassment. 'Please excuse me um … your name again … Morelli, was it?'

'Moretti, Major.'

'Ah yes, Morelli … no … No Moretti, yes of course … Moretti.' The Major blinked his bleary eyes.

Spencer was beginning to get the impression that Watanabe was something of a dreamer, a man trying to relive his past. As the Major rambled on about his vision for Japan, he was becoming more incoherent, Spencer paid close attention to the would-be soldiers drilling on the parade ground. Most of the soldiers were either too old or too young for active service. Was this ragtag army going to be a serious threat, or was it going to be an undisciplined rabble headed by a drunken Colonel Blimp who was all show and bluster?

Buck had drilled Spencer on all of the small arms Watanabe would likely be interested in, as well as what would be a realistic but attractive price for them. He began his spiel. 'The fact is, Major, my organisation can supply virtually unlimited quantities of small arms. In the States, anybody can buy anything as long as he has the cash. I guess you'd want Thompson submachine guns?

'Yes, yes of course Thompsons,' slurred the Major.

'And I imagine, Colt revolvers?'

'Of course, of course,' the Major's voice trailed off.

'Major …'

Spencer laughed out loud; the Major had fallen asleep. Spencer shook his head, as he gazed at the drunken old soldier. *Major Major … wakey wakey.* Spencer prodded the sodden old warrior and was met by a mumbled curse.

Spencer sat bemused, wondering exactly what he should do now; should he try again to arouse the Major? *I think it might be time to go.*

Spencer strolled out of the Watanabe's office; sumo number one was sprawled on a steamer chair, smoking a cigarette.

I think the authoritative approach might be best. 'Our business is complete. I need to go to this address.'

Sumo nodded. '*Hai*,' he said and bowed, throwing his cigarette butt into the flower bed.

A man of few words.

No mention as to what had happened to his companions. The walk back through the forest to the Toyota gave Spencer time to collect his thoughts.

Spencer was relaxed, it seemed as if from here on it was a *fait accompli*, a done deal; no worries, as they might say in Australia.

He was reasonably convinced at some time at the whim of whatever power that had seen fit to choose him for this extraordinary trip through time, he would inextricably be sent back from whence he came. And as on the last two episodes there would be no warning. But what if this time it was different? What if this time he was meant to stay … or even the unthinkable … death at the hands of a thwarted yakuza or an equally unhappy Mafia? These thoughts ran riot through his mind until they arrived at the clearing where the tired old Toyota Crown sat forlornly waiting.

CHAPTER THIRTY-FOUR

OLD FRIENDS

Crunch.

Spencer slammed the Toyota door hard; it closed with the sound of myriad pieces of metal jostling into position. Glancing down, he could see the roadway between the ill-fitting panels.

The afternoon found the Toyota rattling and wheezing its way back through Tokyo, this time without the other overweight yakuza squeezing beside him.

Spencer sat back enjoying the ride, still marvelling at Tokyo's reconstruction. It was hard to believe sixteen square miles had been levelled by US bombers just ten years earlier.

Up ahead Spencer observed the impressive outlines of the Takashimaya department store. on the corner with its distinctive red awnings. The display windows were filled with European-style mannequins attired in the latest American fashion.

The Toyota rumbled to a stop. My God the only thing on this wreck that doesn't seem to make a noise is the horn.

The driver had managed to manoeuvre the car into a small space out the front of a teahouse.

'Follow me.'

They sprinted across the busy street dodging bicycles, ex US military Harley Davidson motorcycles and the most extraordinary collection of largely pre-war Japanese and American cars. Noise and clamour, busy people in a busy city; everyone seemed to be in a hurry. This Tokyo was very different from the Tokyo Spencer was familiar with.

Smoke, smelling of scorched starch, spiralled up from a wood-burning stove on the back of a small truck. 'Sweet potatoes, sweet potatoes straight from the oven,' was the strident call. This was the sweet potato vendor, popular in the 1950s.

Spencer smiled at the sight of the caramel candy man telling tales to a small group of rapt schoolchildren, the hoarse cries of the herb seller, dressed colourfully like a hermit, his rasping voice ringing out above the noise of the traffic.

For a brief moment Spencer was captivated by the scene of Tokyo 1955, but now he was at the front of the warehouse, he wondered if perhaps things weren't going to be quite as easy and straightforward as he had glibly suggested to Savannah.

The warehouse had no markings, drab and nondescript. the old masonry covered with a century of dust and grime.

Obviously allied bombs missed this one.

Spencer's unsmiling guide marched to the unmarked entrance, throwing open the door, motioning Spencer to enter.

Spencer gazed at the vacant office complete with chairs, old teak desks and filing cabinets, a liberal coating of dust suggested the building wasn't operational: no staff, no signage, no indication what the business was or might have been.

The yakuza pressed the button next to a door, then a rare smile. 'Someone will be here in a minute. Wait, please, Moretti *san*.'

The door sprung open, an immaculately attired man stepped forward, his face wreathed in smiles, he bowed. 'Moretti *san*, so glad you could make it. I hope your trip wasn't too arduous? Please, please follow me.'

This guy doesn't appear to be yakuza: no obvious tatts, he seems to have all his fingers.

Spencer followed the garrulous man down a long corridor. Spencer's leather soles clattered noisily on the ancient teak floorboards, the grimy plaster partition displayed cheap lithographs of temples and mountains. A pervasive odour of dust and decay hung heavy in the air. The lathe and plaster walls and ceilings were cracked and yellowed by time.

'How are you enjoying Japan? The weather has been pleasant, don't you think?' The only hint they were in Japan were framed pictures of the emperor Hiro Hito posing on a white horse and photos of Mt Fuji.

'Ah yes, Moretti *san*, I know you'll be happy with our product; absolute pharmaceutical quality, first grade guaranteed.'

'I imagine you work for Mr Takahashi?'

Yes sir. My name is Hibiki."

'And what do you do, Hibiki?'

'My job is public relations, Moretti *san*.'

Once again Spencer was amazed with the corporate structure of the yakuza. It was if the lines drawn between the corporate and the criminal world in Japan were rather blurred.

He smiled to himself as he imagined prospective recruits being told about the yakuza pension plan, and the best way to climb the ladder of success and be granted keys to the executive bathroom. Spencer felt as if he was a potential buyer being given the meet and greet by a reputable international drug company.

Hibiki threw open a door, in front of them were wooden steps leading down to a cavernous warehouse. Light streamed in through dusty windows high up on the soaring walls.

In the room were many wooden crates open at the top, filled with rice. Two compact, hard-looking men opened sacks of the grain, pouring the contents into the crates.

The meet-and-greet guy waved at the scene in front of them. 'I don't think American customs are likely to search a hundred containers of rice for a bit of heroin. What do you think, Moretti *san*?'

Spencer was inclined to agree. 'I'm very impressed.'

The host glanced at his watch. 'The boss will be here in a moment. Can I get you some tea, coffee or perhaps,' and he laughed, '*sake* or beer?'

'A little early for me,' Spencer assured him.

A buzzer rang. 'Ah, that'll be the boss.' He sped to the door, returning with a man smartly attired in a charcoal-grey business suit. 'Moretti *san*, I'd like you to meet Riko Takahashi.'

Riko bowed slightly, fixing Spencer with an unblinking stare.

Spencer gazed at the newcomer. He looked familiar.

Riko Takahashi continued to stare, his eyes narrowing, saying nothing; Spencer began to feel acutely uncomfortable.

Riko gasped. 'Marlowe! You're Spencer Marlowe… your name's not Moretti.' He reached into his jacket pulling out a Nambu automatic pistol.

At the same time Spencer recognised Riko.

Spencer had found himself cast back in time to Hawaii in 1941 prior to the bombing of Pearl Harbor.

Spencer was a journalist on the Chronicle in Honolulu.

Riko Takahashi had picked up he and Roxanne, the Chronicle's photographer in Honolulu, ferrying them to Nakamura's palatial mansion on Molokai.

'Well, well, I don't believe it! Spencer Marlowe!'

The Japanese attack was in 1941, fourteen years earlier. Spencer looked older because of the FBI's aging touches. Riko, he thought had aged well, a little heavier and of course, and with the obligatory yakuza tattoos.

'We thought you and, what was her name?'

'Roxanne.'

'Roxanne … we thought you'd gone up with the munitions when they exploded. Obviously not.' Riko looked thoughtful. 'We found Haru, dead, shot. We couldn't figure out who had done it. I guess you had a hand in that?'

Spencer shrugged.

'You have aged well, Marlowe *san*,' he said conversationally. 'But what I would like to know just what is your part is in all this? Who exactly are you working for?'

Spencer said nothing.

Riko turned to one of his men, 'Daiki, get the wire.' Riko smiled. 'I'm sure you remember the wire, Marlowe *san*?'

Spencer grimaced; he remembered only too well the experience.

'Make sure he's secure, Daiki.'

'Oh yes, don't worry boss, he won't get out of this.'

Spencer had no choice but submit as Daiki took the strips of wire already cut to convenient lengths, expertly securing Spencer to the chair. Spencer winced in pain as the wire cut into his flesh.

'Tight enough, Moretti *san*?' Daiki hissed in his ear, enjoying Spencer's discomfort. 'Well Moretti *san*, alias Spencer Marlowe, I can assure you, you're going to reveal all.' Riko smiled a thin smile. 'Major Nakamura was truly a master at getting people to reveal secrets. And I was a very diligent student.'

CHAPTER THIRTY-FIVE

SAVANNAH ENJOYS THE TEA HOUSE

'Budweiser, you know … Budweiser Beer? Beer from the US of A. The United States … America for Christ's sake! The US. The country that bombed the shit out of you. Good grief. I give up.'

Savannah had figured out which warehouse Spencer was going to arrive at. This wasn't difficult; it was the only building near the famous department store fitting the description. She'd arrived early at the fashionable Tsuen tea house conveniently situated across the road.

The problem for Savannah was the menu, in Japanese. The wait staff didn't speak English and Savannah's patience was wearing thin. The ever-polite girl attempting to serve Savannah was floundering.

'*O-nomimono wa ikaga desu ka*?' (Would you like something to drink?) '*Kōhī o kibōdesu ka.*' (Would you like coffee?)

Boy oh boy, do I need Spencer's Jap-speak about now. Savannah gazed mournfully at the attractive lady in her elaborate kimono.

Savannah made a drinking motion with her hands and pointed to something on the menu. She'd no idea what it was, but she was hungry and thirsty. *God knows what I'll get. But something's better than nothing.*

The woman scuttled off; no doubt glad to be out of range of this difficult American.

While waiting for her food and drink, Savannah observed the Toyota Crown arrive, watching as Spencer and the yakuza made their way to the warehouse. *Now, if they can just wait until I've had something to eat.*

The pretty waitress arrived, nervously placing the food and drink in front of a suspicious Savannah. 'What … er … exactly is this?'

'*Basahi. O tanoshimi kudasai!*'

Savannah stared at the thin slivers, of what appeared to be some sort of flesh, it was red in colour, appearing to be marbled. Savannah had tried Sashimi and quite liked it; on the side was some soy and garlic. *Yeah, that's gotta be sashimi.*

Savannah pointed at the drink.

'*Amazake, kudasai.*'

'Ama what?'

'*Amazake, Okyaku sama,*' the woman said and bowed.

Savannah gazed suspiciously at the milky looking drink. The woman smiled, hesitantly.

Savannah beamed saying the only Japanese word she knew. '*Arigato,*' thank you. She raised her glass in a toast.

Well, it sure as hell isn't as good as a Bud. Savannah drained the last of her Amazake. The sashimi she decided was certainly different but quite tasty. 'Well, this is it girl, time to join their little tea party.'

Savannah dashed across the dusty street, dodging the cars, bicycles, trucks and motor bikes, cautiously entering the warehouse. Once inside, she paused. 'Hello, anyone home?'

Scanning the room, she saw a large brass button, surrounded by chipped porcelain, placed next to the door.

***

Spencer winced as the wire strips cut into his flesh. Riko straddled a chair smoking a cigarette, a half-smile on his face.

'Dammit,' he muttered. 'Who the hell could that be? Daiki, take the pistol and keep our guest covered.'

'What about you, boss?'

Riko held up a finger, opening his coat to reveal a shortened *sai*. 'This is all I need.'

Riko opened the door to the front office not having any idea what to expect, certainly not a well-dressed American woman.

'Oh hello, do you speak English?'

Riko nodded.

'Really, I'm so cross. I'm supposed to be meeting my husband, Mr Moretti, over the road at the teahouse. He told me he'd some business in this warehouse. I just hate business stuff, it's so boring don't you think?' Without pausing for breath, the lady continued.

'This is just so tedious.' She stamped her foot. 'I've got an appointment at the hairdressers for a perm and a colour change. I think this colour is just too buttery. What do you think? I mean if you've seen Grace Kelly at the movies … oh dear I don't even know if you have movies in Japan, well not American ones anyway.'

Savannah pulled a girlish pout. 'You seem like a nice man and honestly Lorenzo, that's Mr Moretti, he's supposed to have finished his silly business by now. Is he here? Could you take me to him?'

Riko was rarely lost for words. He gazed at this foolish apparition before him. Her up-to-the-minute fashion, the dark blue swing dress and slightly retro cloche hat, all suggested money. Her leather bag was a little too big to be stylish. His first thoughts were, *how in hell did these people win the war? Brain dead, absolutely brain dead. Who the hell is she? Is she Marlowe's wife? Has he changed his name? Does he really go by the name Moretti? One thing's for sure, she's going to miss her hairdressing appointment.*

'Yes, Mrs Moretti, it's my fault for keeping your husband tied up for so long. Please follow me. I'll take you to him. And yes, our business meeting has just wound up.' Riko forced himself to smile engagingly. He turned, padding down the corridor, making small talk. 'I do hope you've been enjoying Japan, Mrs Moretti?'

'Oh yes, just wonderful, thank you. All those pretty temples and things. And everyone's just so nice to little old me and Lorenzo. I mean Mr Moretti. And things are just so cheap. I bought this absolutely darling little fan. I mean it's just been so hot, hasn't it? I just hate the heat, don't you?'

As they reached the door leading into the warehouse Riko whirled around, the vicious sai in his hand. 'Now ...'

His sentence remained unfinished. The silly blonde apparition had disappeared and it was as if an alien had somehow taken over the body of the vapid American woman. She held an extremely large revolver confidently in her right hand. Even her voice sounded like it belonged to somebody else.

'Drop the dagger, slant-eye.'

Riko froze, trying to figure out how big a threat she was. In Riko's world, women were subservient. The very idea of a woman pointing a gun at him, Riko Takahashi, a *saiko-koman* in the Yamaguchi-gumi was hard to grasp.

'I won't tell you again.'

Riko dropped the *sai*. It clattered harmlessly onto the wooden floor.

In his most diplomatic voice, he decided a little bit of charm might work. 'Yes, we have Mr Moretti, but not here. I can take you to him. There's no reason for things to become … unpleasant. We still have some more business to conduct … but I suggest you put away the revolver. We can certainly work things out. And at the end we can all be friends and share a *sake*. What do you reckon?' Riko smiled. He was a *charmer*. He spoke perfect English with a slight Californian accent. He'd always prided himself on his bedside manner.

'You don't seem to get it. I know he's here. Take me to him … *now*!'

'Wait a minute. Just wait a minute. Really, he's not here. He went out the back way. Now we both know you're not going to shoot, don't we?' Riko held out his hand, expecting the gun to be handed over.

The magnum exploded, the sound deafening in the narrow passageway. Riko screamed as the round passed through the fleshy part of his upper right arm.

'You bitch,' he howled. Grasping the wound with his other hand, he slumped against the wall, his face ghostly white.

'Now Riko, I think we've established I will use the gun. So, as I said, take me to him.'

'I told you,' Riko snarled 'He's not here.'

'Riko,' she said patiently. 'Are you married?'

'What?'

'Easy question. Are you married?'

'Yes.'

'Do you have children?'

Riko looked decidedly puzzled. 'No, I don't have any children.' Then for the first time Riko's face showed real fear. The colour drained from his face. *How could things have gone so bad, so quickly?*

'Would you like to have children?'

Riko leant against the wall, blood pooling around him. He slumped sullenly, saying nothing.

The magnum exploded once more. This time the round went between his legs, singeing his crotch. He screamed. The heat from the slug burnt his skin. For a second, he didn't know whether or not his manhood had been shot away.

'Are we reaching an understanding?'

Riko nodded his head vigorously as he held his crotch. 'Follow me,' he mumbled miserably, his face twisted in pain.

Riko opened the door to the warehouse, there were five wooden steps leading down. Once through the door Riko jumped off the steps. Flinging himself onto the ground, screaming in Japanese, 'Daiki, shoot the bitch.'

Daiki and the other men had heard the two shots from Savannah's revolver, but hadn't yet formulated a plan of action.

***

Savannah surveyed the scene in front of her. Spencer bound to the chair. A man, obviously Daiki, holding a small Japanese automatic pistol. Another man, well-dressed, looking like he didn't really belong. He stood stunned, as if he had no idea what was happening. A small man, obviously yakuza, stood to one side, saying and doing nothing. Daiki was at least fifty feet away when he fired a shot.

'Are you, ok?' Savannah yelled to Spencer as Daiki's round whistled harmlessly overhead,

'Yeah, but watch it, these men are all trained killers.'

'Oh, really?'

Savannah's smile widened as she saw Daiki adopt a shooter's stance, about to loose off another round. 'Japanese rubbish against a Smith and Wesson? Good luck with that.'

Savannah fired from the hip without appearing to take aim; Daiki was hit in the chest, the destructive hollow point round exploded with devastating effect, spattering Spencer with blood. Daiki's body spun around; he lay face down.

Hibiki up until now had appeared to be a well-dressed company man, unused to violence. He finally showed his yakuza colours. He grabbed a long-bladed knife from the table, stood behind Spencer holding his hair in one hand, the knife against Spencer's throat with the other, while screaming in Japanese.

'What's he saying?'

'Drop the gun, or he's going to cut my throat,' Spencer yelled back.

Riko was now standing, holding his arm, trying to stem the bleeding. 'Listen lady, we can still sort things out. But if you don't drop the gun now, Hibiki will cut his throat.'

Hibiki had quickly understood the American lady was a crack shot, so he made himself into as small a target as possible. He held the knife at Spencer's throat, while crouching, so that only the top of his head was visible.

Savannah took a step closer. Hibiki screamed in Japanese, his voice hoarse with fear.

'What's he saying?' Savannah yelled at Spencer,

'He says, one more step and he's going to do it.'

Riko managed a painful cackle. 'Unless you want Marlowe dead?' His voice wheezed. Riko was clearly in pain, having lost a lot of blood. 'Unless you want him dead, drop your weapon. Hibiki's not going to back off. Face it, if you shoot, you're probably going to hit Marlowe or Moretti or whatever the hell his name is. So just throw down your weapon.'

Savannah stood both hands now on the magnum, as good as she was, she knew this shot was practically impossible.

'Your call, kid.' Spencer winked.

For Savannah the world stood still. There was silence, broken only by the faint drone of traffic. Riko and the others stood as if in suspended animation.

In that brief moment in time Savannah felt as if her whole life had been building up to this moment. The faces of the men she'd killed flashed before her: Henry Kelly with his anchor tattoo, his different coloured eyes, the two hit men in the restaurant. Gino and Louie burning to death in the grey Hudson. The look of fear on the lawyer's face when he realised he was about to die. And of course, Daiki, now sprawled face down on the floor with a hole in his back the size of a soup plate, where the ferocious magnum round had exited his body.

She smiled at the memory of her first FBI instructor suggesting that perhaps she would be better off with a lady's gun. Maybe a 0.22. And her retort, *the magnum round will go through steel, why would you want anything less?*

Savannah was not particularly religious, but she muttered a prayer she remembered from her childhood.

'The Lord is my shepherd … I shall not want … He maketh me to lie down in green pastures, He leadeth me beside the still waters, He restoreth my soul, He leadeth me in the paths of righteousness for His name's sake.'

CHAPTER THIRTY-SIX

THE YAKUZA AND THE LITTLE LADY

The spring threw the hammer forward and hit the primer. The primer exploded, igniting the propellant. The 125 grain 9.07 mm round travelled across the room at 1800 feet per second. The magnum bucked like an angry stallion at a rodeo.

The bullet struck Hibiki's forehead approximately an inch above Spencer's head. Once again Spencer was drenched in a deluge of scorched skin, bone, blood and brain matter. Hibiki fell backwards, he lay there, eyes open, his expression strangely calm.

The other man threw his hands up, babbling incoherently.

'What's he saying?'

Spencer who was still coming to terms with just how lucky he was to be still alive, grimaced as he saw the mess he was covered in.

'Not surprisingly, he's saying "I surrender." Now can you please cut me loose from this bloody wire? I tell you; it hurts.'

'Sure. Will do. I surrender, huh?'

'Yeah, I don't think he's going to be a problem.'

'No, he won't be a problem.'

The revolver roared its deadly message once again, the yakuza's body slumped onto the floor.

'For Christ's sake, Savannah, was that really necessary? That was bloody murder.'

Savannah calmly surveyed the scene. She chambered more rounds into the revolver. 'Do you know,' she murmured, 'you might be right?'

'About what exactly?' Spencer snapped.

'I might stop using these hollow point rounds. They sure make a mess.'

CHAPTER THIRTY-SEVEN

HAPPY DAYS

Spencer rubbed his wrists and ankles; the late Daiki had wired him to the chair with rather more enthusiasm than was necessary. The pain was excruciating as circulation was gradually restored.

Savannah wound the same wire around Riko's legs, leaving his arms free. Spencer wrapped some cloth around Riko's damaged arm to stem the bleeding.

'So, which is it, Moretti or Marlowe?' Riko seemed to have regained his good humour.

'It's Marlowe.'

'Well … Mr Marlowe, would you mind telling me what exactly is going on?'

'First things first. I need to phone a friend,' Spencer said cryptically. 'Back in a minute.'

Spencer sauntered back wearing a beatific smile, he pulled up a chair, 'Ok, where were we? Without letting the cat completely out of the bag, I guess you have realised we are with US law enforcement. I think it's what is known as a sting.'

'And what about Mrs Moretti?' He pointed at Savannah with his uninjured arm.

'Agent Steele at your service.' Savannah managed a smile as she curtsied.

Riko was quiet for a few minutes. 'Things are not going to go well for me. The yakuza are not going to be happy. And I imagine Romano is going to be in trouble with his colleagues in New York.'

'Do you know, you could've knocked me over with a feather when I recognised you. I still have trouble believing it's really you. I mean, that was all those years ago.' He shook his head. 'What's puzzled me, is exactly how you managed to escape from Major Nakamura's warehouse on Molokai and shoot Haru.'

Savannah stared at Spencer. 'Yes, I'd rather like to hear the story. 1941? You must've been rather young … in fact … I don't get it … none of your past makes any sense.'

Riko gazed at Spencer and Savannah in turn, not understanding what was going on.

'Ah, it's a long story.'

Savannah exploded. 'Spencer, I've had it with "it's a long story". Nothing about your past makes any sense. This nonsense about Michiyo and Dorothy Comopo or whatever her name is supposed to be. Your speaking Jap. Your martial arts skills. Your Australian background. Now it seems you were mixed up in some operation in Hawaii, when you couldn't have been any more than … what … sixteen … or … for Chrissake give me a break, seventeen perhaps? God damn Spencer,' Savannah shrieked, 'you're simply going to have to spill the beans.' Both her hands were balled into fists; her face livid, she unclenched a fist, waving a finger in his face. She lowered her voice. 'You think I'm kidding? I'm getting to the bottom of this. No more, "it's a long story," no more lies and no more evasion … got it?'

'For God's sake Savannah, this isn't the time or the place, all right? For all we know there could be more yakuza on their way here. I promise, I'll tell you everything.'

'Yeah, I'll just bet you will. When, eh?'

In the background the insistent wail of sirens grew closer.

Saved by the bell.

'That'll be the police. I've phoned Inspector Yamamoto.'

Spencer had located a phone in the front office.

'Yamamoto?' Riko's face fell.

'Sorry Riko, but you're going to have a lot of explaining to do.'

'I need a cigarette.' Riko mumbled. With his good hand he reached into his top pocket and fished out a fresh packet of Lucky Strikes.'

'You really shouldn't smoke, Riko,' Spencer chided. 'Bad for your health.'

'You're not kidding.' Riko laughed a short bitter laugh. Riko ripped the top off the soft pack with his teeth and shook out a cigarette.

'Do you need me to light it for you?'

Riko smiled at Spencer and said in a quiet voice, 'I won't need a light.'

It took a second for Spencer to realise what was happening. Riko bit the filter off the cigarette and swallowed. He immediately fell forward, his body limp.

Savannah leapt forward. 'What in hell's happened?'

Spencer smelt the odour of bitter almonds once before. 'Cyanide.'

'Why on Earth would he do that?' Savannah was clearly mystified.

Spencer gazed at the limp body the cigarette pack still clutched in his hand. 'I think it was a better choice than to face what the yakuza would have in store for him.'

The noise of the sirens had reached a crescendo. Armed police burst through the doors, screaming, yelling. At their head a dignified older officer with the sort of gold braid that seemed to be the hallmark of every high-ranking police officer around the world. Yamamoto was tall, his shaven head and high cheekbones giving him a sinister, brutal appearance.

Yamamoto studied the scene briefly, viewing the carnage with what Spencer thought was a great deal of aplomb. He turned to Spencer and bowed. 'Mr Marlowe?'

Spencer bowed in return and both men shook hands. Spencer introduced Savannah. Yamamoto gazed questioningly at Spencer. 'Agent ... Steele?'

'Yes, in fact it's Agent Steele who saved the day. I was a prisoner when she arrived.'

Yamamoto surveyed the scene again. He was a senior officer who'd attended countless murder scenes and gang shootouts, but this time he was nonplussed. 'Well, who actually shot these men?'

'Agent Steele.'

'You must do things very differently in the United States than we do in Japan.'

The debrief at police headquarters the following day seemed to take forever. Yamamoto didn't seem to be at all unhappy about the demise of Riko Takahashi and the other villains. The hard, unsmiling demeanour changed as they gathered in the squad room. Yamamoto stood to attention.

'Please Mr Marlowe, Agent Steele, join us in a celebratory beer. This is a good day for Japan. We are in your debt.'

Cold cans of Sapporo Beer were passed around, the officers were grinning and laughing as they toasted Spencer and Savannah.

Savannah beamed as she accepted a beer from a clearly awestruck sergeant. She turned to Spencer. 'Jeepers, this Sapporo beer isn't half bad either.' She poured a healthy measure down her throat, then wiping a hand across her mouth, whispered to Spencer, 'Don't think I've forgotten. You and I are aren't done. You're going to talk. I'm getting to the bottom of your bullshit story. Got it?'

'Yeah, sure, but not now, ok?' Spencer sighed as he gazed at this earnest young woman, who reminded him of a terrier with a juicy bone.

The uniformed officers seemed to be in awe of these two American agents who'd gone up against the might of the yakuza and won. Savannah was treated as if she was a goddess from another planet, imbued with mystical powers.

Spencer chuckled at the attention she was receiving. 'If you were happened to be looking for a new Mr Right, you could have your pick of the Tokyo Police Force.'

'Thanks, but no thanks.'

Spencer explained what needed to be done; the heroin had been stacked in neat five-kilogram cotton bags and hidden in the crates of rice waiting to be shipped to New York. Icing sugar was substituted for the heroin. If the rest of the operation went like clockwork, the crates would be despatched to Port Newark, New Jersey.

CHAPTER THIRTY-EIGHT

HERE COMES THE CAVALRY

Whomp whomp whomp whomp. The next morning found Sikorsky S58 Helicopters making their distinctive sound. Each carried fifteen heavily armed and armoured Rangers as they tracked just above the forest at treetop level. The forest denizens chattered, barked squealed and hissed at the unfamiliar sound.

The helicopters put down in a clearing a mile away from the militia camp. In total silence, the men made their way through the dense forest. These men were, in the main, hardened battle veterans; some had seen service in the Second World War, some in the Korean conflict.

They were led by Colonel Buck Randall. They wore camouflage clothing and greasepaint. They were equipped with the deadly 30 calibre Browning machine gun known as the BAR. Their sidearms were the tried-and-true Colt 0.45. In case they were necessary, they had M2 mortars. Fragmentation grenades were clipped to their battledress.

A marvellously colourful dawn was breaking the first light showed grease paint warriors snaking cautiously through the jungle, weapons at the ready as they came across the compound. They stopped.

Hidden in the undergrowth, they waited. Rangers were good at waiting. Twenty minutes elapsed before the sergeant tapped Colonel Randall on the shoulder.

'Sir, I don't get it. Nothing seems to be happening. You would've thought they'd have heard the choppers?'

'Yes, Sergeant, odd indeed.' He pointed to the guard towers. 'There doesn't seem to be anybody on sentry duty. What sort of Mickey Mouse outfit is this?'

'Sir, could this be some sort of trap?'

'Sergeant, come with me. Tell the corporal to set up the mortars just in case. Select a squad of ten men and we'll go in. The others can keep us covered. Get McKendrick up that tree.' Randall pointed to a wisteria with wide handsome branches. 'He's the best shot. He can keep watch.'

The mortars were set up, the sharpshooter McKendrick was in place, perched comfortably on a wide branch leaning against the trunk. He grinned, giving them the thumbs up.

'Ok, Sergeant, let's go get 'em.'

The squad edged its way forward in total silence weapons at the ready, anticipating an ambush. Perhaps a barrage of bullets from a cleverly camouflaged position. Perhaps an ingenious booby trap, which the Japanese had excelled at in the bloody fighting on the islands, like Iwo Jima. Many Americans had fallen foul of hidden poisonous spikes and tripwires triggering explosives.

The four watchtowers sitting in brooding silence seemed devoid of soldiers. Colonel Buck Randall glanced at his sergeant who shrugged. Both men thinking the same thoughts. Were there armed men crouched down behind the bamboo surround waiting to spring up and spray them with a barrage of bullets from automatic weapons, at the same time shrieking, '*banzai*'?

The men spread apart as they moved further into the compound, nerves as taut as violin strings. In front of them was the still smoking remains of a campfire. Scattered untidily around were empty cans of White Rose pilchards, a wok sat in the middle of the smoking remains, charred lumps of rice clinging to the sides. The sergeant glanced sideways at Randall mouthing. 'What in hell's going on?'

In front of them lay the barracks, serenely quiet. Buck grabbed his Colt, motioning the sergeant and a private to follow him. Lying scattered around the entrance of the barracks were dozens of empty beer bottles. The sergeant held up one to show Randall. American Budweiser beer all the way from St Louis, Missouri. They both grinned.

The barracks didn't have a door, three wooden steps led up to the open entrance. Buck Randall edged his way up the steps peering into the darkened interior. There were at least fifty men fast asleep, as many beer bottles as there were outside, as well as empty bottles of *sake* and Suntory whisky.

Buck Randall, his sergeant and a private stood in the entrance gazing at the sleeping bodies in front of them. Buck stifled a laugh. Pointing his Colt at the thatched ceiling he fired, the round breaking the silence with a deafening roar.

Pandemonium. The men jumped up yelling, screaming, cowering in fright when they saw the heavily armed Rangers.

The sergeant broke into a loud guffaw, observing the men in complete disarray. 'For God's sake,

Colonel, this isn't an army. It's just a rabble. A group of old men and boys. I can't even see any weapons.'

'*Te o agete.*' Buck knew a few useful phrases in Japanese.

Everyone immediately put their hands up apart from two old men who went on snoring, blissfully unaware of what was going on.

He then yelled, '*Anata wa taiho sa rete imasu.* You're all under arrest.'

The men were immediately compliant.

Buck holstered his Colt, yelling. 'Does anyone speak English?' A young boy, no more than fifteen, nervously put his hand up.

'Please, I do, sir.'

'Don't worry, son, you'll be ok. Will you take me to Major Watanabe?' Buck tried to reassure the boy, placing a fatherly hand on his shoulder.

'Certainly, sir, he's my uncle,' he added proudly.

'Sergeant, while I go and sort out the Major,' He said, and couldn't help but chuckle. 'Get some of the men to find out where their armaments are. We better secure those, I guess.'

Buck and the boy whose name was Eiji set off to find the fearsome Major Watanabe.

'Tell me Eiji, do you like baseball?'

'Oh yes, sir I love baseball.'

'Who's your favourite player?'

'Ruth.'

Buck smiled. 'I guess I should have worked that one out. Yep, he was just about the best, the Sultan of Swat.'

They stood outside of the Major's office and quarters.

'You stay here Eiji, I'll go and have a chat with your uncle, ok?'

'Please. sir, don't shoot him.'

Buck put his hand on the boys shoulder. 'Eiji, everything will be ok, but there's no more playing at soldiers, do you understand?'

Eiji looked solemn. 'Yes, sir.' He then added happily, 'I always wanted to be a boy scout, but my uncle wanted me to join his army. All they do is sit around, drink and sing silly songs.'

Buck strode up the steps of the office, cautiously opening the door, his Colt still in its holster. The shade was drawn, a lamp on the desk still burned, slumped with his head in his hands was the Major snoring quietly, a bottle of Johnny Walker Black label on the desk with an inch of the amber fluid still left.

Buck's sight was drawn to a magnificent Japanese gong perched on a wooden chest. His time in Japan had awakened in him an appreciation of the subtleties of Japanese craftsmanship.

Buck paused for a moment, he recognised this was a fine antique from the Edo period when craftsmen were at their peak, specialising in building complex structures without nails. The wood he guessed was maple, the brass gong was held on a crossbeam by two lengths of cord. Hanging from the side was the wooden mallet. As inconsequential as such a simple instrument may have been to the casual observer, Buck recognised this as a valuable classic piece of history.

Buck warmed the gong with a light tap at the bottom, waiting for the rich murmur to subside, he then stuck the gong as it was meant to be struck, firmly and slightly off centre, the sounds resonated through the office, shimmering, dancing off the walls, beauty and grandeur in a single breathtaking stroke.

Major Watanabe, at that moment, wasn't thinking about the beauty of the gong, he woke with a start only to see a smiling Buck Randall standing with two hands leaning on his desk.

'Wake up, Major. The war's over.'

Major Watanabe reached for his sword, hanging over his chair, swiftly wrenching it from its scabbard, and raising it above his head, screaming, 'Banzai!'

Buck pulled his 0.45 from its holster, drawing a bead directly at the Major's head before he got more than two steps. 'Put it down you old fool. I told your nephew I wasn't going to hurt you. Now drop it. The war is over. Ok?'

The Major's sword slid from his fingers, clanging as it bounced off the hardwood floor. He sat, his head resting on his folded arms, quietly sobbing. Then in English. 'I knew it was all over. I knew we could never resurrect the glory of Japan.' He lifted his tear-streaked face. 'But… these men they needed me. They needed me to give them hope, but…' He shook his head. Watanabe then seemed to pull himself together; he stood to attention and bowed.

'I'm your prisoner, Colonel. If it's your plan to execute me, I request a firing squad in front of my men.'

Buck gazed at the pathetic sight of the old soldier. *I really think he'd be relieved if we lined him up and shot him and he could yell some stupid patriotic slogan before he was cut down.*

'Major. no one is going to be executed. We'll confiscate your weapons, destroy your buildings, your watchtowers and sadly, your office. Then you'll be free to go, but … if I hear a peep from you, or anyone like you, starting this nationalist rubbish up again, it'll be a different story, ok?'

CHAPTER THIRTY-NINE

DALE FLETCHER SMILES

Spencer requested the use of a phone so he could call Dale Fletcher. Spencer told Dale an abridged version of the story.

'Fantastic,' Dale chortled. 'We've got the bastards.'

Spencer explained the shipping arrangements.

'Great stuff, Spencer. Now send a telegram to Romano and tell him to transfer the million. I'll read you the all-important numbers of our Swiss account.'

Spencer and Savannah travelled by taxi to the telegram office. Savannah was uncharacteristically subdued. 'Don't think I've forgotten about what Riko said before he died. I'm going to get to the bottom of your bullshit story, ok?'

'I told you before I would tell all and I meant It. How about this: we drop it for now. I'll tell you everything when we're on the flight back to the US.' Savannah lapsed into a gloomy silence.

Spencer felt as if he was caught like a rat in a trap. He knew Savannah was like a terrier. She wouldn't let go. *Well, I'll tell her the truth. She either believes it, or she'll think I'm a raving lunatic.*

Spencer dictated the telegram to the clerk, 'TONY, RICE CARGO ON ITS WAY. TRANSFER MONEY IMMEDIATELY. NUMBERS

CH842609MMM281TOH822.   REGARDS MORETTI.'

Spencer smiled at Savannah. 'Do you realise that telegram is probably Tony Romano's death warrant?'

CHAPTER FORTY

THE KING IS DEAD. LONG LIVE THE KING

Tony Romano relaxed in his study, savouring a twenty-one-year-old malt scotch and puffing contentedly on a Romeo y Julieta Cuban cigar.

Life didn't get much better than this. The heads of the other families would look up to him. They were all going to make a fortune from the heroin. *This should shut up those whingeing old men. Giuseppe the Lip will be as jealous as hell that I was the one that organised the deal. That old moustache Pete is way past his prime anyway.*

Moretti had displayed ruthless efficiency in dealing with the District Attorney. The charge had been reduced to murder in the second degree. Romano was impressed with Moretti's authoritative manner. The trial date was set for the middle of next year. Bail hadn't been quite as straightforward as Moretti had initially thought, due to two prior felony convictions. It was set at $50,000 and the surrender of Romano's passport. He had complete confidence in his new lawyer; the trial was a done deal, he told himself.

He rose from his latest acquisition, his antique Italian, walnut desk. With his crystal tumbler in one hand and his cigar in the other, he gazed down from his apartment window at West 57th Street and Central Park. The lights had just come on. He could see people walking their dogs, lovers walking hand in hand and office workers scurrying to catch cabs or the subway.

'My God,' he sighed. 'Life doesn't get much better than this.

Clang, clang, clang. The insistent and annoying sound of the phone interrupted his thoughts, *dammit, who the fuck could this be?* 'Yeah, who is it?'

'Boss, boss it's me, Angelo.'

Angelo Fazio hadn't been in Romero's good books since Spencer had smacked him around in the restaurant. 'Angelo, this better be good.'

'Boss,' his voice was accompanied by racking sobs. In that moment, Romano instinctively knew his world was crumbling down around him.

'Get a hold of yourself man,' Tony snapped.

'Boss, it was a setup. Me and the guys had just unpacked the rice and let me tell ya, there was no smack. And then the Feds rushed in. I was able to hide behind some crates. The others were all arrested. I've only just been able to get away.'

Romano felt the cold steel of an invisible hand grasping his insides. 'Marlowe.'

Without another word Tony Romano hung up the phone and plonked heavily onto a carved oak chair. Pride of place on his desk was a highly polished wooden case, heavy, but small enough to be carried under his arm. Tony Romano removed his Patek Philippe watch, carefully writing a note to his wife. *My darling, I have always loved you and Tony junior. Give him this watch on his eighteenth birthday. Tell him how much he means to me.*

Tony Romano picked up the wooden case and padded quietly out of the front door, catching the lift to the lobby.

'Good evening, Mr Romano, can I get you a cab?'

Tony Romano ignored the doorman and strolled out of the building to where his Cadillac waited. Tony reflected it had been a long time since he had driven an automobile. *I don't think I'll need a chauffeur tonight.*

He turned for a last glance at his apartment block, stacked with strangers deep in slumber, unaware that one of their neighbours was striding beneath them in the shadows. Some windows gave out white and yellow light but the others were pitch black. The tantalising aroma of grilled steak wafted from a nearby restaurant, mingling with the smell of car exhaust.

Pausing, he reached into his pocket and grabbed the fob and for the first time noticed the embossed leather, the custom silver surround, and the Cadillac emblem; the black against the gold symbolising riches and wisdom, the red meaning boldness and prowess in action, silver to symbolise purity, virtue, plenty and charity. And blue to stand for knightly valour. Tony vaguely remembered this GMH bullshit when he read the brochure. The lock clicked gently, he swung the heavy door open, and the interior light shone a soft glow over the warm leather upholstery. Sliding behind the wheel, he ran his fingers over the dash searching for the ignition. The big V8 emitted its quiet burble.

He drove aimlessly along Central Park, then on a whim he drove down Broadway and through Times Square, *God, how I love this city, it's really got it all.* He reflected on his life, the grinding poverty of Hell's Kitchen, the brutal fight clawing his way to the top, a journey littered with bodies and the occasional periods of incarceration. Was it worth it? Right now he wasn't sure. *Hell, what else was there? Maybe I could've driven a cab, owned a deli… nah, that was never going to be me.*

As if controlled by invisible hands he found himself driving towards Greenwich Village. He saw the arch, so much a part of Greenwich. He turned into Morton Street, the Cadillac gliding to a halt outside of the blackened ruin that had been Spencer's Restaurant. *If only you had accepted my offer … if only.*

Romano paused for a minute before clipping open the brass clasp and opening the wooden case. Nestled inside on bed of crimson velvet was a present from Police Commissioner Francesco Martino. This was probably the most famous handgun in America, Wyatt Earp's Colt 0.45 revolver, the mythical Buntline Special that'd been used in the gunfight at the O.K. Corral.

Romano reflected as he had done many times before, *how ironic a gun used by America's most famous law man now owned by one of America's most famous crime lords.* He spun the chamber, admiring the mechanical click of the cylinder as it spun around.

Tony Romano gazed once more at the ruins of the restaurant as he put the barrel of the gun into his mouth.

CHAPTER FORTY-ONE

UNFINISHED BUSINESS

In a walled villa high atop Mt Kumotori, with splendid views of Mt Fuji in the far distance, the yakuza were in conference. The meeting room was an impressive sight, modernistic with soaring ceilings. A huge picture window gave the impression they were perched—without support—on a steep cliff overlooking a forest. A stream zig-zagged through the trees.

A very worried Akihito chaired the meeting. He knew unless he could produce a miracle worthy of the gods he was a dead man. After many hours, amidst rumblings of discontent, a plan was hatched.

'Well Special Agent Steele, our flight back home is in three days. Yamamoto has suggested it'd be a good idea if we don't leave the hotel.'

'Blast, I wanted to do some last-minute shopping in the Ginza,' Savannah grumbled.

'Cmon, we have a few enemies in town. Sit back and relax. Watch TV. Drink some Asahi. Order room service.'

'Yeah, right, and now would be a real good time for a little bit of explaining. I'm not letting go of all this Spencer Marlowe bullshit, now talk, damn you.'

Spencer knew he had run out of excuses. Their conversation was interrupted by the insistent sounds of the telephone.

Saved by the bell. 'I'd better answer.' Spencer grabbed the phone.

'Yes, this is Marlowe *san*. What … really … when? Now? I see … How much time do we have?' Spencer hung up the phone.

'What in hell was that all about?' Savannah demanded.

'That was an inspector Kobayashi.'

'Who's he when he's at home?' Savannah asked peevishly.

'He's one of Yamamoto's officers.'

'And?'

'Apparently this hotel is no longer safe. Yamamoto has sent a car and a police escort, they're taking us to a safe house until we're ready to fly out.'

'That's all I need. When exactly?'

'He said there's no time to lose. They have been tipped off. The yakuza have hatched some sort of plan. He means, like, right away. Pack your things. Don't forget your passport.'

Spencer wasn't unduly concerned; they were packed and ready when the phone rang again.

'Moretti *san*,' the sweet-voiced receptionist said, 'There is an Inspector Kobayashi and several police waiting for you in the lobby. I understand you're checking out. I'll send the porter.'

Spencer was on high alert as they accompanied the porter into the lift and down to the lobby. Spencer scanned the lobby, relieved to see a phalanx of armed uniformed police standing grim faced in the lobby. A senior police officer dripping with gold braid stepped forward and bowed.

'Moretti *san*, my name is Kobayashi. My apologies for this development, but we deem it necessary.'

'No apology needed, Inspector.' Spencer bowed.

The inspector motioned to one of his officers who grabbed their bags. They strode through the lobby as bemused customers and staff looked on.

Savannah gasped at the sight of a magnificent gleaming six door black Mercedes Pullman limousine waiting at the entrance. In front and behind were four police Rikuo motorcycles, their motors idling with a slow rumble.

'God almighty, I'll feel like the Queen of England. What a car.' Savannah ogled the vehicle.

A helmeted motorcycle cop dismounted his machine and with a bow, opened the rear door. Without a word the inspector and another officer climbed into the front seats. Another officer deposited their luggage in the cavernous trunk.

Spencer grinned at Savannah, 'As we would say in Australia, "this's the duck's nuts".'

The rear of the Mercedes had two rows of seats, facing each other, all in black leather. A glass partition separated them from the driver and Kobayashi. The motorcycle sirens blared as they roared off into the Tokyo traffic.

'This could be a good time for our little chat,' Savannah glared.

'Tokyo really is a magnificent city, isn't it?' Spencer yawned.

'Stop yawning, and start talking. Dammit, you're making me yawn.'

Spencer could feel a gentle lethargy starting to take over. He wondered how long their journey would be. He tapped on the glass divider. The last thing he remembered was a smiling Kobayashi who turned and grinned. He noticed the edge of a black tattoo peeping above the inspector's collar.

# CHAPTER FORTY-TWO

OUT OF THE WOK AND INTO THE FIRE

'My God damn head hurts. Shit, I feel like I have a hangover. What in hell…' Spencer rolled onto his back and opened his eyes, gazing at steel bars. His bed was a hard, narrow bunk, the mattress a worn, bleached white futon. Beyond that he could see a tiled corridor in bland, institution style grey. The other walls appeared to be made of thick grey stone. The window was a barred opening with no glass. The only furnishings were a worn, teak table, two chairs and a bucket in the corner. Ignoring his pounding headache, Spencer listened. Total silence, apart from a whispering breeze from his cell window. Climbing to his feet, he grasped the window bars and hoisting himself up, peering out at a mountain view of astonishing beauty. In the distance lay a snow-capped mountain. *That's Mount Fuji!*

Spencer sat forlornly on the bunk, trying to remember just what had happened as he held his throbbing head in his hands. The last thing he remembered was a grinning Inspector Kobayashi.

'A tattoo! The bastard had a tatt.' Spencer knew that in Japan tattoos were frowned upon, and most public swimming pools, spas and gyms banned the display of tattoos. Why? 'Bloody yakuza. All yakuza were inked. No, this can't be right. What's going on, and where's Savannah?'

He climbed unsteadily to his feet and stumbled over to the bars of his cell, and in Japanese yelled, 'Anybody there?'

'Thank God, are you ok?' Savannah's shrill voice rang out.

Spencer tried to peer down the corridor. He had the impression they were in some sort of prison, and Savannah was in an adjoining cell.

'What do you think's going on? And where the hell are we?' Savannah yelled.

'No need to yell. I can hear you. I reckon we're in the mountains, probably a couple of hours away from Tokyo. That's an educated guess, but still a guess. Maybe Yamamoto has stuck us in a jail for our own protection?'

'Oh yeah, and Santa Claus is real. You don't believe that do you?' Savannah snapped.

'No. Something is definitely off. I gather you fell asleep in the car?'

'You got it. And I woke up in this blasted cell about twenty minutes ago. How the hell does that work? Christ, I feel ill.'

'Hey, listen.' The sound of stout shoe leather echoed along the corridor. Spencer gasped at the sight of the last man in the world he expected to see. 'Akahito.'

'Yes, Moretti *san*, if that's really your name. And in answer to your associate's question: methyl propyl-ether.'

A smiling Akahito smoked a cigarette, impeccably dressed in a fashionable blue rayon single breasted suit with long wide lapels. Accompanying him was a surly looking guard, wearing a peasant-style black cotton 'pyjama' outfit topped by a conical bamboo hat and armed with a British Sten gun. Strapped to his waist, a walnut-handled pistol rested in a leather holster.

Spencer quickly studied the guard, momentarily bemused by his height and round eyes. He was unusually tall, his round, flat face showing no emotion.

'I'm sorry. Come again?' Spencer queried.

Akahito laughed. Not a pleasant sound. 'Methyl propyl-ether. It's a gas that puts you to sleep. Leaves you with quite a hangover I'm told. The Mercedes has been modified so that recalcitrant passengers don't prove to be a problem. All Kobayashi had to do was flick a switch and the appropriate amount of the gas seeped in. Clever, don't you think?' Akahito beamed.

'So … Kobayashi, the police, the motorcycles…?'

'Ah yes. All loyal yakuza.'

'Listen, you creep, you better let us out. You hear me, you son of a bitch?' Savannah bellowed.

Akihito ignored Savannah. 'Now Mr Moretti, please extend your hands through the bars and Shinda will place you in handcuffs. I wish to have a conversation with you and I have seen your formidable martial arts skills. One false move and he'll shoot.'

Spencer thrust his hands through a rectangular opening in the bars. The steel cuffs clicked.

'If you please, Mr Moretti, take a seat at the table, and we can talk like civilised men.'

Shinda produced a large steel key from a ring on his belt. The lock ratchetted open and he slid the barred cell door open. The two men entered the cell,

Shinda withdrew the pistol from its holster, pointing it at Spencer. The Sten dangled from a strap over his shoulder.

Spencer pulled back a chair and sat awkwardly and watched as Akahito dusted his seat with a handkerchief and carefully draped himself onto the other chair.

'We will speak in English if you don't mind.' Akahito put his flawlessly manicured hands together as if in prayer.

Spencer had never heard Akahito converse in anything other than Japanese and was surprised to hear a cultured Atlantic English accent, suggesting a higher-level education.

'First, I will explain my position.' Akahito reached into his pocket and produced a packet of Chesterfields in a soft packet and a gold Ronson lighter.

'Smoke?' he offered the packet to Spencer, who shook his head. 'Our position is well … you know what it is. We have despatched our heroin as agreed, and we don't have our money.'

Spencer shrugged.

Akahito continued. 'What we don't know: is this a double cross by that barbarian Romano? Is it possibly something you and your, whatever your lady friend is, has engineered? Or is it something that's been orchestrated by … let's say the FBI, for instance?'

Spencer's mind was in a whirl. *They don't have any real idea. How can I turn this to our advantage?* 'Akahito *san*, my bona-fides are easily established. I'm sure you have already checked me out. My name is Moretti. I am Tony Romano's lawyer. I have been entrusted with this transaction. Making sure the merchandise was as agreed and then advising Mr Romano to forward the money. It's simply inconceivable that Romano and his associates have been involved in any sort of double cross. This is the first I have heard that you haven't received your money. I don't wish to be insulting, but how do I know what you say is true? I know absolutely this was to be an ongoing, mutually beneficial business arrangement. And let me add, if Mr Romano or his colleagues in any way suspected me or my companion of being involved in any double dealing, we would be dead. Have you not spoken to Mr Romano?'

'No, we have held off phoning America until we questioned you and your companion.'

'Savannah knows nothing. She's my mistress, nothing more, nothing less. In fact, I was going to dump her when we got back to the US. You understand Akahito *san*, I'm a married man and … well. In America divorce is costly and she has threatened to confront my wife. I'm sure you understand. That aside I'm not at all happy at my treatment by you and your people. I don't understand why you didn't contact me when you discovered your money hadn't arrived. I have found this whole experience to be quite distressing, and frankly I'm not at all sure that I would advise Romano and the rest of his associates to enter into another business transaction with you or your organisation. I have told you everything I know, and I expect you to release me and Miss Steele immediately and take us back to our hotel. Do I make myself quite clear?'

Spencer was sure Akahito would be able to hear his heart hammering in his chest. *We are in with a chance.*

Akahito was silent for a brief moment. 'I understand, that originally you were meant to be travelling with another man, I forget his name. Tell me why this was not so?'

Spencer rolled his eyes, 'That was Carmine Ferrera, nasty little brute.'

'And why the late change?' Akahito asked.

Spencer steepled his fingers. 'This is a little delicate, Akahito *san*. I am Mr Romano's lawyer but I am not privy to the inner workings of his business. At the last minute I was told that Ferrera's employment had been terminated, which I'm sure you understand…'

'You think he was perhaps—'

'It's not my position to speculate, but given the late change in arrangements, I suspect that Mr Ferrera is now probably the *late* Mr Ferrera. He was an uncouth individual, so I decided to avail myself of a far more attractive companion.'

Spencer sweated. Akahito seemed to be falling for it.

'We have other concerns.'

'And what would they be, Akahito *san*?'

'You went to see Major Watanabe, to arrange an arms deal. Yes?'

'You know I did.'

'The very next day Watanabe *san* was attacked by a squad of American Rangers. A bit of a coincidence?'

Spencer snorted. 'I know nothing about any American soldiers. C'mon seriously, just who the hell do you think I am? Do you think the US Army is at my beck and call? The reality is, I was very annoyed you wasted my valuable time in sending me to see that old drunk who was simply playing soldiers with a group of geriatrics and boys. He was never going to buy guns. Why the Americans would be interested in him, I really can't imagine.'

Akahito stared with cool intensity 'I had heard rumours that what you say is true. However, there is one other, rather more serious issue.'

Spencer's stomach lurched. He had an idea what that might be.

'Riko Takahashi, Mr Moretti. Remember him?' Akahito fixed him now with a decidedly hard stare. Spencer returned his gaze. It felt like a competition.

'Remember him, Akahito? Why wouldn't I remember him?' Spencer deliberately left off the honorific suffix 'san'. His best move now was to be more assertive.

'You saw him, where exactly?'

'Stop playing around, Akahito. You know where I saw him. In your warehouse opposite the Takashimaya department store. Along with someone named Hibiki and another. Satisfied? Now suppose you tell me what's this's all about? Frankly I'm fed up with it all. I've done everything required of me and my colleagues and you seem to be playing some sort of mind game.'

'What if I was to tell you Takahashi and the others are missing?'

'What if you did tell me, Akahito? And for God's sake, what's it got to do with me? What on Earth are you suggesting? Somehow with no contacts in Japan and no weapons, I have somehow kidnapped or liquidated some of your men? This gets sillier by the minute. On the surface it seems as if you have solved your mystery, but you don't like the answers. It would seem obvious Takahashi and maybe the others are behind some sort of con. That's where you should be looking.'

Akahito held his hands over his face. As he removed them, Spencer saw they were shaking. 'Mr Moretti, if I don't retrieve the money or the heroin, I'm a dead man. *Seppuka.*'

Spencer knew all about *seppuka* or *hari-kari* as it was also known.

'Once again, Akahito, I insist you let my friend and I go. We are not your problem.'

'Mr Moretti, at the moment you and your lady are the only leverage I have. You will be my guests until I get to the bottom of this.'

'And just how long is that likely to take?'

'How long, Mr Moretti? It will take as long as it takes.'

'And then what?'

'And then, Mr Moretti, if I'm not convinced you are innocent, your deaths will be infinitely more painful than *seppuka.*'

CHAPTER FORTY-THREE

DESPERATION

The retreating footsteps of Akahito and the guard clip-clopped down the bleached tile corridor. Spencer rubbed his wrists, relieved that Akahito had ordered the cuffs to be removed. *Just how long do we have? Just a few days probably.*

Spencer gripped the bars, listening to the sounds of silence, 'Savannah,' he whispered, 'Can you hear me?

'Yeah, what's going down?'

Spencer gave an abridged version of the discussion, hoping the cell wasn't wired for sound. 'Our only hope is an escape or we're dead. I have an idea, it's a bit tricky. But just stay alert.'

'Try not to kill anyone, Spencer dear.' Spencer smiled at Savannah's sarcasm.

Just as the last rays of sunlight drained away, Shinda appeared bearing miso soup, silently depositing a bowl under Spencer's cell door. Spencer heard a gentle thunk as another bowl was placed in Savannah's cell. Spencer greedily consumed every last drop of the thin beverage. After wishing Savannah a good night, he lay on his bunk.

He awakened after a bad night. The dour Shinda appeared with bowls of steaming rice and natto, the stinky ammonia-smelling fermented soybean dish.

'What the hell's this crap, Spencer?' Savannah called.

'Eat it. It's nutritious and you're going to need your strength.'

Spencer waited and listened. Absolute silence. *Well, here goes.*

'Guard, guard, help me,' Spencer's plaintive cry echoed through the building. He lay on the floor in a foetal position, groaning. Running feet clattered along the passageway. He sensed Shinda standing by the bars. The guard's panicked voice rang out in the Ainu dialect, similar to Japanese, calling for assistance. Another guard ran in.

The two guards then discussed the situation, the second man warning it could be a trap. After thirty seconds Spencer heard the click of the lock. He groaned with more enthusiasm. Shinda bent down, rolling a whimpering Spencer on to his back.

'I think it's my appendix.' He bared his teeth and clutched his stomach. Spencer quickly assessed the situation; the second man, short but muscular, leant against one wall munching an apple, Sten gun in the other hand.

'Where does it hurt?'

'Oh, my stomach. It's on fire!' Spencer screamed in Japanese. 'I need a doctor.'

Shinda addressed his partner. 'Auta, if he dies, we're in trouble.'

Hauling Spencer up by his jacket lapels, Shinda roughly hoisted him to his feet. The other guard, now behind Shinda, looked on with disinterest. Swiftly

Spencer jerked himself upright, grabbing Shinda by the head and skilfully twisting. *Crack.* The vertebrae snapped.

Auta cursed, dropping his apple. Spencer tore the Sten from Shinda's lifeless body and slammed the steel stock into Auta's face. The Sten buckled, but the damage was done. Auta slumped to the floor. Blood squirted from his broken nose as he tried to unbutton his holster. Spencer clubbed Auta over the head with the Sten until the gun shattered.

Breathing heavily, Spencer surveyed the situation. Blood painted the floor in messy strokes. Auta had no pulse. Spencer carefully removed Shinta's black pyjama-like costume and unbuckled the holster.

Now clad in black and wearing the holster and pistol, Spencer grabbed Shinda's straw hat, jamming it on his head. Scooping up keys and handcuffs in one hand he fled through the open cell door, speaking softly. 'Time to go, Savannah.'

Fortunately, there were only four keys. The second opened Savannah's door. She grinned, looking calm and ready for anything.

'Now, what about the guards? I couldn't hear much. Oh dear, you've killed them, haven't you? We just can't take you anywhere, can we?' Savannah smiled sweetly.

'All right, smarty pants, we still have to get out of here.'

'What now, killer?' Savannah asked.

'Slip these handcuffs around your wrists. Don't lock them.'

'I'm getting the picture. You've given this some thought, haven't you, Boy Wonder?'

Spencer cautiously stuck his head out of the cell, checking the passageway.

'All clear.'

One end of the passage led to a stairwell going down, at the other end, a similar stairwell going up.

'I think down will lead to outside. Let's just wing it.'

With a seemingly handcuffed Savannah, Spencer prodded her along, Auta's Sten at her back.

'Hey, Savannah.'

Peering through a rectangular barred window they found themselves looking down on a carpark and a curved driveway that led to a road winding scenically down the mountain.

'Spencer, look. In that corner.'

A boy, no more than sixteen chamois in hand, diligently cleaned the Mercedes.

'Isn't that nice. He didn't have to do that for us.' Savannah chuckled.

As they bound down the stairs and stepped outside, the unaccustomed sunlight hurt their eyes.

'Oh hell, Spencer. Over there.'

In the far corner of the carpark two yakuza sat at a small table, drinking coffee and playing cards. Two Stens lay next to them. Spencer and Savannah strolled over to the Mercedes.

'Get out of here,' Spencer snarled at the boy who yelled, dropping his chamois as he fled. Coffee mugs smashed on the ground. A wicker table went flying. The yakuza yelled as they grabbed their sub machine guns.

'I'll drive,' Savannah shrieked.

As they slammed the solid Mercedes doors shut, Spencer cursed. 'We're in Japan, remember? Right hand drive. Looks like I'm driving. Lock the bloody doors.'

Spencer knew the key had to be there as the radio was on, spouting a trite Johnny Ray song about a cloud. In the seconds before he realised the ignition was in the centre of the dash, the two yakuza furiously banged on the side of the car, screaming and grabbing at the door handles.

'What are they saying?' Savannah gasped.

'Get out or they'll shoot.'

'Well, I'd sooner be shot than be tortured by these bastards. Drive, damn you, just drive.'

Spencer turned the key, the engine turned over. 'See you on the other side.'

The engine roared, and Spencer planted his foot on the accelerator. Two sub-machine guns erupted, 9MM rounds bouncing off the glass. The Mercedes fishtailed wildly as the tyres grabbed for purchase on the loose gravel. The car headed straight for a wall.

'Spencer, turn the God damn wheel.'

Spencer spun the steering wheel and the car powered through the gates, machine gun rounds bouncing off the bodywork.

'I should have guessed.' Savannah laughed hysterically. 'Damn well armour plated. Of course, it is. My God. Doesn't that just beat all?'

'Do you know what day it is?' Spencer asked.

'Tuesday, I think?'

'I think you're right. And that's the day we're due to fly out. The clock says it's 9:12 am and our flight was at 3:30 pm. I've just seen some signs … we've just left Mount Kumatori. I sort of know where we are. How about we drive straight to the airport?'

'Great idea, but no passports, tickets, ID, anything.'

'I'm going to head to Haneda Airport. Let's see if we can sort something out when we get there. Meanwhile keep your eyes peeled for mobsters.'

The black limousine rocketed down the narrow mountain road. The sky was now tar black. As they flew through the first village, they heard the first few drops splatter on the window, then a pitter patter. People ran for cover outside. Umbrellas unfurled as the clouds unleashed a veritable torrent.

'For Christ's sake, Spencer, slow down,' Savannah shrieked as the car momentarily lost traction and slithered towards the stone walls of an ancient bridge.

Spencer cursed. Taking his foot off the pedal, the car rolled gently to a stop. 'Bloody hell that was close.'

Grinning at Savannah, he accelerated smoothly around the next bend. As suddenly as the cloudburst had descended, it dissipated to a slow drizzle.

Three uneventful hours later the black limousine pulled into a parking bay at Haneda International Airport.

'I've had a thought.' Spencer grabbed the keys, climbed out of the limo and opened the trunk. Savannah followed. 'Oh, Savannah…'

There before them, they saw their bags neatly stacked, just as they had been when Kobayashi picked them up.

'There really is a God.' Savannah murmured as she gazed at the contents.

CHAPTER FORTY-FOUR

TIME TO GO

Bloodied black pyjamas now discarded, Spencer thought he looked like an urbane international traveller in his grey business suit, black brogues, white shirt and pale blue silk tie.

'Jesus, I never want to come back to this God damn country again.' Savannah took a hearty swig of her beer as they waited nervously in the bar. She'd changed into a conservative tweed swing dress and comfortable saddle shoes.

'Well, we'll sure have a story for Dale,' Spencer said, sipping any icy Coca Cola. He continued to scan the busy airport for anyone who might have been a threat.

'We probably should have phoned Yamamoto and told him about our little adventure, I guess,' Savannah said moodily.

'The hell with that. It would have meant a bloody de-brief and probably another day or two in Japan, and that could give the yakuza another crack at us. Dale can sort that out.'

'Now Spencer. Superhero and slayer of evil men. I haven't forgotten.'

'Forgotten what?' Spencer asked innocently.

'You know damn well what. I want to know just what the hell is going on. Hawaii? Riko whatisname?

He knew you back in 1941. I want to know about your mysterious wife. I'm not letting go of this. I mean now, right now!'

A melodic Japanese voice sung out from the Tannoy.

'Time to board, Savannah. This'll have to wait.'

Clutching his airline bag Spencer strode out to the tarmac with Savannah trailing behind, swearing under her breath.

'What's wrong with TWA or Pan Am?' Savannah hissed to Spencer as they were escorted to their seat on the Japan Airlines Douglas DC-3, heading back to New York via *San* Francisco.

The faithful DC-3 had been the stalwart of transport aircraft during World War Two and was noisy and cramped with its Pratt and Whitney turbo prop engines, far noisier than the engines of the Super Constellation they'd arrived in.

'Ok, now's the time to spill the beans. You promised to tell all,' Savannah demanded.

'Can we at least have a drink? They're going to be serving a meal shortly. How about we wait until after dinner?' Spencer couldn't see an alternative; he was dreading this moment.

'Alright, but don't think you can wriggle out of it.' Savannah fixed him with a fierce gaze.

There's no getting out of this.

Spencer sighed and spoke to their hostess, a charming Japanese lady in her smart navy suit with gold buttons and blue military style side cap.

'Could I please have a glass of champagne and a Budweiser for my friend?'

'Oh, ah excuse me,' Savannah interrupted. 'Could you make mine an Asahi please?'

'My God,' he chided, 'What next?' Spencer raised an eyebrow.

'Yeah ok, I've decided I don't mind Jap food and drink.'

Menus were handed out Spencer had chosen the *hanaichi*, which was curried chicken with rice and shrimp.

Dinner arrived both Spencer and Savannah were ravenous, Spencer glanced at Savannah's dish, 'What is that?' pointing his chopsticks at her plate.

'This is called *basahi*, I had it in Tokyo, it's really good, you should try it sometime.'

Spencer stifled a laugh.

'What?'

'Nothing,' He was now completely unsuccessful at stifling his mirth.

'Ok, give … what's the joke?'

Spencer concentrated on his *hanaichi* which had arrived, its fragrant odour tantalising his taste buds. 'Savannah, did you like the movies when you were a kid?'

'You know I did, I told you that.'

'I forget, tell me again … who was your favourite?'

'You know … I just loved the Cisco Kid and his faithful … Oh no,' Savannah wailed 'don't tell me I'm eating Diablo?' Savannah's face screwed up.

'Well probably not Diablo, but it could be one of his close relatives.' Spencer attempted to placate Savannah.

'That's barbaric, but … hey it tastes ok.'

Spencer reluctantly swallowed the last delicious morsel of his *hanaichi*, he pressed the button for a stewardess. 'May I have a large cognac please?' Resigned to the inevitable discussion with Savannah he'd decided to fortify himself with a glass of Fine Champagne Cognac. *Bloody coward,* he remonstrated himself.

'There's one other thing.' Savannah took a swig of her Asahi, 'Not bad, not bad at all.'

'That would be?'

'Well, apart from your bullshit that we are … and I mean *we are going* to get to the bottom of. What are your plans?'

'I'm sorry. I don't follow.'

'Well, this little op is over. Are you going to stick with me and we find out just what Dale has planned for us? Are you happy to stay in New York? What I mean, boy wonder, is what's next for you?'

Spencer stared out of the window. What's next? He hadn't a clue. *Is this it? Am I stuck in the 50's?*

'I … I … don't know,' he stammered. 'I guess I'll see what Dale has in mind. I must confess New York isn't my idea of home. Too cold in winter. Too hot in summer.'

'I know exactly where you should be.'

'Really. Where?'

'California,' Savanna said triumphantly. 'You are definitely a West Coaster.'

'I am?'

'You bet. I can just see you now. Santa Monica, Carmel, Santa Barbara. The beach, the surf. That's you to a T.'

Spencer had put thoughts of his future on hold. He didn't want to confront the reality he was faced with.

'You may be right. California has appeal. Well, let's see what Dale comes up with.'

He felt in his pocket for the *cornicello*, he grabbed it, examining it as he had done so many times before. *Well, I wonder, are you my lucky charm?* He smiled as he put it back into his pocket, as always comforted by this strange talisman.

As he sipped the superb Remy Martin offering, his mind flashed back to the very start of this fantastic adventure, in April. His first meeting with Tony Romano and Dale Fletcher, his fear, the pain at the savage beating inflicted by Louis and Gino, his induction into the FBI. He also remembered the simple pleasures of running the restaurant 'Spencer's.'

The faces of all the players that had starring roles in this tumultuous episode in his life. His other life all appeared in and out of sequence. He remembered Riko's face when he had recognised him as Spencer Marlowe. He unconsciously grimaced at the memory of his introduction to Savannah's intended, Seth Alvah. And Michiyo … he choked back a tear and reached out.

Everything flashed past him, like a drowning man that sees his life before him. The brandy balloon slipped from his fingers. The faces and places whirled around ever faster. He felt himself sliding, slipping. Piercing screams. Yells, intensifying. Engulfing his senses in a terrifying confusion of noise. Someone trying to get his attention. Someone shaking him.

CHAPTER FORTY-FIVE

REUNITED

'Spencer, please wake up. You've been asleep for hours. Would you believe it's 7:04 in the evening? I've been shopping. I've explored Saks and Macy's. I've bought the sexiest lingerie and I'm starving. I read in the Best New York Eateries about a pizza restaurant in Greenwich Village called John's. It's in Bleecker Street. How about we give it a try tonight?'

Spencer gazed at his beautiful wife. He put his arms around her, clinging to her as if his life depended on it,

'Michiyo, I haven't told you for a very, very long time just how much I love you.'

Michiyo freed herself from his embrace and stroked his cheek. 'Have you been away?'

Spencer nodded. 'Yes, but I'm back now.'

***

Akahito glanced at his watch. It was almost time. In the great hall downstairs, the yakuza waited.

Donning a scarlet silk kimono, a *wakizashi* in his hand, he shuddered as he tested the keenness of its blade and glanced around his sumptuous apartment for the last time. As he walked with measured tread towards the apartment door, he turned.

Through the open balcony doors, he could see Mt Fuji in the distance. He imagined the bitter fragrance of the cherry blossoms. He grabbed a small oak stool and carried it to the balcony. Placing his feet on the stool, he climbed up on to the railing. Way below him meandered the stream, bordered by rocks of rough granite. He gazed momentarily at the last sight to meet his eyes. *Just who are you, Moretti?*

EPILOGUE

Savannah mooched around the brownstone apartment in Brooklyn Heights she now shared with her fiancé, Seth. It was a lazy Sunday afternoon some years after she'd returned from Japan. Seth was due to return from yet another weekend away with his drinking, card-playing buddies in a remote cabin in the Catskills. As Seth was leaving, Savannah had commented it was a curious outing as Seth neither drank nor appeared to be interested in gambling.

'Darling, it's just the chance to appreciate nature and let my hair down, I guess,' he said with a shrug.

Once she'd put Marlowe into the unsolved cases bin and got back to living her life, she could finally appreciate living with her fiancé, and just life in general.

Savannah just adored this apartment. Built in 1895, it had broad concrete steps that led down to the sidewalk. Magnificent wrought iron railings stood like sentinels on either side, handy to clutch onto when the steps were iced over. The windows were large, adding a dignified, timeless and aloof expression of past grandeur.

Inside, Seth had tastefully decorated the apartment in muted sepia tones. The ceilings were the highest Savannah had ever seen. The wide, oak timber floorboards had a lustre that added warmth and a touch of history to the spacious rooms that had played host to generations of families. Savannah loved everything about this solid, charming residence. All it needed, she thought with a smile, was the pitter-patter…

Through the windows she admired the last gasps of beauty before the death of the day The red maple with its glorious colourings added a splash of warmth to the scene. The traffic whispered below, a hazy murmur in the background; the solid old brownstone walls filtering out the harsh sounds of the busy metropolis.

Savannah wandered into Seth's darkroom. He was an avid photographer and had taken many photos of his young patients.

He sure loves kids. Savannah couldn't help but smile at the snaps of trusting children safe in the care of the doctors and nursing staff at Bellevue Hospital. In the corner of the room stood an old combination safe.

Seth had explained it was just there when he'd moved in. Apparently, he kept his passport and a small amount of cash tucked inside.

Savannah sat down at Seth's desk, idly glancing at the doodling and scribbles on his blotter. Amidst the jumble of dates, names, etcetera, in the top right-hand corner was printed 051229. That would be Seth's birthday, she thought.

Feeling a little guilty, she applied these numbers to the safe's combination lock. What made her decide to open the safe, this solid steel keeper of secrets, impressive in its black livery with the faded gold lettering proudly proclaiming 'Wells Fargo 1852' she didn't quite know.

Neatly stacked, collated and numbered, were dozens of eight by ten inch glossy black and white photos. Savannah picked up the first stack and peered in the half light at the pictures. She gasped in horror. The stack fell from her hands. She raced to the bathroom, kneeling over the toilet, retching until there was nothing left.

Climbing unsteadily to her feet she shuffled back to the room, the room of horror. Savannah turned on the light and forced herself to look at the images. There she found multiple photos of Seth, naked with a little girl, from different angles. Then another several photos with a boy no more than six years of age, then more of the boy in a room with other men. Savannah recognised the men as Seth's friends he went away with on weekends.

Savannah had seen horrific photos of death, destruction, violence and murder since she'd been with the FBI, but this level of depravity eclipsed anything that she'd ever witnessed. All of a sudden, the photos Seth had of his patients took on a new significance. She recoiled again at the memory of him saying how much he loved children. Up until now Henry Kelly, the man who cold-bloodedly murdered her father had been the epitome of evil.

My God, my God, in part she was blaming herself, *how could I have got it so wrong?* It occurred to Savannah; Henry Kelly's crimes were practically wholesome compared to the sickening images spread out before her. As Savannah forced herself to pore over the photos, she formulated a plan. The grotesque horror spread in front of her in graphic black and white, only served to harden her resolve. She knew these images told only half the story and could never tell the full horror of destroyed lives and damage that would be generational.

Savannah was aware more than most that people with money could distort and delay the judicial process. More importantly, she knew this evil needed to be stopped, exterminated, obliterated. She knew what she had to do.

Savannah sat heavily on the old bentwood chair she'd placed next to the small wooden table at the end of the hallway, facing the front door. She held in her hand a High Standard LR semi-automatic pistol, forsaking the Magnum for the stealth of the low calibre 0.22. There was, she decided, something authoritative about the weapon; an instrument of evil in the wrong hands but equally an instrument of emphatic justice.

She removed the silencer from her handbag, methodically screwing it into place. She waited.

At 7:04 pm the door swung open and Seth backed in, carrying his suitcase.

'Hi honey, I'm home.' He turned, light heartedly kicking the door shut with his foot. 'Terrific weekend. The guys and I had a great ...'

His suitcase fell to the ground with a thud. The colour drained from his face as he saw the photos strewn on the floor. A hundred death warrants. All bearing his name. Before him was Savannah, perched on the chair and gripping the automatic, her face a blank mask.

'Darling, please, I ... I can explain ...'

Savannah stared at the cadaverous features, the anchor tattoo and the odd-coloured eyes. 'Goodbye, Henry.'

THE END

An excerpt from Spencer Marlowe's next time
traveling adventure, coming soon:

L.A.
CONFRONTATION

CHAPTER ONE

THE LADY FROM TEXAS

The heat of the sun scorched the man's body, penetrating, it seemed, to his very soul. It callously sucked the last drops of moisture from every fibre of his being. Sweat bathed his brow, trickling down his parched cheeks then mixing with the arid dust that coated his face as it evaporated.

Oh my god, this has to be just about as hot as it could get without the world going up in flames. So, is this how I'm going to die? He leant against a wooden pole supporting a sign, emblazoned with the words "Pione … oon Good Spri gs Nevada thi ty mil s." Riddled with bullet holes, the sign left its complete message up to weary traveller's imagination.

The man removed his Stetson, wiping his brow with a bandana that'd been wrapped around his neck.

I reckon that sign is meant to say 'Pioneer Saloon'. He found himself trying to laugh as he deciphered the wording, but his throat was so dry nothing but a hoarse wheezing sound sputtered out of his chapped lips.

I could sure use a drink of water, and something to eat … when did I last eat? He glanced at his wrist. *My watch, what on Earth happened to my watch?*

He felt unease bubbled up inside him. Where in hell am I? And the watch? Momentarily forgetting his hunger and thirst he tried to remember. The watch dammit, it was valuable, it was a gift … Who from? Can't quite … think … think …

A faint sliver of memory flashed in an out of his mind, elusive. When he tried to focus the memory ran and hid like a child, yelling 'you can't see me, you can't see me'. A moment of triumph—he could see the watch, he could remember the man—the old man saying, 'Happy birthday, son.'

He could see it now, gold and steel, the words on the bezel 'Rolex'. Rubbing his sweaty hands against his grimy jeans then rummaging through a pocket, he discovered a ten dollar note. *That should buy me a cold drink, something to eat, surely.* Delving further into the pocket his fingers grasped a small metallic object. He pulled it out, examining it: silver, embossed. What was it?

Well, it's old. He held it up, it glinted in the morning sun. *I remember this I've seen it before. I think it may be important.* The man tried to remember. *What is it? I just know it's significant, but why?*

In the distance he could see a cloud of dust spring up from the road the only sign of life or movement in the surrounding inhospitable desert. As the swirling dust drew nearer, he could see it was an automobile.

The candy red Chevrolet Impala convertible jerked to a stop beside him, throwing up a splash of dust, like water from a roadside puddle. He observed an attractive lady, her Titian hair largely concealed by a black and silver scarf, her face partially concealed by the biggest sunglasses the man had ever seen. In a slow Texan drawl, the lady spoke in that soft Southern accent that sounded like an invitation even when it wasn't.

'I'll just bet y'all are fixen to head to the Pioneer?'

The man smiled, the relief on his face like a man who had been thrown a life belt, after spending twenty-four hours in shark infested waters. 'You're a lifesaver.'

'Priscilla. My friends call me Prissy.' The lady held out a hand.'

The man smiled and shook the proffered hand. 'Hi my name's …'

CHAPTER TWO

REALISATION

'Yeah honey, your name is?'

Oh my God. 'I don't know.'

Priscilla eyed him suspiciously. 'What do you mean, you don't know? I figured your automobile must have broken down. I mean, you're miles from anywhere? You don't have any luggage? You sure as hell don't sound American? Are you English or what?' she said sharply.

The man gazed around at the desert surroundings. An unending vista of cracked land and crumbling rock. Tumbleweeds and dust devils, scattering as if they possessed a demonic life force making them run as the Chevrolet passed by. Cactus and impressive granite formations loomed in the distance.

He was starting to see snatches of images. The Qantas A380 aircraft, the smiling hostess handing him a menu. An airport, with a multitude of signs, and the relentless hustle and bustle of people on the move. What did the signs say? '*LA International Airport. Customs, going through customs, a mild argument with an official. Resolved ... all resolved ... welcome to the USA. Michiyo oh no ... where's Michiyo?*' A moment of panic. *Where's Michiyo?*

'I'm from Australia. Perth, Western Australia.'

'Waal, welcome tall handsome Australian from, where did you say?' Again, the broad Texan drawl.

'Perth. Western Australia.'

'Uh ha, now … all we need is a name.'

The man felt the outline of a hard metal object sticking into his leg. Thrusting his hand into his pocket he pushed the trinket into a more comfortable position. Touching the metal this time felt like a shock, a live current coursing through his body, a current, switching on the previously darkened recesses of his mind.

Oh. Thank God, the cornicello. The silver talisman given to Spencer by Bert Weadley, now sat reassuringly in his hand. Spencer breathed a sigh of relief. Recall was now complete. Frightening but complete. The *cornicello* given to Spencer by a grateful Bert when Spencer had been cast back in time to wartime Australia 1942.

'My name's Spencer Marlowe. I think I must have had some type of amnesia. I'm from Australia and I know I've recently flown into LAX.'

'What's an LAX?'

'You know, LA international airport. Just about the biggest airport in the US.'

Priscilla looked at him curiously. 'Ok … if you say so. Sorry if I seem a little suspicious. But you know with all this stuff going on in Cuba, we've all been warned about commie spies. And you must admit your circumstances are a little odd.'

'Cuba, what's up with Cuba? I haven't heard.'

'You gotta be kidding me. Bay of Pigs. Kennedy, Castro. C'mon even in outback Australia you must've heard about this stuff?'

Spencer gazed at the lady as the full horror of the situation hit him like a thousand-pound weight, squashing him, he'd been there before, he knew now what was happening. 'What year's this?'

'Pal you're starting to scare me. It's June, 1961.'

The colour drained from Spencer's face. He now knew exactly what had happened. He shook his head, gazing around. The Chevrolet was clearly near new, big and bold with its pedestrian slicer fins. The lady looked like an extra in an Annette Funicello and Frankie Avalon beach party movie.

Memories now flooded back, cascading through his mind, jostling to find a place as image upon image thrust themselves forward.

Spencer, Michiyo and their beautiful five-year-old daughter Trilby had flown into LAX on holiday.

It had been over five years since Spencer had found himself cast back in time. He and FBI agent Savannah Steele had been instrumental in dealing a mortal blow to the Romano crime family in New York. Dale Fletcher, the boyishly enthusiastic FBI chief had labelled the operation the' Manhattan Sting.'

As the years passed and Spencer's vivid and disturbing dreams vanished, both he and his wife Michiyo hadn't spoken of his time travel episodes. Try as she might, Michiyo had never been able to completely grasp the enormity of Spencer's journeys into the past.

Spencer would go to bed as usual, be transported to another time and be involved in life threatening situations, then when least he expected, he would wake up next to Michiyo, having been gone sometimes for years. But in real time he'd never been away. He would awake and pour out his hair-raising tale to a confused and scared Michiyo, who tried to believe and accept what Spencer had to say. But in the end, she could only compartmentalise it, effectively put it into the too hard basket.

Spencer had some business in LA. He was now a senior partner in the Perth firm Dynamic Marketing. When the business was complete, Spencer, Michiyo, and Trilby were going to do LA. Disneyland, Universal Studios, the Farmers Market and Hollywood Boulevard, they were going to do it all.

If you have enjoyed the latest Spencer Marlowe story a kind review on Amazon or Goodreads would be appreciated.

The Chicago Story, once again featuring FBI special agent Savannah Steele, and of course Spencer Marlowe, will be out soon.

ABOUT THE AUTHOR

I am a Western Australian author, having been born in Perth and living in WA for most of my life. Like so many authors, my background is littered with many and varied careers; taxi driver, musician, roof tiler, shoe salesman and a plethora of others I attempted when young.

Being an avid reader prompted my desire to put pen to paper. I have three self-published novels, the first being 'Oh, How We Rocked', my musical memoir published 2021. This sold quite well in local Perth and Fremantle bookshops, as well as internationally on Amazon and other on-line sales outlets.

My 'Spencer Marlowe' adventure stories, 'The Singapore Saga' and 'The Hawaiian Intervention', published in 2021, have sold in twelve countries as well as Perth and Albany bookshops. They have received excellent reviews on Amazon and Goodreads.

My latest story 'Birthright', a crime novel co-authored with Perth author Bruce Russell was a change of direction and draws on my experience as a taxi driver in Perth in the 1990's.